"Stacey Ballis manages to be irreverent, unflinching, sexy, and somehow very sweet.
She is truly a writer to watch."
—Laura Caldwell,
author of *The Night I Got Lucky* and *Look Closely*

PRAISE FOR
Room for Improvement

"I adored everything about it—best of all, the humor is pervasive throughout the book. For those who say chick lit is played out, all I can say is, think again. Stacey Ballis proves the genre can be funny, honest, clever, real, and most importantly, totally fresh."
—Jennifer Lancaster, author of *Bitter is the New Black*

"More fun than a *Trading Spaces* marathon. One of the season's best."
—*The Washington Post Book World*

"Rife with humor—always earthy, often bawdy, unwaveringly forthright humor."
—*Chicago Sun-Times*

"Self-proclaimed home-improvement junkie and author Ballis has written a laugh-out-loud novel that will appeal to HGTV devotees as well as those who like their chick lit on the sexy side. One of the summer's hot reads for the beach." —*Library Journal*

"In her third outing, Ballis offers up a frothy, fun send-up of reality TV. Readers will have a blast watching Lily and her friends try to figure out what their priorities are in this lighthearted tale."
—*Booklist*

continued . . .

Sleeping Over

"Ballis presents a refreshingly realistic approach to relationships and the things that test (and often break) them. Ballis's sophomore effort will please readers who want something more than fairy-tale romance."
                                                                    —*Booklist*

"*Sleeping Over* will have you laughing, crying, and planning your next girl's night out. This is the first novel I have read by Stacey Ballis, but I guarantee it won't be the last!"
                                                    —*Romance Reader at Heart*

"This engaging story delivers everything you ask from a great read: it makes you laugh, it makes you cry, it makes you *feel*. *Sleeping Over* gets my highest recommendation."
                                                                —*Romance Divas*

Inappropriate Men

"An insightful and hilarious journey into the life and mind of Chicagoan Sidney Stein."   —*Today's Chicago Woman*

"Ballis's debut is a witty tale of a thirtysomething who unexpectedly has to start the search for love all over again."   —*Booklist*

"Stacey Ballis's debut novel is a funny, smart book about love, heartbreak, and all the experiences in between."
                    —*Chatelaine* (also named *Inappropriate Men* one of their
                                        Seven Sizzling Summer Reads for 2004)

"Without a doubt, *Inappropriate Men* is one of the best books of 2004. Stacey Ballis has a way with words. Effortlessly, she makes them exciting and pulls the reader into the life of one of the most engaging characters ever created, Sidney Stein."
                                                            —*A Romance Review*

The *Spinster* Sisters

STACEY BALLIS

BERKLEY BOOKS, NEW YORK

THE BERKLEY PUBLISHING GROUP
Published by the Penguin Group
Penguin Group (USA) Inc.
375 Hudson Street, New York, New York 10014, USA
Penguin Group (Canada), 90 Eglinton Avenue East, Suite 700, Toronto, Ontario M4P 2Y3, Canada
(a division of Pearson Penguin Canada Inc.)
Penguin Books Ltd., 80 Strand, London WC2R 0RL, England
Penguin Group Ireland, 25 St. Stephen's Green, Dublin 2, Ireland (a division of Penguin Books Ltd.)
Penguin Group (Australia), 250 Camberwell Road, Camberwell, Victoria 3124, Australia
(a division of Pearson Australia Group Pty. Ltd.)
Penguin Books India Pvt. Ltd., 11 Community Centre, Panchsheel Park, New Delhi—110 017, India
Penguin Group (NZ), 67 Apollo Drive, Mairangi Bay, Auckland 1311, New Zealand
(a division of Pearson New Zealand Ltd.)
Penguin Books (South Africa) (Pty.) Ltd., 24 Sturdee Avenue, Rosebank, Johannesburg 2196,
South Africa

Penguin Books Ltd., Registered Offices: 80 Strand, London WC2R 0RL, England

This book is an original publication of The Berkley Publishing Group.

This is a work of fiction. Names, characters, places, and incidents either are the product of the author's imagination or are used fictitiously, and any resemblance to actual persons, living or dead, business establishments, events, or locales is entirely coincidental. The publisher does not have any control over and does not assume any responsibility for author or third-party websites or their content.

PRINTING HISTORY
Berkley trade paperback edition / March 2007

Library of Congress Cataloging-in-Publication Data

Ballis, Stacey.
    The spinster sisters / Stacey Ballis.—Berkley trade paperback ed.
        p. cm.
    ISBN: 978-0-425-21356-8 (trade pbk.)   1. Single women—Fiction.   2. Sisters—Fiction.
3. Dating services—Fiction.   I. Title.

    PS3602.A624S65 2007
    813'.6—dc22   2006031997

PRINTED IN THE UNITED STATES OF AMERICA

10   9   8   7   6   5   4   3   2   1

This book is dedicated with much love to my parents,
Stephen and Elizabeth Ballis.

You have always embodied the best in
what it means to be a family,
including the addition of friends who feel like family.
You gave me the best gift anyone ever has,
you made me a sister.
Everything there is, there is because of you.
Everything I do, I do because you empower me.
The heart and soul of all my words begins with you both.
LAS

For Deborah,
Who has always been my best friend, my strongest supporter,
my most challenging opponent, and my conscience.
Whatever else I do, my favorite job is being your older, shorter, sister.

For Peggy,
Sister by Choice since 1973.
Thanks for over thirty years of love and encouragement,
for scratching all those damn mosquito bites
and teaching me double solitaire
and a couple of adventures at Northern we probably
shouldn't talk about.
This particular adventure began with your title,
and I hope I did you proud.

ACKNOWLEDGMENTS

Is anyone still reading these? Really? I thought not. I could thank just about anyone here, including Archduke Ferdinand, and I doubt it would cause a ripple.

But, for those of you who I do know actually stop here . . . a couple of heartfelt thanks.

To my amazing family, Mom and Dad, Deborah and Jonnie, you all know how much I love you. Ditto friends.

Scott Mendel, the world's best agent and dear friend and partner . . . what a delight to have you with me on this journey.

Christine Zika, über-patient editor, for making the ladies real as well as lovely.

Jennifer Novak, for working miracles.

And for all my "sisters," and you know who you are, thank you for everything!

The *Spinster* Sisters
The New Face of Single

by Bethany Jacobs

Jodi and Jill Spingold know a lot about being single. In fact, these siblings have made a career out of it. Jodi (thirty-four, with a degree in journalism), and Jill (thirty-two, with a degree in marketing and business), are riding the very lucrative self-help wave, and their mission is to empower single women everywhere. Their four-year-old corporation, Spinster Inc., is in fact made up of several different smaller business ventures. Their noon-to-two satellite radio show, *Lunch with the Spinster Sisters*, keeps women all over the country glued to their XM radios every Thursday. Their lines of T-shirts, office accessories, and gift items are sold nationwide. The Spinster Sisters Seal of Approval stickers on everything from pajamas to wine in a box have become a coveted marketing tool, and companies vie for their products to be one of the select few. (They choose just one item per month, and the products are always items that the sisters themselves use and enjoy.) And last, but certainly not least, their books are bestsellers in eight languages.

In the new conservatism era, when the average age of newlyweds is on the decrease and three children have supplanted two as the ever-increasing norm in the middle class, the self-proclaimed Spinster Sisters are touting empowered singlehood, and women all over the world are listening. I've been invited to meet with the moguls in their offices in Chicago. Their director of PR sends me an extensive press kit before my visit, which includes everything from copies of their coverage in *Chicago* magazine's Most Eligible issue, to a joint bio, which reads almost like a Grimm's fairy tale.

Nothing in my independent research deviates at all from what is iterated for me in the press materials. And the story is a compelling one. In a spectacular understatement, it hasn't always been easy for the Spingold girls. At the tender ages of six and four, they lost both of their parents in a tragic car crash. Their mother had no family to speak of, but their father had two older sisters, neither married, who lived together in a ramshackle house in Palmer Square, a quiet residential neighborhood on the near northwest side of Chicago. These women, in their early forties at the time, took in their nieces and raised them well, if unconventionally. Ruth and Shirley Spingold, referred to as the "Original Spinster Sisters" by Jodi and Jill, are a throwback to another age. Never married, the two lived with their elderly parents until their deaths six months apart, and then assumed joint care of the house they had grown up in. Neither had ever moved out of her

childhood bedroom. After the tragedy, the master bedroom was converted into a little girls' paradise, with canopy beds, pink carpeting, and clouds painted on a blue ceiling. Jodi and Jill would remain together in this room, altering the decor as they aged, until Jodi left for college. Their parents had left a small amount of life insurance and savings, and their deceased maternal grandparents had established education trusts for them both, but the girls were mostly supported by income generated by Ruth and Shirley.

Ruth earns her unconventional, but by no means negligible, salary by serving as a self-proclaimed "curator of Chicago." She can tell you the place to get the best Chicago-style hot dogs and the finest five-star meals. She knows the urban legends and the proven history and is hired by wealthy visitors to guide them around the city, helping them explore the less touristy attractions and serving as a sort of private concierge. Her services are entirely based on word of mouth and apparently have no set rate. According to Jodi, "Oh, whatever you feel appropriate . . ." is her only acknowledgment that she is supposed to be paid. And apparently this tactic works very well, with the flustered clients desperate to not appear cheap by offering too little. She takes the month of July off every year to travel, noting that her type of clientele tend to be at their own beach houses and cabin getaways that month anyway, and admitting to not completely adoring the weekly festivals that Chicago celebrates in the summer.

Shirley serves as a cookbook recipe tester for several publishing houses, who send her galleys of new cookbooks and have her try out the recipes to see if they are suitable for a home kitchen. She is quoted as saying, "There was much less joy in the *Joy of Cooking* before I fixed it." The elder pair of Spingold sisters hold a monthly salon of local artists, writers, intellectuals, and a smattering of paying guests, who gather to eat and talk and participate in everything from traditional Native American drum circles to lessons in self-defense, and one misbegotten snake charming experiment. (About that incident, all that the elder and younger Spingolds will say is that both an ambulance and Animal Rescue had to be called in but that neither humans nor reptiles were seriously injured.)

Sitting in the large office Jodi and Jill share in the West Loop area of Chicago, I ask them about their upbringing. Aunt Ruth and Aunt Shirley are, according to the girls, the perfect pair of surrogates.

"Aunt Ruth has always been full of adventures and wild ideas and grand plans," Jodi reminisces. "And Aunt Shirley is calmer, more logical, with excellent organization skills and a mean hand in the kitchen. Aunt Shirley was like having a stay-at-home mom—she was always there when we got home from school—and Aunt Ruth breezed in and out a little more haphazardly." Apparently Ruth took them to strange, exotic restaurants, introducing them to the cuisines of Vietnam and Ecuador, and Shirley taught the girls how to make delicious and nutritious meals at home and trained them in the recipes of Bubbe Spingold, their great-grandmother. Ruth planned outings to tea ceremonies at the Midwest Buddhist Temple, and Shirley took them to high tea at the Drake Hotel.

"It was like being raised by Auntie Mame and Mrs. Piggle Wiggle!" Jill says. "But it was also a place of security and great love. They were both amazing about keeping our parents alive for us; we celebrated their birthdays and kept loads of photos around, and they would tell us as many stories as they could remember. Aunt Shirley even made each of us a small quilt with scraps from their clothes."

"And they showed us how to rely on each other and ourselves," Jodi offers.

"True." Jill nods in agreement. "They made it very clear that they liked their independence and were self-reliant, but they also allowed themselves to depend on each other. Clearly, we took that lesson to heart."

I ask about their aunts' attitudes about relationships, wondering if it might have influenced their own ideas regarding matrimony.

"Aunt Shirley was engaged to be married when she was in her early twenties," Jodi says, twirling a piece of hair around her forefinger. "But she called it off because she didn't feel deeply in love with him. I think she dated here and there, but never anyone that seriously."

"And Aunt Ruth is a total player!" Jill jumps in. "She has always had a small stable of regular beaus and seems to manage her time with each of them with Swiss precision."

"But they were always very conscious of being honest with us about their opinions while encouraging us to have our own. And

they have always been very supportive of our relationships," Jodi says, presumably to dispel the myth that the aunts might have encouraged the girls to stay single.

"That's very true." Jill nods emphatically. "It didn't matter if it was about politics or personal choice; they always told us to follow the path that made the most sense for us."

It is clear from the way these women interact that the bond between them is extraordinary. The energy that comes from them is unified and clear, and while one starts to get the idea that Jodi is more of a creative, big-picture idea gal and Jill a savvy and organized businesswoman, without a doubt, this is a partnership of loving equals.

Growing up, to hear them tell it, they were just as devoted. Jodi was offered a double promotion from the fourth grade to sixth, which she declined, telling Ruth and Shirley that she didn't want to be more than two grades ahead of Jill. Jill dropped out of the high school yearbook committee when Jodi was passed over for editor. More than sisters, best friends, and helpmates, the girls stayed together through thick and thin. Jodi chose the University of Chicago so that she could be close to home for college, and Jill joined her there two years later, passing up a scholarship to the University of Pennsylvania.

Their entrepreneurial spirit became apparent when they were still in college. Surprised at the girls in her classes, who all seemed bound and determined to find one steady boyfriend, Jodi started writing a weekly anonymous column called "The Spin" for the *Maroon*, the campus paper, a fun series of essays on the joys of dating lots of different people, including, shockingly, university staff, assistant professors, and visiting dignitaries. Jill, meanwhile, studying marketing, recognized a potential business opportunity among the young women of the campus and began selling notepads, T-shirts, and other paraphernalia with tongue-in-cheek "girl power/boys are stupid" phrases. Jodi shocked everyone, including herself, when she fell for the quiet guy that computer services sent to fix her system when it crashed in the beginning of her senior year. They moved in together right after her graduation and were married within the year.

"Jill never really liked Brant much," Jodi says. "But she supported me in all things, even if that included suffering an irritating brother-in-law."

"I wanted her to be happy, and while Brant was making her happy, I had to support that." Jill shrugs.

"And when he stopped making me happy, she supported me in my decision to divorce," Jodi admits.

Five years ago, the spunky sisters were in very different places in their lives. Jill was tackling the world of marketing from the bottom, leading focus groups for a research firm. Jodi was cobbling together a living from freelance writing for local Chicago print media and teaching journalism at Columbia College. Jodi's marriage to her college sweetheart had crumbled, and she found herself suddenly single before her thirtieth birthday.

"It was frightening," Jodi says. She is a short, curvaceous woman with wild brown curls and piercing blue eyes, and she is simple and frank in her delivery. "I'd never expected to be back out in the dating world. But I found that while I had no regrets about my marriage, I significantly regretted the feeling that I had lost my twenties focused so exclusively on a relationship. I felt perhaps I would have made smarter choices had I been more independent."

Jill is a taller, slimmer version of her older sister, with hair more wavy than curly, and eyes a shade closer to green than blue, but with the same porcelain skin and the same wide smile. There is an identical cadence to their speech, Jill's voice a hair deeper in tone. "We went to a family friend's wedding, the bride and groom both twenty-five. Jodi looks at me during the reception and says that she feels like grabbing them and telling them not to do it, to live twenty-five first."

Jodi interrupts her sister. "So Jill asks me what I meant by that, and I started this mini rant about what I would have done differently. By the time the reception was over, we had outlined the idea for a book."

Their first literary collaboration, *Living Twenty-five*, was written in the evenings and on weekends and celebrated being young and adventurous and playing the field; encouraged devotion to one's career but not one man; and suggested that women put matrimony on the back burner. They gave it to their aunts for content advice (Ruth) and editing (Shirley). When the elder Spingolds gave their final approval, Jodi and Jill put together a proposal and sent it to a publishing magnate who had spent a week in Chicago under Ruth's tutelage some twenty years earlier and had

stayed in touch ever since. The publisher jumped on the book, and the sisters embarked on their new adventure.

The real whirlwind began when they were invited, shortly after the publication, to appear as guest speakers for a local Jewish twenty-something charity event. One of the attendees was a well-connected socialite visiting from New York, who upon returning to the East Coast touted the sisters as her own little discovery to all of her wealthy and powerful friends. Within weeks there were invitations to appear at similar events in New York, Boston, and D.C., and the word of mouth began to take hold.

Their easy banter and complementary public speaking styles made them a hot ticket on the lecture circuit and landed them the radio show with a small Internet station. A call to fill in last minute for an AWOL celebrity on the Oprah show did what it does for any book—sent it rocketing up the bestseller charts and selling out at bookstores. The business grew exponentially over the next two years, with the second book debuting at number seven on the *New York Times* bestseller list. "No new Harry Potter book that week," Jodi makes a point of noting. The show got picked up by satellite radio, Jill's merchandising fetish returned with a lucrative vengeance, and Spinster Inc. was quickly an industry to reckon with.

The second book, *The Thirty Commandments*, became a bible to single women in their thirties. The company name is both alliterative (Spingold/Spinster) and a way of reclaiming the moniker and taking the negative connotation out of it. Jodi and Jill are having the time of their lives. "Chicago is a great playground for two successful women in the prime of life," Jodi says with a wink. And things are only looking up. There is some discussion of a possible television show, and the third book, *Facing Down Forty* (targeted at women in their mid to late thirties and encouraging them to create a list of forty things they want to do before turning forty, and then finding ways to do them), is coming together smoothly and will be out in time for the summer. Both sisters were listed in *Chicago* magazine's annual Most Eligible issue last summer but are closemouthed about their romantic lives.

"You'll just have to see if we're in there again next summer!" Jill says with a twinkle in her eye.

This charmed life for charming women doesn't come without a price. Conservative family values organizations claim that the Spinster Inc. message is antimarriage and pro-promiscuity and undermines the importance of the stay-at-home mother as a representation of all that is right with the American family. For every message of thanks received from the Spinster website, there is at least one calling their work shameful, and at least a few times per week, one that is actually threatening. "We have appropriate security measures in place." Jodi shrugs off the hate-mail issue. "We believe in our message, a part of which is that every woman should make up her own mind and be her own person. We aren't antimarriage; we are simply against women feeling as if they are a failure or less than a woman if they choose *not* to marry. We aren't against women being stay-at-home mothers, as long as it is their choice and desire to pursue it, and not because they feel it is expected of them. Anytime you attempt to empower someone, there will be someone who would prefer them submissive. And in this country, the right to publicly disagree with an opinion is sacred. We respect these organizations' right to voice their message and wish they were more respectful of our right to voice ours."

Detractors or no, the business continues to be lucrative and offers a nice lifestyle for all four Spingold women. They were able to purchase a gorgeous three-flat up the block from the house they grew up in and, after an extensive renovation, moved everyone into the new digs: Jodi on the top floor, Jill on the second floor, and the aunts, now in their early seventies, on the first floor. It is a house full of independent women, depending on each other.

I accept a coveted invite to meet the aunts at the Palmer Square residence and find myself immediately drawn to these very different women.

"We couldn't be prouder of them," says Ruth, a tall, slim, elegant woman with short, spiky red hair and strands of chunky beads over a long, black dress. "We know their parents are watching over them."

"Goodness, yes," pipes in Shirley, a good six inches shorter than her sister, with a grandmotherly air and silver hair in a neat chignon. "They work harder than you can imagine, sometimes twelve, fourteen hours a day. Frankly, I don't know how they do it."

We don't know how they do it either, but their fans are sure glad they do.

"They give you permission to put yourself and your need for personal development ahead of creating your identity in relation to other people, especially romantic partners," says Paige Andrews, who started as a shared executive assistant for both sisters and has moved up within the organization and now serves as the director of operations for the company. Paige approached the sisters after hearing them speak shortly after the first book was released, and offered her services. The sisters took a chance on the young woman, who was just a year out of college. Now twenty-eight and in a position usually reserved for people with both graduate-level educations and years of practical experience, the pretty redhead is humble about her meteoric rise.

"They took me at my word when I promised to work very hard, not just for them but also true to the spirit that the company was started with. They have supported me, encouraged me, and inspired me."

This sort of loyalty seems par for the course. Everyone one encounters with even the smallest professional connection to the Spinster Sisters has shown a fierce respect for both women. Their primary business philosophy, to hire strong, intelligent women and then let them do their jobs without micromanagement, seems to be paying off. The fact that they pay at the high end of the industry scale for all positions, offer full benefits to all employees, tuition reimbursement for continuing education, and a healthy bonus structure doesn't hurt their reputation as good employers.

For Jodi and Jill, it seems that they are taking the whole thing in stride.

"We are so blessed," Jill says. "We do what we love, there are constantly new challenges to keep things interesting, and we get to do it as a team."

"We wonder sometimes if we'd have ended up here if the accident hadn't happened," Jodi says, "but we like to think that we would have! As it stands, we know we have pretty powerful guardian angels, and we just hope we're doing them proud."

I think there's little doubt of that.

For information on their speaking engagements, to read excerpts from the books, or to check in on the Spinster blog, log on to their website, www.spinstersisters inc.com.

The End of an Era

How many times have you suppressed your own will in the beginning
of a relationship, just to find that down the road it has rendered you
powerless to change the pattern? It is essential from the beginning of a
relationship to be clear about what is important to you. If you want
sleepovers, buy him a spare toothbrush and make your wants known. If
you need your space, don't respond to every phone call and e-mail in
the beginning; he'll think you're pulling away when you stop in a few
weeks. Human behaviorists say it only takes three weeks to establish a
habit. Use the first three weeks of any new relationship, romantic or
platonic, to create habits that won't need to be undone later.

—From The Thirty Commandments by Jill and Jodi Spingold

The alarm on my cell phone sounds a shrill beeping, which
wakes me with a start. I roll over to shut it off and look at the
time: 4:30. Crap. I roll back over and nudge the snoring gentleman next to me.

"Abbot. Wake up. You gotta go."

He grunts and throws an arm over his head.

I poke him in the ribs. "Abbot, I mean it. I have to get ready."

He bolts up, rolls over quickly, and traps me beneath him.
Then he kisses me deeply. "You're delicious, you know that? I
have half a mind to make you my prisoner." He kisses the side of
my neck, below my ear. Sigh. He's pretty delicious himself. I poke
him again.

"I'd credit you with less than half a mind at the moment. You know the rules, mister. If I'm going to let you drag me away from work in the middle of the afternoon, then I have to be able to keep my evening free to catch up. Besides, I have to be downstairs for cocktail hour in thirty minutes, and with what you've just done to my hair, I need primp time." I push him off me and throw back the covers.

"Yikes!" He yelps, snatching at the blankets. "No fair!"

"Up you get, lover. No fooling." I grin at him and then get out of the bed, stretching.

"Fine, fine. I give up." He gets out of bed. "First dibs on your bathroom."

"Of course." On his way by, he kisses the side of my neck and smacks me on the ass.

I throw the blankets back over the bed and put on my bathrobe. I have to admit, there is something so wonderfully decadent about a midafternoon romp, I feel perfectly wicked. The fact that Abbot is a skilled lover doesn't hurt matters. Never underestimate those banker types, ladies, they may seem stuffy and conservative, but I find they can be shockingly delightful in the bedroom. But despite his numerous charms, I do have to make sure Abbot knows that my rules aren't made to be broken. Not even by someone who knows where my G-spot is.

I hear the toilet flush and the sink running. Moments later, he reappears, salt-and-pepper hair slightly damp, face pink, grin as wide as all get-out. Boys, even forty-eight-year-old boys, always get that cat-that-swallowed-the-canary look after sex. It is at once adorable and infuriating.

"Where are my briefs?" he asks, wandering around my bedroom.

"Psst," I say. He turns to see me dangling them off one finger.

"Thanks, darling." He dresses while I watch. Abbot Elling IV is a classic mergers and acquisitions guy. Conservative in dress, moderate in politics, sort of pasty from spending all his time in boardrooms, fit enough but not overly muscled. He looks like Anderson Cooper's older brother. Well, maybe cousin. He doesn't have Anderson's chiseled handsomeness; he's more like a Xerox of a Xerox, a little fuzzy around the edges. Not bad-looking, just not striking. But smart as anything, quick-witted, and excellent company. He shares my passions for theater, old movies, Impressionist art, and Sunday crossword puzzles. He makes a perfect martini. He's more devoted to my orgasm than his own. The only thing he can cook is an amazing spaghetti Bolognese, which is about the best thing I ever ate postfling at midnight or for a hangover-cure breakfast. Plus he spoils me rotten.

I've been seeing him for four months, ever since he ran into me in the lobby of my bank. Literally. Came around a corner like a bat out of hell, juggling a briefcase and a BlackBerry, and slammed into me. Lucky for me, I'm only five three and far from a lightweight, so my center of gravity is close to the ground. This makes me something like a Weeble, and Weebles wobble, but they don't fall down. They do, however, shriek like a banshee and lose control of their overstuffed purse-cum-briefcases. The shrieking echoes off the bank walls with a decibel level somewhere in the U2 concert range, and the bags send their contents skittering across the marble floors with astonishing speed. Abbot, to his enormous credit, made sure I was all right and then assisted me in collecting my personal items, including fetching my tampon case from under the chair of a bemused security guard.

I liked his efficiency and his warm hazel eyes, and when he offered coffee to make it up to me, I suggested that it was at least worth a dinner. He agreed and took me to Kiki's Bistro the next night, and over Dijon stewed rabbit and a perfectly chilled Côtes de Provence, we began. So far he has been lovely. A little pushy at times, and with a tendency to be unknowingly condescending, but I always call him on both, and he's quick to apologize. Plus, he sends flowers the next day every time we sleep together, which, tough broad though I may be, makes me all gooey. I think he's got Robert Daniel's florist on retainer.

He finishes dressing, folds his tie and puts it in his pocket, then looks at me. "Tell me again why I can't come to the sacred, super-secret cocktail hour? I'm dying to meet these aunts of yours."

"Sorry, family only. Besides, you know the aunts are off-limits. I'm not interested in sharing you." It's my standard reply. I learned early on in my reentry into dating that bringing boys home to meet Ruth and Shirley was not a good plan. My aunts are the kind of older women whose laughter is so infectious, stories so enter-taining, cooking so delicious, that they seduce everyone who meets them, and that makes giving a guy the boot that much more difficult. Guys always tried to win over the aunts in order to more firmly ensconce themselves in my life, and that makes things messy when you tire of their attentions. I hate messy.

I made the rule hard and fast after I came home one afternoon to find a recently exed boy sitting in my aunts' parlor, playing three-handed gin and scarfing down vanilla tea cakes with Ruth smirking and Shirley beaming. I think, though they would never tell me so, that they are split on their hopes for my romantic future. Ruth, I believe, is thrilled that I am following in her stilettoed foot-steps, never without a decent bit of male companionship but not attempting to secure a permanent future for anyone but myself. Shirley was sadder to see my marriage end and would like to have me find someone the way Jill has, someone she can cook for. I think deep down she may be somewhat regretful that after breaking off her engagement to Mr. Not Right Enough, that the one she was saving herself for never showed.

"Fine, fine," Abbot says, resigned. "You make the rules." He smirks at me, as if he knows that someday he will break me down.

"Yep, I do." I smirk back at him, knowing that he won't ever succeed. "C'mon lover, I'll walk you out."

I escort him to the back door off my kitchen. He shakes his head.

"Really, darling, this back door business bothers me. Why on earth can't I leave from the front like a normal human being? It makes the whole thing feel so illicit."

"First, because the last thing I need is Jill bumping into you when she gets home from work or the aunts catching you on your way out. And for your information, sex at three o'clock in the afternoon on a Thursday is reasonably illicit for those of us running businesses. Walk it off." I kiss him and open the door. Then I put my tough-girl persona aside for a moment. "Thanks for a lovely afternoon, Abbot, really. You are the best abductor ever." I turn my face up to him.

He leans over and kisses my lips softly. "Thank you back. I rely heavily on the Stockholm syndrome for your complicity. Dinner Saturday?"

I mentally look at my BlackBerry screen for Saturday. Full up. "Can't. How about Tuesday?"

He shakes his head, assuming appropriately that I have another date, but with the good taste not to pry. "Done. I'll make us a reservation at MK."

"My favorite. I'll speak with you over the weekend sometime." I hold the door open for him.

"Okay. Have a good cocktail hour."

"Will do." He cups my face in his hands, kisses me deeply, then turns away. I watch his silvery hair disappear down the back stairs and then head back inside.

My own hair, a mop of brown curls, has not fared nearly so well from the afternoon's attentions. It looks very much as if I have attempted to comb it with an electric mixer. I check the clock: 4:42. Gotta boogie. I jump in the shower, wet my hair down, and give myself a thorough scrub. I have that slightly bruised postsex feeling that makes me feel so alive. As if every inch of my skin is attuned to some mild electric charge in the air. After a quick towel-dry, the hair goes up in a ponytail, I jump into a pair of lounging pants and a sweater, throw on my slippers, and head downstairs. On the second-floor landing, I knock on Jill's door.

"It's open . . . ," she calls out. I open the door.

"Cocktail time, let's go," I say. She appears from out of her bedroom. She is wearing a cute outfit: little gray tweed skirt, lavender blouse, fabulous bronzed leather boots. Her hair, which unlike mine is just sort of gently and perfectly wavy and never, damn her eyes, frizzy, is tucked behind her ears as usual. Simple makeup, our mom's diamond studs. It makes me feel very frumpy. Actually, Jill frequently makes me feel a little frumpy. She is built like Dad was, tall, long legs. She has the most amazing clavicle I've ever seen and never struggles with her weight. I, on the other hand, seem to most favor Grandma Spingold, short, round, heavy of hip and breast, like a Russian farmwife, and just sniffing too deeply as I walk by a bakery can add a pound to my ample frame. The fact that Jill also got the good hair seems like insult to injury. It's a good thing she is my favorite person and best friend, or I might have to hate her.

"You and Hunter going out tonight?" I ask her, faking innocence. Hunter is her boyfriend of almost one year. He's a really great guy, definitely the best boyfriend she's ever had, and the only one I've ever approved of without reservations or caveats. The aunts are madly in love with him.

"Yep. He's picking me up in an hour." She grabs her purse and jacket. "Shall we?"

We leave her apartment and head down the stairs to the first floor. I love this building. Buying it was Jill's genius idea. It's a great old three-flat brownstone in Palmer Square, just a few blocks from where we grew up. And while the aunts were sad to leave the old family place, having grown up in it themselves, the idea of us all living in the same building again was too tempting. The fact that the old family place garnered nearly two million dollars, allowing them both a tidy annual income and securing their golden years, didn't hurt.

I have the third-floor apartment, Jill has the second floor, and the aunts are on the first floor. We have laundry and storage in the basement. All the benefits of living together, but with plenty of privacy. Even if it does mean having to sneak boys out the back door for the sake of decorum.

Aunt Ruth opens the door in a haze of Shalimar, her spiky burgundy-colored hair pushed off her forehead with a pair of black-rimmed glasses. "Hello, darlings," she says, kissing us on both cheeks. "Shirley is just pulling the nibbles out of the oven, and I'm manning the bar."

We head inside and flop on the overstuffed couch in the front parlor. Something savory and buttery smelling is wafting in the air. We can hear the ice rattle in the cocktail shaker. All is right with the world.

Jill leans into me and whispers, "Where'd you run off to after the show today? I finished talking to John, and you were gone." John is the producer of our Thursday satellite radio show, *Lunch with the Spinster Sisters*, coming to you live from twelve to two central time at number 187 on your XM dial.

"I got abducted." I grin at her.

"I thought you looked happy. Sneaky bitch. Ben?" she asks.

Ben is my other beau at the moment, my aforementioned Saturday night conflict, and the antithesis of Abbot. He's brand-new, just met him a few weeks ago, and he is wooing me like crazy, which, I have to say, feeds my ego enormously. Twenty-eight, graphic designer, rides a bike everywhere. Fun, spontaneous, a little bit of ADD but not in an annoying way. "Nope, Abbot."

"The Silver Fox? Really? In the afternoon? On a workday? I'd have thought he'd be too busy scaling some corporate walls to plunder and pillage. You must have him really smitten."

"What can I say? The man can't stop thinking about me."

"Well, who could blame him?" She winks. "No wonder your cheeks are so pink and glowing. When did he leave?"

"About twenty minutes ago."

"You and your back-door Johnnies." We giggle. Lucky for me, Jill doesn't think I'm a slut. She knows that since Brant and I split I need to keep my relationships noncommittal and varied. And that I'm a little bit of a slut.

Aunt Ruth reappears with the cocktail tray.

"Darlings, today we are sampling a classic Gibson, made with Skyy vodka, dry vermouth, and your aunt Shirley's homemade pickled onions." She deftly fills the four chilled martini glasses.

Aunt Shirley comes in from the kitchen with her own tray, her candy floss hair in its usual chignon, slightly flushed from the heat of the kitchen. "Hello, sweethearts. Let me put this down." She rests the tray on the coffee table in front of us, and we rise to kiss her powdery cheeks.

"What are we eating?" Jill asks Aunt Shirley, after the four of us clink glasses and take a simultaneous long sip of the ice-cold drinks.

"Cheese gougères," she says, pointing at crispy-looking puffs. "Artichoke bundles with Boursin, and asparagus wrapped with bresaola." It's a mini feast, and we dive in with hearty appetites. Of course, I always have a hearty appetite, hence the size-sixteen pants I'm currently sporting. But in light of the afternoon's indulgences, I figure I'm entitled to some sustenance.

"The show was very good today," Aunt Shirley says, delicately placing an asparagus spear on her plate. "I approved of the advice you gave that girl who was afraid to break up with her boyfriend, very sage."

We had encouraged the girl, who didn't love her guy but was afraid to be alone, to test her potential for joy in freedom by taking a short vacation by herself, to someplace she'd always wanted to go.

"I'm not so sure," Aunt Ruth pipes in. "After all, she would still have him waiting for her at the other end. She would still have the backup plan in place; she wouldn't really be free. She wouldn't really be challenging herself to be independent."

The two of them begin a quick discourse on the pros and cons, and Jill and I wink at each other and stuff our faces. They always do this. It's a comforting sound, the two of them debating.

"Oh, hush now, Ruthie, I want to hear from the girls." Aunt Shirley, who at age seventy-one is the younger of the two by nearly three years, always treats Aunt Ruth with the slight impatience usually reserved for an older sibling. And to her credit, despite her fiery personality, Ruth shows particular deference to her sister most of the time. Shirley turns to us.

"More importantly," she says, getting serious, "I want to know about the security issue. Has it been handled?"

Last week we had a series of e-mails from some wacko who appeared to be threatening to "cleanse the earth of our sinful propaganda" by utilizing an explosive device in his possession.

"They got him this morning," Jill says. "Turns out it was some seventeen-year-old kid whose parents are a part of that Family First organization that was protesting at the station last month. He seemed to think it would make him look cool to some of the younger women in the group if he were to really make us sweat. The cops' Internet division tracked him down and searched the home, but the parents were genuinely horrified, and they didn't find any bomb-making stuff, so it sounds like he'll do some community service. The lawyers said they won't need us to appear at the hearing."

"Well, thank goodness for that," Ruth says. "I swear, I worry sometimes about you girls, with all the crazies out there."

"Don't even get me started," I say. "I've been trying to tell Jill we need to pay more attention and consider a broader protection plan for this place and the office—"

"We can't live in fear of a couple of twisted idiots who get off by writing nasty e-mails." Jill is very dismissive of the security issue, generally, and I'm in too good a mood to push it tonight.

"On to happier subjects," I say.

"Quite right," Aunt Shirley says. "Jill, are you going out this evening?"

"Yep. Hunter's coming to get me at six." Jill pops another pouf of cheesy goodness into her mouth.

"You will let the boy come in for a cocktail this time, won't you?" Aunt Ruth asks. "We haven't seen very much of him lately."

Jill nods. "He's been traveling a lot, you know, the new job and all. But he misses you, and of course he'll come in for a drink. Our reservations aren't until seven." Hunter's architectural firm recently won a bid to design a small art museum in St. Louis, and Hunter is the lead architect on the project, so he's been back and forth every week for the last couple of months.

"Well, as long as he's happy," Shirley says.

"And as long as he's still keeping you happy," Ruth adds.

"He's great, we're great, everything is great."

"These asparagus things are great," I say. "What are they wrapped in again?"

"Bresaola," Shirley says. "Italian, spiced, air-cured beef."

"Are you still working on that appetizer cookbook, then? Good Lord, it's been ages!" Ruth exclaims.

"Sadly, yes. I never thought I'd get so bored of hors d'oeuvres, but this cookbook has no originality." Shirley sighs deeply, as if the lack of creativity in the catering guru who put together the book is a personal insult. "The gougères are delicious, but nothing new in the world about them. Artichokes and cheese in puff pastry is hardly revolutionary, and the asparagus called for prosciutto, but I just couldn't bear it." When Aunt Shirley is testing recipes, she can't help but fix them to make them better. Not in the usual way, adjusting salt or cooking times, but actually reworking recipes materially more often than not. If anyone had a real idea of how many cookbooks would be filled with inedible food were it not for her diligence, she'd win a goddamned Beard award.

These Thursday night cocktail hours began when Jill joined me at the U of C, a way to lure us home once a week, as if we needed reason beyond laundry and a hot meal. But the tradition became a sacred obligation after I married Brant, since it was a way to ensure that the four of us had some quality girl time, no matter what. The only time we ever miss it is when we go on vacation; the rule has become that no business travel can happen over a Thursday night. All four of us are equally committed to keeping it in place, the most important hour of every week.

We are in the middle of our allotted half a refill (a lady never gets tipsy at cocktail hour; we are restricted to one and a half drinks each) when the doorbell rings.

"I'll get it," I say, getting up and heading to the front door. I smile at Hunter through the mottled glass.

"You're early," I say, kissing him on the cheek.

"I couldn't help myself," he says. "She have any idea?"

"None," I say, grinning. "Your surprise is safe with me."

"Shall we?" He offers me his arm.

I take his arm. "Absolutely."

Hunter escorts me back into the parlor, where Aunt Ruth is already pouring him a cocktail. Aunt Shirley rises from her overstuffed chair to greet him.

"Hello, Hunter dear," she says, offering her cheek, which he kisses. "It's so lovely to see you. Please eat something." Aunt Shirley is only happy if you are eating something.

"Let the boy get inside, Shirley," Ruth says, handing over the martini glass. "And for Lord sakes, let him sit down and have a cocktail before you try to feed him." Hunter kisses Aunt Ruth and accepts the glass gratefully. He crosses to Jill, who is beaming at him.

"Hello, you," she says, as he leans in to her.

"Hello, you," he says, after planting a soft kiss on her lips.

"You're early," she admonishes him.

"I had something very important I needed to discuss with your hands," he says.

"My hands?" she asks.

"Not just yours, all four of you," he says.

"All four of us?" Shirley asks.

"Our hands?" Ruth asks.

"Hunter, what on earth are you talking about?" Jill asks.

Hunter gestures for us to sit down, and even though I know what's coming, I can feel my heart thumping in my chest.

He takes a deep draw on his drink, places the glass on the table, and clears his throat gently.

"I'm a pretty traditional guy," Hunter begins. "And one of the things that I've always appreciated about Jill is not only her traditional nature but the specific traditions that the four of you uphold. The comfortable rituals in your holidays and celebrations, how important it is for all of you to maintain your strong connection to each other. Even these Thursday-night events, which on the surface can seem like such a simple thing, how serious the four of you take it, how you don't let anyone or anything get in the way of your time together. That is a rare and special quality in all of you. And it is just one of the rare and special qualities I see in Jill." Hunter reaches for his glass, takes another deep sip, replaces it on the table, and turns to Aunt Ruth and Aunt Shirley. "The two of you have embraced me as a part of Jill's life and have made me feel very welcome in your home." He turns to me. "And Jodi, even though it's your first instinct to protect Jill, you've always made me feel as if you were on my side and in my corner, and I've come to view you as a good friend." Then he turns to face Jill, who is sporting a very confused look.

"Jill, you are the most extraordinary woman I have ever met. Every day I know you, I like you more. Every day I know you, I'm amazed by your intelligence. Your strength, your humor, your commitment to your family, and more importantly, your commitment to me. I have never loved anyone the way I love you. The four of you are an incredible family, and I'm not so naive as to think that I could just ask for Jill's hand in marriage. I know that this is a package deal. And so I'm asking for all four of your hands, to embrace me and let me join your family by allowing me to spend my life with Jill."

We all have tears in our eyes as he drops to one knee, reaches in his pocket, and pulls out a small, black velvet box. Ruth and Shirley reach for each other's hands, their heads nodding delightedly up and down in perfect unison. He nudges it open, and even from my place across the room, I can see the bright sparkle of the ring. I don't need to see it up close. I helped him pick it out over a month ago. Jill's face lights up in a wide grin as she nods vigorously, and Hunter places the ring on her finger.

Hunter rises, and they embrace tightly, Jill laughing delightedly, as Aunt Shirley holds her arms out to me. I fall into them, burying my face in her neck, soft as fresh bread dough. There is tightness in my throat that goes beyond simple emotion. My head is filled with a dozen images at once. The joy on Jill's face. Hunter's eagerness at the jeweler to find the perfect ring. How much Ruth and Shirley approve, and how open they have been about their opinion that my parents would have approved; more, that they had sent Hunter to Jill. When we expanded and re-designed our offices, Hunter was our architect. By the time we approved the final plans, it was clear he and Jill had amazing chemistry. And by the time we checked the last item off the punch list, they were well on the way to falling in love. And while I missed having Jill as my constant companion in our dating adventures, I loved how happy Hunter made her so quickly, how joyous she was to take herself off the market, despite the delightful array of possible men on her roster when they met. I only poached two of them, which I thought very restrained of me.

Aunt Shirley releases me, and I turn around to see my sister, my best friend, my business partner, grinning and weeping behind me. We throw our arms around each other and start to laugh.

"Did you know?" she says through her joyous tears.

"Of course. You know I know everything," I admit.

"I needed help with the ring," Hunter says, smothered by the attentions of two very happy aunts, who are trying to hug and kiss him nigh to death.

"He did not, actually," I say. "He had already picked that one out; he just wanted my stamp of approval on it."

A three-and-a-half-carat flawless cushion cut, in a beautiful filigreed platinum setting with pavé diamonds all around. Elegant, unusual, and very Jill. She has an old-world sensibility that I appreciate but cannot fathom. We are as different in taste as two people could be. Her apartment is a slightly less dusty version of the aunts': all antiques and lush rugs and eighty-five thousand throw pillows. I'm more of a minimalist myself: clean lines, spare, simple furniture, nothing froufrou. My apartment looks more like a high-end spa in Sweden meets a chic lounge, and hers looks like a cozy B and B in New England meets a cozy B and B in old England. She's a little bit country, and I'm a little bit rock and roll.

Aunt Ruth fetches a bottle of champagne and five glasses. A cardinal Spingold rule is that one should never have fewer than two bottles of decent champagne in the fridge. Another is that one should never hesitate to open one just because it is Wednesday and you're thirsty.

Aunt Ruth pours our flutes full to the top and hands them around. "I know I speak not only for Shirley but for Alan and Melissa as well when I say that you are most welcome into our family, Hunter. The joy you have brought into Jill's life has spilled into ours; you are already a part of this family in terribly essential ways. We wish you both all continued happiness. When Alan proposed to Melissa, it was at a family evening much like this one, and so much of his calm and kind sensibility is present in you, Hunter. And Jill, you have the same glow about you that your mother had on that magical night. They were as well-matched as the two of you, and I know that we are all surrounded by their love and approval on this night." She raises a glass for herself and my parents. "Mazel tov." Jill and I both well up afresh.

We all clink glasses, drink, and talk excitedly, and finally Hunter gets up.

"We have to be going; dinner awaits. But my parents are planning on coming in next weekend, and we'd love to have a celebratory engagement dinner with everyone on Saturday night."

"Of course, you go have a lovely, quiet dinner and enjoy the night," Shirley clucks.

"Congratulations again to you both, darlings. Have a wonderful evening," Ruth says, handing Hunter his coat while Jill gets her bag.

I hug Jill and whisper in her ear, "I love you, Moose Face."

She hugs back and whispers, "I love you, too, Butthead."

I kiss Hunter. "You did good, little brother."

"I like the sound of that. Thanks again for your help."

"Get out, go eat!" I shoo them toward the door. Jill will soon find out that he booked Le Bouchon, where they had their first date, and that they will have the whole restaurant to themselves, with a special menu prepared just for them.

I wave them good-bye at the door and head back into the parlor. The aunts are talking animatedly. I flop on the floor near Aunt Shirley's chair and put my head in her lap. She scratches my scalp like she used to do to help me sleep.

"What a lot of excitement!" she says. Then she pinches my ear.

"Ow! What was that for?" I ask, rubbing the wound.

"I can't believe you kept it a secret from us!" she says. "Such a big thing, and you're supposed to keep us informed."

"Oh Lord, Shirley," Ruth says. "You can't keep a secret to save your life. You'd have flubbed it in front of Jill within twelve hours."

Shirley hits her in the arm with a throw pillow. I laugh. She hits me on the head with it.

"Hey, I didn't say anything!" I say.

"I could hear you thinking," she says.

"So how do you feel about all this, Jodala? I'm sure you have some opinions," Ruth asks me. I sit up and hug my knees.

"I'm thrilled, of course," I say. "I love Hunter, he's the perfect guy for Jill, and I know they want all the same things. I think he'll be a wonderful husband and father and brother, and I know he'll make Jill very happy."

"But . . ." Ruth prods.

"But, nothing," I say. I do have a weird feeling in the pit of my stomach, but I'm not ready to put it into words yet.

"Oh, Ruthie, leave the child alone. Her sister just got engaged fifteen minutes ago. Give her a chance to feel her feelings before having to articulate them for your amusement, really," Aunt Shirley upbraids her.

"I don't mean to push, darling, I just know when your eyes go that particular shade of midnight blue that you are thinking serious thoughts." Ruth backs off, knowing full well that when I'm ready, I'll talk about it.

"Well, I don't know about the two of you, but all this excitement is making me hungry. Who wants pizza?" Aunt Shirley, for a gourmet, always knows when greasy comfort takeout is in order.

"Stuffed. With sausage," Ruth says in her clipped, definitive manner, making a decision as opposed to offering an option.

"That will do admirably," Aunt Shirley says, getting up to clear the cocktail glasses.

"I'll order from Bacino's and go pick it up," I say. "I'll be back in an hour."

I kiss them both and head up to my apartment. I order the pizza, then go to my library and sit on the low, wide chaise. Jill's getting married. To a perfect guy and for all the right reasons. Which only leaves one question. How can we be the Spinster Sisters if one of us isn't a spinster? And if we aren't the Spinster Sisters, what the hell happens to our business?

In the business of helping people to help themselves, you have to practice what you preach; you have to live the advice you give. Our whole corporation is based on the "do as we do" philosophy. What single woman in her right mind is going to listen to a married woman tell her to enjoy being single?

And for all Jill's glib bravery when it comes to this current rash of anti-Spinster sentiment, I worry even more for the PR mess it is going to create.

My phone rings. "Hello?"

"Hey Boss Lady Number One." It's Paige.

"Hey, Paige."

"I hear Boss Lady Number Two just got affianced." Paige has become an adopted little sister to us since she joined the company four years ago.

"Word travels fast. Who called you?"

"Jill did. She wanted to see if I could cover the marketing meeting in the morning, since apparently Hunter got them a suite at the Peninsula, and they want to sleep in."

"It's been pretty exciting for a Thursday. You okay on that meeting? Want me in on it?"

"I've got it. Come if you want, but don't shift anything for it. It's just an update on the new branding survey anyway. If anything exciting happens, I can brief you guys later."

"You're the best," I say. Which she is.

"I learned from the best," she says. Can't argue with that logic.

"Okay, Paige, anything else exciting?"

"Nope. Actually a slow day. Well, Benna has some new guy she's all jazzed about, but that doesn't really count."

Benna is our office manager and receptionist, and for a smart, organized girl, she is always embroiled in boy trouble.

"Great. I should be in around eight or so. Let's try and have lunch, and you can fill me in on the marketing stuff then."

"Cool. I'll have Benna make a late reservation. Jill said she should be in by one; we can take her to celebrate."

"Let's have Benna join us. She'll only make us repeat everything when we get back to the office. We can cut out the middleman if we bring her with."

"Good idea. Where should we go?" Paige asks.

"Let's go to Naniwa. Jill's been on a sushi kick lately. And Paige, tell Kim she should start thinking about how we present the news to the public."

"Done. I'll see you tomorrow. And congrats, sister of the bride!"

"Thanks, Paige. See you in the morning, colleague of the bride."

Paige laughs. "Bye."

Sister of the bride. That one is going to take a minute to sink in. When I got married, Jill was great, even though she didn't really approve. But she supported me a thousand percent, and whatever my concerns about the effect of this marriage on the business, I have to be sure I support her with the same enthusiasm.

I grab my coat and head out to pick up ten pounds of cheesy-sausagey goodness. Tomorrow I'll think about Jill and the future of our family and our business; tonight there is pizza.

Guess Who's Coming to Visit?

It isn't impossible to remain friends with an ex. But it can also be unhealthy, so it is important to look closely at how the relationship ended when determining if you are a candidate for staying friends, particularly if the relationship was your first serious one. Was the desire to break up mutual, or did one of you fight to stay together? Did one of you do something particularly hurtful like lying, cheating, or being abusive? Were you friends first, or did the relationship begin as a romantic one? Who are the other stakeholders in the relationship: friends, family, children? If the relationship simply ran its natural course, and no one broke trust, you can retain a comfortable friendship, provided both parties agree to be conscientious about appropriate communication and interaction.

—*From* Living Twenty-five *by Jill and Jodi Spingold*

The first week of Jill's engagement passes in a flurry of activity and excitement. Bouquets of flowers and engagement gifts pour into the office on a regular basis. Over half of the phone calls that come through the main line are friends offering words of congratulations. Jill, much to her credit, seems to be keeping a level head about the whole thing. She accepts everybody's words and offerings with grace and dignity and does not at this point seem to be getting too caught up in bride mania.

I've done my best to show outward signs of excitement, belying the little feeling in the pit of my stomach that signifies uncertainty and distress. I'm trying very hard not to worry about the big issues: the future of the business, how it will impact our relationship. We will be meeting in the next week with our publicist to figure out the best way to spin it, and so far, it hasn't leaked into the press. I've quietly told everyone to keep as much of the negative stuff as possible out of Jill's path. If someone major covers it, we won't be able to protect her, but I'm damned if I'm going to let her see every snarky e-mail that comes in.

So in spite of the engagement, the week flows pretty smoothly. Work gets done, meetings are held, and all in all, everything is good. Tonight, Jill and Hunter are going to the airport to pick up his parents and brother and then they are having a quiet meal together. We'll all be celebrating tomorrow night, the families meeting for the first time.

I had offers from Abbot and Ben for this evening but turned them both down. I had dinner with Abbot on Tuesday as promised, a lovely, quiet evening. He seemed very excited about Jill's engagement, and I couldn't help but wonder if he thought that perhaps being around wedding plans might make me more inclined to take our relationship seriously. Not likely. After marrying someone I never should have married, I'm not exactly eager to get terribly serious about anyone right now. As much as I like Abbot, I'm still awfully self-protective of my heart, and it is going to take a very special man to make me consider matrimony again.

Ben took me out on Wednesday night. We went to an event at Translucent Chocolates in the South Loop, sort of an art opening slash cocktail party. It was a fine evening, lots of laughter; I love how uncomplicated and easy it is with him. A semiperfect pair, my current suitors. Abbot makes me feel so taken care of, and Ben makes me feel young and alive. Abbot pampers me, and Ben tickles my funny bone. Abbot makes love to me with all the skill of an experienced and attentive partner, and Ben and I romp like a couple of puppies in a basket, with utter abandon.

Of course, neither of them is ideal in any sort of important way. Abbot is too set in his ways; he likes what he wants and isn't often inclined to compromise. Fine for our current situation; we plan our time together around the things we both enjoy, and all goes well. But I can tell that we would be incompatible roommates. His meticulousness would make me crazy. The man wipes the water droplets out of the sink after washing dishes and squeegees his shower door after every shower—even if he has a naked woman trying to get him to come to bed.

I met Ben a few weeks ago. I got a flat tire at the gym, and by the time AAA got there, Ben had changed the tire and acquired my phone number. I've never dated a younger man before, and while I enjoy his company tremendously, I still admit to some embarrassment about the six-year age difference. I know it shouldn't matter, but I can't help how self-conscious I am when we are in public, especially since he is so affectionate. And tall. I was always a sucker for a tall guy, and Ben Kohn is the tallest guy I have ever dated. A full six feet three and three-quarters inches. Yum. With that lean biker's body that just makes me feel like the Pillsbury Dough Girl, even though he does nothing but praise my curves. He's very creative, which sparks my own artistic tendencies, and he is encouraging of everything I do without reserve. But he won't argue with me, not even to debate an issue of the day. And I need that back and forth to keep my intellect feeling honed. He isn't at all interested in any of the more elegant or luxurious or sophisticated things in life, and there seems to be a slight air of disapproval when I express a desire to indulge. But he does make me feel powerful and beautiful and strong, and his deeply held belief that I can do whatever I set my mind to and achieve excellence has a tendency to keep my spine straighter these days.

Unfortunately, the physical chemistry isn't quite there for me. I slept with him a couple of times when we first met, but while he is a fantastic kisser, the sex wasn't really amazing. And since this coincided with Abbot stepping up his courting of me, I told Ben we needed to slow down and back away from the physical intimacy. We'll kiss a bit at the end of an evening; we've even spent a couple of nights together, just cuddling. And he is very sweet about not pressuring me for more. In some ways, I think the fact that I'm not sleeping with him is making him pursue me even more doggedly.

But for whatever reason, neither Abbot's sophistication and intelligence nor Ben's infectious energy seemed the right Friday night entertainment this week. Lucky for me, Paige had been available, and we made plans that involved Thai food and a showing of the documentary *March of the Penguins*, which I had never seen.

"Some more stuff came in today about the wedding," Paige says, handing me a folder.

"How bad?" I ask, riffling through a small stack of papers, mostly e-mails and letters.

"No death threats today, but we are starting to get some of the communication the PR people were worried about. Not the people who always hated us, but women who are feeling betrayed by the marriage."

My eye falls on the top page of the packet.

I read your books and heard you speak and turned down the only marriage proposal I ever got in my life. So now I live alone, and I was feeling pretty righteous about it, even though I have been very lonely, because I believed that I was being strong. I'm sure you and your new husband will be very happy, but I have to say I feel like you have slapped me in the face. Slapped all women in the face who trusted you that living single was the way to go. You won't have to live alone, but what about the rest of us? How can you still go on the

air week after week and tell us to be strong and independent while
all the while you're planning your wedding? How dare you? I hope
you are ashamed.

"Oh boy. That's not good," I say. "Are they all like this one?"

"Not all. Some are just mean-spirited. Some are calling you
guys frauds and saying that you just did it for the money. But they
are coming in at a rate that makes me think actual press isn't far
behind."

"Let's have another meeting with the PR people, see what we
need to do. Maybe we need to plant a couple of features with the
journalists that like us to be proactive."

"Should I get Jill in on this one?" Paige asks in a tone that im-
plies she thinks yes.

"Not yet." I shake my head. "I don't want her troubled by this.
Let's try to take care of it quietly. And keep this shit out of her
box, okay? She doesn't need to see it."

Paige shrugs. I know she disagrees with how I am handling
this, but I'm not in the mood. Luckily, the buzzer rings, and I go
downstairs to get the food.

The two of us are curled up on my couch, full of cucumber
salad and pad see eiw from Sai Mai, and about two-thirds of the
way through the movie, when my buzzer rings.

"I wonder who that could be?" I say.

"You don't suppose it's one of your boys?" asks Paige.

"They know better than to show up without calling first," I
say as I walk over to the intercom. "Hello?"

"Hey. It's Brant."

Oh, good Lord. What is he doing here? "Hey, come on up." I
press the buzzer to let him in.

Brant and I have had a reasonably amicable divorced life.
Brant fought the divorce pretty vehemently at first, but once he

realized I was determined, he was resolute about the whole thing. Since neither of us owned anything, including the apartment in which we were living, and since we didn't have any children, we decided to do it ourselves and not use lawyers. It went very smoothly, without any fighting, which I believe saved the friendship. He kept the apartment, and I moved in with Jill. He kept the cats, which had been his anyway. I was never much of a cat person. We split the joint assets right down the middle and divvied up the material possessions fairly easily. And while we both gave each other plenty of space in our lives, we do still have a presence. That is undeniable. But he can be something of a schmuck, and the longer we are divorced, the less time I spend invested in maintaining the friendship. He simply hasn't ever really grown up, and I'm less and less interested in hearing about computer crap and how angry the new Star Wars movies make him. He can be sweet, and he is always nice to me, so I'm hard-pressed to cut him out completely. However, he should know better than to arrive unexpectedly at ten P.M. on a Friday evening.

I go to the door and open it, waiting to see him appear around the stair bend. But the first head I see isn't Brant's. Instead, I'm faced with a tiny woman with large breasts, long, straight, auburn hair, and cat's-eye glasses. Two steps behind her is Brant, smiling at me.

She reaches the landing. "Hi Jodi, I'm Mallory," the redhead announces, thrusting a hand at me excitedly. Super.

"We were on our way back from dinner and noticed the lights on," says Brant. "Figured we'd stop by to say hello." What a dumb idea that was.

Mallory pushes past me into my apartment, while Brant greets me with a kiss on the cheek.

"Wow," says Mallory. "Some place you have here."

"Hey, Paige," says Brant, waving at her.

Paige raises one arched eyebrow. "Hey, Brant."

Brant walks into the living room and sits on a chair. Mallory is looking longingly down my hallway.

"It really is a beautiful apartment," she says.

I can't fucking believe it. "Would you like a tour?" I ask her.

Mallory is Brant's new girlfriend. They've been dating approximately two months and, according to Brant, have not slept together yet. I don't really relish being the recipient of Brant's dating information. But he doesn't have very many friends, and since my business has become a success, everybody focuses on how great it is for me to be single, so I sort of feel like I owe him one. After all, he's become even less than a footnote in my public persona, which he's taken in stride, and even though I make no attempt to hide the fact that I have been married, most people assume I've always been single.

Apparently, Mallory used to work for a PR firm here in Chicago before going back to law school. She's had some trouble passing the bar exam and is working as a paralegal for a large firm while studying to take her third stab at it. They met at a birthday party for a mutual friend, and Brant is very excited about the new relationship. So I feel like I have to be supportive. After all, just because he wasn't the right guy for me doesn't mean he should have to spend his life alone. Brant stays in the living room talking to Paige while I walk Mallory through my apartment.

Usually I'm very proud of my place. I designed it myself, painstakingly picking out furniture and fixtures. Every compliment usually goes straight to my ego. But this time is different; every kind word that Mallory offers makes me uncomfortable. She comments about the size of the apartment, the expansiveness of the rooms, the quality of the furniture and the artwork, the details in the kitchen and the bathrooms. I can just see her comparing it to my old apartment where Brant still lives. A third the size, in a lesser neighborhood, with hand-me-down furniture, and bookshelves made of planks and cement blocks. Not that Brant couldn't afford better. Computer network guys always manage to make a pretty decent living. Brant never cared about aesthetics the same way that I did. If he has a roof over his head that doesn't leak, heat in the winter and air-conditioning units in the summer, and the couch doesn't fall apart when he sits down, that is good enough for him. But five minutes with Mallory makes one thing patently clear. She is ambitious. And I can practically hear the running tally in her head as she fingers the cherry cabinets and stainless appliances in my kitchen. We return to the living room, where the movie is clearly paused on my flat-screen television. Paige makes pointed eye contact with me as Mallory kicks off her shoes and curls up in a corner of the couch. I guess we're having a real visit.

"So Brant tells me you're an expert on relationships," Mallory says.

"Well, I'd hardly say that," I say. "The work my sister and I do has less to do with relationships to other people and more to do with the relationship you have with yourself. It's about how to embrace your life no matter what your relationship status. And if you are in a relationship, how to not lose yourself. Our primary philosophy is that you can't be a good partner to somebody else unless you've clearly defined who you are and what you want in the future."

"Wow," Mallory says. "I'm just lucky you didn't have all that relationship expertise when you were married to Brant, or maybe I'd still be alone!"

Sweet Cap'n Crunch. What the hell is this bitch aiming at?

"Well," I say, "I couldn't ask for a better ex-husband. I'm probably one of the only people who can honestly say that getting married was one of the best things that ever happened to me, and getting divorced was one of the best things that ever happened to me."

Brant smiles. "See? That's why you're my favorite ex-wife."

"What's that I smell?" asks Mallory. "Vietnamese food?"

"No." says Paige. "We had Thai."

"Oh," says Mallory. "I was just wondering because I'm very knowledgeable about Vietnamese culture. I lived in Vietnam for over a year. I speak the language. Do you speak any languages?"

"French," I say.

I can't look Paige in the eye. I know she's got a look about her that says, *Who the hell is this woman?*

"Actually, there's a lot of French influence in Vietnam," Mallory begins. And then proceeds to regale us for a full twenty minutes about her life in Vietnam, her study of the culture, her desire to return with Brant and show him her village. She talks a blue streak. And she has one primary topic: herself. We hear the entire story of how she and Brant met. We hear how she was a clarinet player of such caliber that she was recruited by the army to play in one of their orchestras, and that was how she paid for college. We heard about her privileged Jewish upbringing in Savannah, Georgia, and her subsequent estrangement from her family. She flops around on my couch, posing and posturing and letting one bit of information about herself lead into the next in a manner that practically sucks all the oxygen from the room. Brant sits on the chair, this strange look of pride and nervousness on his face.

What the hell is he thinking? I look at the clock over the television. It's ten thirty. They've been here for a half hour. Mallory has not asked either Paige or me anything about ourselves. Nor has Brant participated in the conversation. It's been a monologue on the wonders of Mallory and her exciting and dramatic life. All I want is to find out if the mother penguins make it back to the daddy penguins in time to feed the baby penguins so that they don't die. Mallory pauses to take a breath, and I jump on the break to say, "That's very interesting. You know, I feel bad; I invited Paige over to watch this movie, and we still have a half hour left. You guys are welcome to stay and watch with us, but I think we'll get back to it."

"Oh no, we couldn't," says Mallory. "We have shul in the morning."

"Shul?" I ask Brant.

"Shul," he says.

"Orthodox shul? With the curtain down the middle and all the Hebrew?" I ask.

"Yes," he says.

"What's that mean?" asks Paige.

"Apparently, it means my ex-husband has converted to Judaism," I say.

Actually, Brant is technically Jewish. His mother was the granddaughter of a rabbi. But she gave it up when she married his Episcopalian father, and he was raised essentially without religion. He always referred to his family as humanist agnostic. He absorbed the Spingold traditions while we were married, celebrating the holidays with our usual focus on food and not so much on God. But still, it was more observant than he had been growing up. Looks like Mallory is having an even greater spiritual influence.

"Well then, don't let us keep you," I say, rising to walk Brant and Mallory to the door.

"It was very nice to meet you," she says, slipping back into her clogs.

"Likewise," I say. "I'm sure I'll see you again."

"Thanks, Jodi," says Brant. "I'll call you this week."

"Okay, talk to you later," I say.

I close the door and hear them heading down the stairs. Brant always walked like a herd of elephants, so I can hear his footsteps all the way down to the bottom. I go to the front window and see them exit the building and head out to Brant's beat-up car. I go back to the living room and sit down.

"What. The fuck. Was that?" says Paige.

"I have no idea." I sigh.

"Did you know they were coming?"

"Of course not. Don't you think I would've mentioned it?"

"So he just showed up here unannounced with his new girl-friend. At ten P.M. on a Friday night." Paige looks gobsmacked.

"It certainly looks that way."

"You realize she did everything except piss on your furniture," Paige says.

"Yes, I noticed that."

"And what the hell was that big long speech about her life and her fabulous years as the queen of Vietnam, and how smart she is and how everything has been difficult for her, but she's risen above it?" Paige is building a head of steam.

"I couldn't begin to tell you."

"And what was with needing to have a tour? And taking her shoes off and flopping all over your couch?" Paige takes a breath. "Jodi. I swear to God, if you would've come in to work on Monday and explained what just happened, word for word, without any embellishment, I would've thought you had lost your mind. I would've thought you were exaggerating to make the story funnier. I would've thought that you are perhaps feeling a little strange that your ex-husband has this new girlfriend in light of how hard he fought the divorce and vowed that you had ruined him for other women. In a million years I never would have believed you, had I not just seen it for myself."

"Yeah, I know. Kind of amazing, isn't it?"

"What the hell was he thinking, bringing her here?"

"You know Brant. He's a great guy deep down, but he's totally socially inept. I'm sure that he thinks it makes him look very cool and progressive to have such a comfortable, friendly relationship with his ex-wife. I think he was showing off for her. Announcing that we have the kind of relationship where he can just drop by because he saw the light on. That I would be welcoming and warm and want to meet her and be friendly and she could see us banter back and forth, and isn't it all one big happy family? But he and I are going to have to have a little talk about the point at which it is appropriate for me to meet the woman in his life. I mean, Jesus Christ. They're not even sleeping together yet! I don't need to be part of his weird seduction plan. I don't think it's too much to ask that he wait until a relationship is really serious before he drags me into it."

"And they're going to temple together?" Paige says.

"What can I do? He is who he is. If he thinks rediscovering his Judaism with her will be a good thing, who am I to argue?"

"You're being too good!" Paige gets up onto the couch and props herself on her knees in a pinup-girl pose with her chest thrust out. "Have you met me? I'm Mallory, and these are my breasts and I'm sort of a lawyer and I used to be in the army and I lived in Vietnam and I invented the Internet and I'm so wonderful and fabulous and I'm making your ex-husband become a rabbi since I wrote the Torah, and I've decided that he'll be my new husband and I hate that you have a nicer apartment than he does, and so I'm going to try to make you as uncomfortable as possible in your own living room."

We start to laugh. Paige rolls over onto her back, unbuttons two buttons on her shirt, throws her legs up into the air, and starts doing little ballet maneuvers with her feet. "And do you drink pop, because I invented pop. I'm the first one that ever thought you should put a flavor and sugar into sparkling water, and that makes me a genius and did I mention that I have lovely breasts and like for you to look at them? I notice that you have furniture in your house, and I think that's fascinating, as I build all my own furniture from scratch." Paige allows the front half of her body to slide off the couch so that she sprawls gracefully onto the floor. She strikes another provocative pose. "I think it's so cool that you're watching a movie. I starred in a movie, and I wrote it myself and I directed it and I produced it and I designed all of the sets, and I sewed all the costumes myself and it was going to be called *Me Me Me: A Retrospective* and shown at Cannes and Sundance, which was an idea I gave to Robert Redford a long time ago, but my funding fell through because nothing good ever really happens to me, I have to make it happen myself, and I come from a terrible family, my father beat me as a child with my mother's shoe, and she popped pills, and every bit of success that anyone in the world has ever had is somehow related directly to me and my perseverance, and even though I cannot pass the bar, I'm still the super-duper genius girl of the universe." Paige collapses, spent and out of breath.

By this time, the two of us are laughing so hard we're practically peeing in our pants. On the one hand, I feel a little bad making fun of Mallory, who was clearly so uncomfortable with the idea of my having a continuing relationship with Brant that she needed to stake out her territory. On the other hand, her behavior had been so appalling that I am hard-pressed not to feel justified in having a little amusement at their expense.

I open another bottle of wine, and Paige and I watch the last twenty-five minutes of the penguin movie. When it's over, she asks me what I think.

"Well, first of all," I say, "these are not Jewish birds."

Paige starts to laugh. "Why not?"

"Really? With the walking seventy miles over the ice, and no food and the wind chill a hundred and eighty below zero and the egg on the feet and it could fall and it could freeze and then there's a two-day window where the mother has to get back if she hasn't been eaten by a leopard seal. The poor father, four months in the cold, no food, and one little piece of phlegm to sustain the kid, if it actually hatches. I mean, honestly."

"But it's so heartwarming. And it's so sweet, their relationship with each other," says Paige. "And it's amazing, their ability to survive."

"Look, I'm trying not to be a cynic about this. And I'm trying to get past one of my least favorite things, which is the strange desire for filmmakers to anthropomorphize animals. I mean, ten minutes on the mating ritual as if it's some nightclub, and everybody's finding the perfect dance partner. I could even get past that. And Lord knows I would listen to Morgan Freeman read out of a phone book for two hours most happily. But I'm going to be honest here. I think these may be the second-dumbest creatures on the face of the earth."

"So which are the first?" Paige asks.

"That's easy," I say, "the goddamn filmmakers!"

She snorts wine through her nose.

She laughs, and I start laughing, too. I know that I'm taking out some of my frustration with Brant on the poor penguin movie.

We chitchat for a little while until Paige starts to yawn. "Sorry, Boss Lady," she says, "I'm fading."

"Me, too."

"I should probably go home."

I walk her to the door and then go back inside to clean up the wineglasses. Maybe I was wrong. Maybe there is a creature dumber than the penguins and the filmmakers. If there is, my ex-husband is definitely in the running.

We Are Family

Nothing is more important than family. Whether it is the family you were born into or the family you create around you with your good friends, that support system is essential to a good life. But two of the most difficult things to manage can be your family's involvement in your relationship and the relationship you have to your lover's family. There are all sorts of pitfalls to be aware of, and family can often be a significant factor in relationships going awry. If one partner's family doesn't approve, it can bring enough tension into the relationship as to be detrimental to good communication. And respecting the feelings, traditions, and needs of both families is the only way to keep your partnership strong.

—*From a speech delivered by Jodi Spingold at the Scottsdale JCC Jewish Book Club Girls' Night Out event, November 2006*

We have reserved the private dining suite at One Sixty Blue for dinner, to celebrate Jill and Hunter's engagement and meet his family. Aunt Ruth and Aunt Shirley and I got here a little early to ensure that everything is set up to our exacting standards. This meant that within ten minutes of our arrival, Aunt Ruth was delivering a lengthy set of directions to the waitstaff, and Aunt Shirley had weaseled her way into the kitchen to meet the chef. I'm taking a quiet moment in the sitting room attached to the dining area to gather my thoughts.

Jill hasn't said too much about Hunter's family. She's only met them twice before, and even then just for short weekends. All she has said is that they are pretty conservative, sort of B-list Philadelphia Main Line types, not gazillionaires, but definitely wealthy, and that they have always been very polite to her, if not necessarily what one would call warm. And the brother, some sort of Wall Street wunderkind, apparently spends most of his time disappearing to talk on the phone. Jill confessed earlier today to a small bit of apprehension about tonight, worried that Hunter's family will find the aunts a little too strange to like, and that the whole Jewish thing will rear its ugly head. Not to mention the fact that they have been known to give money to some of the very groups that are currently making our professional life hell. Hunter swears that they don't have a problem with the Jewish thing, especially since it isn't like he is planning on converting, but Jill thinks he is a little bit myopic about his family in general. He also thinks that when they attend the galas hosted by their cronies to fundraise for candidates who are pro-life that it isn't making a statement about their own feelings about the abortion issue; they are just supporting their friends. God bless Hunter. I hope he is as clueless about our many faults and foibles.

"Well, I think the meal is going to be lovely," Aunt Shirley says as she glides into the room to join me. "The chef was delightful, and the kitchen is immaculate and humming."

"They've never disappointed us before," I say, just as Aunt Ruth appears. She folds her long legs into one of the chairs.

"Well, are we ready to meet the in-laws?" Ruth asks.

"Ready as I'll ever be," says Shirley, shaking her head. "Why should I be so nervous?"

"It's just natural," I say, reaching over to pat her arm. "I'm nervous, too. These people are becoming family, and our family has always consisted of just us. Suddenly we have to take a whole other group of people into account."

"And they're WASPs," says Ruth bluntly.

"Ruthie, that's terrible!" Shirley flashes her eyes at her sister. "You must behave yourself. Tonight is very important to all of us."

"I didn't mean it in a derogatory way, simply a statement of fact. They are WASPs. We are not. There won't be a common footing. It's likely to be awkward in the beginning, and since we know that, it makes us nervous."

"Our common footing is Jill and Hunter," I jump in. "These people created Hunter, and we love him, right? So there is no reason to expect that we won't love his family."

"Of course, dear," Ruth says.

"You're so right," Shirley offers. "I'm sure they'll be lovely."

"For WASPs," adds Ruth.

"Well then, smile, because here they come," I say as the glass doors open and Jill leads her soon-to-be new family into the room.

"This is my sister, Jodi, and my aunts, Ruth and Shirley." Jill points to us each in turn. "Everyone, this is Hunter's father, Cleveland." Jill gestures to a tall, ruddy-faced man with oddly greenish blond hair and broad shoulders.

"Everyone calls me Cleve," he says, stepping forward to shake hands.

"And this is my mother, Grace." Hunter escorts his mother by the elbow. She has a helmet of perfectly frosted hair, a slim figure, and the placid lack of expression that seems to come with BOTOX or Xanax or both. She offers her hand to me first, which is ice cold. I instinctively grasp it in both of my hands, if nothing else to warm it up.

"It's lovely to meet you, Mrs. Charles," I say.

"Please, do call me Grace," she says in a breathy, nasal voice that makes me wonder if the perfectly upturned button nose is original or a reproduction.

"And this is Hunter's brother, Stallworth. But everyone calls him Worth." Jill points to a slightly taller version of Hunter, but instead of Hunter's golden hazel eyes, Worth's are the piercing ice-blue of those dogsled dogs. I step forward with my hand extended, but he raises one finger at me and reaches inside his jacket pocket for his phone, which he flips open with one hand as he sidles back out the door.

Cleve laughs. "That's my boy! Something always cooking. You'll have to excuse him, ladies. He means no disrespect; he's just an important fellow with pressing business obligations is all."

Aunt Ruth snorts softly, and Aunt Shirley shoots her a look that expresses her extreme displeasure. A waiter arrives with a tray of champagne flutes and hands them around. Worth reenters the room.

"So sorry, everyone. I have a deal on the line that is sort of tenuous at the moment. But I've informed my assistant not to forward any more calls until after dinner, so hopefully we won't be disturbed again." He walks around the room, kissing first Aunt Ruth, then Shirley, then me. The waiter hands him a glass of champagne.

"I'd like to propose a toast," he says. "To my little brother and soon-to-be sister. There is nothing nobler or more admirable than when two people who see eye to eye keep house as man and wife, confounding their enemies and delighting their friends. Homer."

"Hear, hear!" says Cleve.

"In life you are sometimes the chicken in the henhouse, and sometimes the chicken in the soup. May you never both be in the soup on the same day. Bubbe Spingold," Shirley says. Cleve and Grace raise their glasses, puzzled looks on their faces, and sip quietly.

The waiter comes back to let us know that we can repair to the dining room, and we file out of the sitting room quietly and take our seats at the large, round table. The waiter tops off our champagne glasses. Hunter and his family are on one side of the table and the four of us on the other. I'm not the only one who notices this.

"Well, this is no way to get to know one another," Ruth says. "Everyone stand up again."

Grace and Cleve peer sidelong at one another.

"Come on, up!" Ruth insists. We all rise obediently.

"Now, Hunter, you move to the other side of Jill."

He walks around to where Aunt Shirley is sitting.

"Shirley, you there, next to Worth."

She heads over.

"Cleve, you here, next to me, then Jodi, then Grace. Now, sit!"

We all look around. She has alternated Spingold/Charles all the way around the table. Doesn't matter which way one turns, there are in-laws everywhere.

"How smart, Ruthie, so much better for us all to get to know one another." Aunt Shirley beams.

Two new servers enter the room with our original waiter and begin to pass out small plates.

"An *amuse-bouche* from the chef, chilled artichoke soup with tuna tartare crouton," the headwaiter announces, and the three of them disappear. We all pick up our spoons and begin to eat.

⅋

"So, we'd love to talk a little about the wedding, if that's all right with you kids," Cleve says, as the desserts begin to arrive.

"Of course, Dad," Hunter says.

"Well, first off, we'd like to pay for half."

Aunt Shirley purses her lips together. Aunt Ruth pats the corner of her mouth with her napkin and clears her throat.

"That is a very generous offer, Cleve," Aunt Ruth says.

"However, Shirley and I are very committed to covering the costs of this wedding. It is something we were thrilled to do for Jodi when she married, and something we are thrilled to be in a position to do for Jill. Thank you very much for the thought; however, we will have to decline."

"Well, I'm sure you ladies have things under control, but from all accounts, Jodi's wedding was a small affair, and you all have no additional family to speak of. What with the size of our family and personal obligations, it just wouldn't feel right for you to shoulder that burden," Cleve presses on. He clearly didn't anticipate that his money wouldn't be wanted.

"Um, Dad . . ." Hunter is spurred into action by Jill's elbow. And from experience, it is quite an elbow. Pointed almost to the brink of being sharpened and with a homing device for the sensitive area between ribs.

"Now, son, no need to thank us; your mother and I are very happy to do this for you both."

"No, Dad, I mean, Jill and I aren't looking to do a really big wedding. We're keeping the guest list really tight. Probably under a hundred people."

Cleve looks at Hunter. Then he looks at Grace. He clears his throat.

"Son, I'm saying there's no need for that now. We're happy to cover the costs. You don't need to limit yourselves anymore. Under a hundred people, nonsense! Our list alone is nearly two hundred." Cleve says this as if he is making a proclamation. I can't stand it any longer.

"Cleve, I think what Hunter is trying to say is that he and Jill don't want a big wedding. It isn't a function of cost; it is a function of personal taste and desire. They prefer the idea of a small, intimate gathering of their closest friends and relatives." I've adopted the same tone of voice I have heard my friends with kids use when explaining to their toddler that the peanut butter and jelly sandwich doesn't belong in the DVD player.

"But, darling, think of all of our friends and your father's business associates. All of them have invited your father and me to the weddings of their children. How will it look?" Grace says. It is the longest sentence she has uttered all evening.

"It will look like you are honoring the wishes of your son and his bride," Aunt Shirley says. "I'm sure everyone will understand that."

Cleve places his large hands on the table. "Weddings are a big deal where we come from. They make a statement. Who is invited is important. Now, you gals may not have any sense of what the protocol is on such matters, what with your little home projects and such. But in the world of real business, there are obligations." He turns to Jill. "Now, surely you had some dreams of being a bride at a big, fancy wedding once upon a time. We are going to make that dream come true."

Uh-oh. Here it comes. I see Jill's spine straighten, making her instantly look six inches taller. Her jaw works subtly, which means that she is literally chewing on the words she wants to use. Mr. Cleveland Charles has no idea that what he just said is going to be his undoing.

Jill meets Cleve's eyes. "My dreams, to be clear, were to find a wonderful, kind, loving man with whom to spend my life. To be a wife, not a bride. And now that I've found him, my dream is to gather the people around us who know us well and love us deeply, and to solemnize our union in the center of that love. I find it insulting that you assume that every woman wants some huge, luxurious affair for her wedding. Jodi and I often find in our business that the women who dream of lavish weddings are the ones who want to get married, not the ones who want to be married. I'm sorry you feel that it will be a slight to your colleagues to not invite them to the wedding; however, Hunter and I have agreed between us what the day will be, and that isn't up for debate. Hunter has created a list that includes the immediate family, selected extended family members, and family friends with whom he feels close. I have done the same. Neither of us is inviting any of our business associates, save the ones with whom we socialize separate from work-related occasions. You may notice we have not solicited a list from you of any size, since we have created the entire invitation list on our own. My aunts can confirm that we didn't ask for their input either where that was concerned."

"That's true, they haven't," Ruth says in a clipped, low voice.

"Well, why would they? It isn't our wedding," Shirley adds.

"But we've already told everyone!" Cleve sputters.

"I announced it at the last meeting of the DAR!" Grace is practically whimpering.

"The what?" Aunt Shirley asks.

"Daughters of the American Revolution," says Worth, clearly amused at the dramatic proceedings. "I was thinking of sending out a memo to everyone at the New York Stock Exchange." I kind of like him for that. But Jill is seething, and the aunts are building a case to hate these people, and Hunter has been cowed speechless. Time to step in.

"Okay, let's all take a deep breath for just a moment," I start. "Now, obviously we have a conflict, but we're all rational adults, and I am sure there is a compromise to be made here."

"Well, honestly, Jill here seems very inflexible . . ." Cleve starts. "Not that I'm surprised, your whole little enterprise seems to be about undermining marriage in general. No wonder you want to downplay the wedding."

"Dad . . ." Hunter says in the defeated tone of a child who has long given up trying to get a parent to not embarrass him.

"I'm sorry you feel that way about me and about my business,"

Jill says through clenched teeth. "But I know who I am and what I believe, and I'm afraid I won't be bullied on this."

"Cleve, Jill, please. Bear with me." I turn to Jill and place my right finger on my right temple. This is our secret sign to just follow the other person's lead. We have used it since high school for everything from getting out of a boring party to negotiating a major business contract. "Jill, have you and Hunter made final plans about your honeymoon as of yet?"

"No, we thought we would wait until after the wedding to plan the trip. We are just going to get a suite somewhere in town for a couple of nights after the wedding, and then probably go somewhere later in the summer or early fall."

"Good. Good idea. Now, the weekend after the wedding is Memorial Day weekend. I seem to remember that last year, Jill attended a wonderful barbecue at your home on that holiday." It was her first meeting with Hunter's family, and there were so many other guests and party preparations that she barely got to speak with them at all over the weekend.

"Yes," Cleve says through gritted teeth. "We've been hosting that party annually for over thirty-five years."

"I assume this year will be no different."

"Of course. It's a tradition," Grace says, as if not having the party would be the end of democracy.

"Hunter, Jill, would the two of you be available to attend that event again this year?" I nod at Jill, who immediately sees where I'm headed.

"Of course," she says. Then she turns to Cleve and says demurely, "It was a wonderful weekend and a fantastic party."

His nostrils flare, but he stays silent.

I continue on my way. "Weddings are hard. They are at once very personal and very public. Everyone has different expectations and needs. But I think we can use the geography of the situation and the timing of the wedding to our advantage. Jill and Hunter will have their wedding as they want it here, and the rest of us will attend with our hearts full of joy and send them into their life together with all the love we can bring into that room." I see both Cleve and Grace tense, so I speed into the next part of my plan. "But the following weekend the five of us will come out to attend your annual Memorial Day party, which can serve as a sort of East Coast wedding reception for Jill and Hunter. All of the people who might be slighted by not being invited here will be invited there. They will get to meet Jill and her small family. You can say that the decision was made to save everyone the trip to Chicago, and even claim that we were too proud to accept financial assistance but couldn't afford a larger event, whatever you need to do to save face on your end."

There is a huge silence. And to my great shock, Grace speaks first.

"Would I get to plan the party as a real reception?" she asks me.

Jill speaks up. "Of course, Grace. It can be anything you want it to be."

"Would you help me make the decisions, food and such?" Grace turns to Jill.

"I'd love that," Jill says, smiling.

"Well, um, I . . ." Cleve seems somehow deflated.

"Oh relax, Cleve. Your lovely wife is going to put together a bash that will make you look like the grand fucking Poo-Bah of Pennsylvania. All your cronies will be thrilled," Ruth says.

There is a brief pause, and then Cleve bursts into a large, deep-throated laugh.

"Grand fucking Poo-Bah," he repeats.

Aunt Shirley waves over a waiter who is passing by the glass doors. He enters the room and walks around to her chair. "Dear, please bring over a bottle of single malt whiskey and eight glasses, would you?" The waiter nods and leaves again.

"Son, I've got to hand it to you," Cleve says, turning to Hunter. "You've got yourself a smart, strong woman there. No hard feelings, right, Jill?"

Jill smiles her winningest smile. "None here if you have none."

Cleve shrugs. "I'm beginning to see why this business of yours is so successful. The two of you are some team. Grace, we never had a chance!"

The whiskey arrives, glasses are distributed, raised, and drunk. Hunter leaves to take his family back to their hotel, with kisses all around except for Worth, who got back on the phone the moment the bill was paid and waves to us while doing whatever business one can do at ten P.M. on a Saturday night. Aunt Ruth's midnight blue Mercedes arrives from the valet, and we all pile in.

"Jodi, you saved the day," Aunt Shirley says, buckling her seat belt.

"You sure did. I thought I was going to have to kill my future in-laws," Jill says. "Thank God they live so far away. Can you imagine having to put up with that all the time?"

"I'm sure they feel the same about us," Ruth says, deftly guiding the car through traffic. "Us little ladies with our *home projects*." Her voice oozes contempt. "What an ass."

"Well, don't forget how disappointed the women of the DAR are going to be!" Aunt Shirley says.

We all start to laugh.

"Oh, God, they are going to be the grandparents of my children!" Jill says in mock horror.

"Wait till they want to throw your first daughter a coming-out cotillion!" I say.

"Lord help me." Jill is laughing again, and I'm relieved that she isn't retaining too much anger. "How on earth did Hunter end up so normal?"

"I'm assuming intelligence and fortitude," Aunt Ruth says. "That poor boy."

"Well, at least the ice is broken!" I say.

"Yep. Almost an iceberg's worth!" Aunt Shirley says.

Ruth pulls up in front of the house. "All right, I have a late appointment, so I'm heading right out." Trust Aunt Ruth to line up an eleven P.M. date.

"Have a good time, Ruthie," Aunt Shirley says, getting out of the car.

"Thanks for all your support tonight, and for the wedding in general." Jill kisses her on the cheek.

"You're welcome, honey."

I lean over the seat and kiss her as well. "Have fun!"

"I will. Good night." Aunt Ruth pulls back out and heads off to her rendezvous. The three of us climb the stairs to the front door, drained and very glad to be home.

"Wanna come down and keep me company till Hunter gets back?" Jill asks me on our way upstairs.

"I'll be there as soon as I get in my pajamas."

I head upstairs and mull over the evening as I undress and take my makeup off. We have, for our family pleasure, one pompous blowhard of a father, a shrinking violet socialite of a mother, and a supercilious ass of a brother. What a hat trick.

I jump into a set of gray flannel pajamas, slip into some cushy socks, and head downstairs. Jill is in her bedroom, hanging up her outfit from the evening. She is so good about stuff like that, often getting three wears out of a piece of clothing before it needs dry cleaning. I can't seem to prevent myself from leaving everything in a pile on the floor next to the hamper. Every time I have a beau coming over, I'm frantically shoving clothes and towels under the bed and stacks of accumulated crap into the guest room for hiding. I'm a secret slob and always envious of Jill's natural organization and neatness.

"So, that was some dinner . . ." I start.

Jill closes the closet door and flops on the bed next to me. "Why do I feel like this is just the first of many such negotiations?" she says, pouting.

I reach over and pat her hair. "Because you know people, and people are what they are. And these people are used to things being done in a certain way, and you are very unlikely to want to do things in that way. But I don't think they're malicious, just a little thick. You'll be fine."

Jill lays her arm across my lap for me to tickle, like she used to do when she was little. I run the very tips of my fingers and my fingernails all over her forearm, and she smiles. "Thank God they didn't bring it up last night. I don't know what I would have done without you there to moderate!"

"You would have been fine. You will be fine. Hunter is an amazing guy, and he loves you just the way you are. He doesn't want you to be the person his parents would have dreamed of or he would have chosen a girl like that. Just remember that."

"Gosh," she says in mock deference. "You should write a book or something."

I pinch her arm. "Bitch. See if I pull your ass out of the fire next time."

"You know I love you oodles and squinches."

"And I love you, too. Even if you are foisting the world's most irritating in-laws upon me."

"Oh, no, you don't," she says, sitting up. "Not after all those visits with Brant's crazy family."

Brant's family had an aversion to hotels and would descend upon us for a week at a time from California. If it was just his folks, it was okay, since we had a guest room. And if only one of his siblings came, then we had a pull-out couch. But if his sister and his brother and his sister-in-law all decided to meet in Chicago for a vacation, Jill had to take the overflow.

"At least they don't expect to stay with you," I say.

"Or with you, for that matter." Jill laughs. "And I win in the husband category for sure."

"That you do. Poor Brant."

"Poor Jill! All those mind-numbing evenings of technical discussions about computers."

"Brant couldn't help his own strangeness. He was still the most normal person in that family."

"This is not the most rousing recommendation I ever heard," she says.

"Hey, if it weren't for Brant, we wouldn't be where we are, so let's at least give him some credit."

She tilts her head. "Jesus, you're right. I never thought about it that way. I wonder what we'd be doing if you hadn't married a mouth-breathing Trekkie!"

I pounce on her and pin her arms. "Say Shruth!"

"Never."

I lean over and wiggle my hair over her face.

"Okay, okay. Shruth! *Shruth!*" she yells, and I roll back off her. *Shruth* is our alternative to *uncle*. We never had an uncle, so it never seemed to make sense, and we didn't want to discriminate between the aunts, so we blended their names instead.

"You ever think about getting married again?" she asks when we catch our breath. "Now that you know what not to do?"

I think about it for a second before answering. "I don't know. I mean, I'd like to think that someday I might find someone I would trust to be a good life partner. But I'm never going to settle ever again, not for anything, and it's a pretty tall order. I think that's why I like dating more than one guy at a time. I can pick and choose what I need from someone and assemble a sort of Frankenstein man out of the best parts of them."

"But aren't you ever tempted to just stick with one and try to move forward?"

"Not yet. I suppose if I meet the right guy, then I will. But in the meantime, I get everything I want and need without being responsible for anyone else."

"Not everything," she says.

"What am I missing? Look at Ben and Abbot. Abbot is urbane, sophisticated, perfect in social situations, owns two tuxedos, and makes me feel like a princess. Ben is crazy and funny and takes me on adventures. Abbot is pretty sage about advice and is a good guy to debate things with. Ben is handy and fixes stuff and does the heavy lifting. Abbot is great in bed, and Ben doesn't seem to mind that I won't sleep with him."

"And who says 'I love you' last thing before you go to bed?"

"You do. That's enough for now."

"And I do love you, and you know it doesn't matter to me one bit if you ever get married again. I just don't want you to feel like you can't consider it just because you've taken a sabbatical from serious commitment."

"I know. And I appreciate it. And trust me, if someone comes along who seems like he wouldn't be settling, I'll take the plunge again."

"I have dreamt about this so often," a husky voice comes from the doorway. We look up to find Hunter grinning lasciviously at us. "Two women at once, and sisters, no less." He takes a flying leap and lands on the bed between us. "Am I interrupting serious girl talk?" He kisses Jill's hip and tickles my knee at the same time.

I get up off the bed and rumple his eminently rumpleable hair. "Not at all. I was just headed up to bed."

"You don't have to leave on my account, sis," he says.

"Not at all," I say.

"Hey, thanks for handling my family tonight. That was a great idea about the party out East. You saved our wedding day," he says.

"Anytime," I say.

"I know they're a little weird and pompous and Republican, but I've given up on trying to change them. And they did say how much they were impressed by all of you in the car."

Interesting. They mentioned being impressed by us. Not liking us, but being impressed. Very different things. "We were impressed by them as well. Brunch still on for tomorrow at the Bongo Room?" I ask.

"Yep. Eleven o'clock," he says.

"Okay. Good night, little brother. Good night, Moose Face," I say.

"Good night, Butthead," Jill says.

"Good night, Possum Toes," Hunter says.

Jill and I both look at him.

"What? I need a good-night insult, too. No good?"

"Keep working," I say and leave them to the rest of their evening.

When I get upstairs, I have a message from Abbot. I call him back, and when he suggests that he might be in a position to be at my beck and call for the remains of the evening, I tell him to come on over, and I go to unlock the back door. We might not be in love, but his good night is still pretty sweet.

The Holy Trinity

Don't get in a people rut. Bringing new people into your life can be exhilarating and helps keeps your interpersonal skills honed. There is no trick to maintaining relationships with the friends and family and colleagues you've known for years. But being open to new people can expand your interests and make you a well-rounded individual. Don't be afraid to strike up conversation in an exercise class or at the bookstore. Don't be afraid to invite someone to share your table at Starbucks. If your flight gets delayed, look around for someone reading a book by an author you like, and introduce yourself. You never know who you might meet in the strangest of circumstances. At the very least you can have some interesting conversations, and you just might find a new friend or lover in the process.

—*From* The Thirty Commandments *by Jill and Jodi Spingold*

I pull my car into the parking lot at Dominick's. It's a 1957 Plymouth Fury in cherry red, which I bought for myself when the first book hit the *New York Times* bestseller list. I couldn't believe how reasonably priced it was, considering. It had been a show car, so it had fewer than 50,000 miles on it and was in pristine condition. Since Jill drives us to work most days in her very sensible BMW sedan, I get to tool around in Stella only evenings and weekends, which helps ensure she keeps purring. And I love how unexpected she is on Chicago streets; I always get honks and waves. I get out, lock the door, and run through the brisk winds into the brightly lit store. I'm mentally praying, *Please let them have them. Please let them have them.* This is my fourth stop of the evening, looking for the final ingredient for tomorrow's Thanksgiving feast. And so far, every place I go, the stores are out of mini marshmallows. I'm a decent cook, nothing spectacular, but Aunt Shirley has trained both Jill and me in the basic culinary arts.

Lord knows that for tomorrow, all the major food groups are being covered by Shirley. But the one thing I do better than almost anybody is sweet potato casserole with marshmallow topping. I remember being maybe three or four the first time I made it with my mom. She let me arrange the mini marshmallows all over the top. I don't have many clear memories of my parents, but Thanksgiving was always our family's favorite holiday. Always back at the aunts' house, and the casserole the only thing my mom was allowed to bring. And the key to the recipe is that the marshmallows have to be the mini kind. The normal-sized ones add too much sweet goo. The sweet potato casserole is my only responsibility for tomorrow, and Jill will plant her foot in my butt if it doesn't have the mini marshmallows on top.

I run down the baking aisle toward the marshmallows, and I notice there is a man standing right in front of them. He reaches for a bag. I peer over his shoulder. He is taking the last bag of mini marshmallows. Sweet Charlie the Tuna.

"Oh crap," I say.

"Pardon me?" he asks.

"I'm sorry. You just took the last bag of mini marshmallows. I've been looking for them all over town." *You bastard!* I'm mentally shaking a fist at him.

"Are you trying to guilt me out of my mini marshmallows?" He smirks at me.

"Wouldn't dream of it," I say. "I assume that you, like me,

have only one sacred Thanksgiving memory of your dead mother that involves putting mini marshmallows on the sweet potato casserole."

He laughs. "Well then, I'm glad there's no guilt."

"Sorry," I say. "That was really unforgivably bitchy of me. It's been a long day."

"No worries," he replies. "Thanksgiving is stressful."

"Sweet potatoes are hard," I agree.

"Math is hard," he says.

"Heidegger is hard."

"You win."

"I didn't realize we were in competition." He's quick, this one.

"Tell you what. I'll make you a deal," he says very seriously.

"Yeah? What's that?"

"I'll let you have the last bag of mini marshmallows, but you have to buy me a drink."

I take a closer look at him. He's probably fortyish, thick, dark hair, hazel eyes, strong jaw. Definitely cute. An interesting scar on his chin. Not overly tall, maybe five ten or five eleven. Can't tell much about the bod—he's sporting a thick, puffy jacket—but the legs look good in faded jeans.

"Buy you a drink, huh?" I say.

"Yep."

"When?"

"Right now."

I try to look sweet and needy. "I really ought to go home and finish the sweet potato casserole." If I'm going to have a drink with this new prospect, I'd like to be a lot cuter than I am at the moment. I'm fine in my long trench coat, but underneath is a not-so-pristine U of C sweatshirt and a pair of black leggings. Not exactly dishy.

He waggles the bag at me. "That's going to be kind of hard without these, isn't it?"

"You have a point," I say.

"Do it for your sainted mother," he continues. "I'm pretty sure she'd approve. For the sake of Thanksgiving, and all."

"Well, if you put it like that. I'm Jodi."

"Connor." He puts out his hand. "Nice to meet you, Jodi."

"Where should we go?" I ask.

"There's a little neighborhood tavern not far from here. Quenchers. Do you know it?"

"Fullerton and Western?"

"Exactly."

"I'll meet you there." I hold my hand out for the bag. He shakes his head at me.

"Sorry," he says. "I'll have to hold them hostage. I wouldn't want you running off on me."

"Of course not."

"Glad to hear it."

"Did you have more shopping you need to do?" I ask.

"Nope. We can go." I follow him to the front checkout and ask if he will let me pay for the marshmallows.

"You can get the beer, but the marshmallows are on me."

We step outside, and he says, "I'll see you in a few minutes, Jodi."

"I'll meet you there." I walk over to my car and get in. I'm definitely intrigued. I've never been picked up in a grocery store before. I like his brash confidence, the look in his eyes that seemed very sure that I would say yes to the drink. I drive the few blocks to Quenchers, a tiny little place known for having over a hundred different types of beer. By the time I find parking and head inside, he is already there, marshmallows sitting on the bar next to him.

"Can I buy you a drink?" I ask.

"Absolutely," he says.

"I was talking to the marshmallows."

He laughs. It's a nice sound, kind of low and baritone and genuine, not like he's laughing to impress me or to make me feel good, but because he actually finds me amusing. I have a deep appreciation for boys that find me amusing.

He orders some obscure Belgian brew, and I ask for the same. We clink beer mugs and start to talk. Connor Duncan is a commercial real estate developer. The second-oldest of six boys in his Irish Catholic family. He started his career in real estate by flipping houses with three friends from college. The four of them would buy a run-down place, rehab it themselves, and sell it as quickly as possible. Their first commercial venture happened when they bought an old former bakery on the northwest side and converted it into office space, with retail stores on the first floor. One of the original guys eventually moved to the East Coast to be close to his family. But the other two and Connor continue to grow and develop their business. They now specialize in the development and management of commercial property, and the occasional residential project.

I always like to ask a lot of questions right in the beginning when I meet someone new. One of the unexpected hazards of making your living in the way that I do is that the minute people find out what your job is, they have a million questions. Everybody wants to know how hard it is to write a book, if you have met famous people, how the radio show works. It's always better to get as much information about them and be as interested in them as possible in the beginning so that you have some frame of reference to go back to, to make sure that the conversation is evenhanded. But eventually, my digging for information on Connor leads him to retaliate.

"That's enough about me. I didn't ask you to buy me a drink so that I could sit here letting it get warm while I talk about myself. What about you? Do you make your living putting mini marshmallows on top of sweet potato casseroles?"

"No. I make my living telling other people how to live their lives."

"Nice. Is that a lucrative business?" he asks.

"Being bossy is surprisingly financially rewarding."

"So, what? Do people just call you up and say, 'Tell me how to live my life'?" he asks.

I laugh. "Only on Thursdays from noon to two."

He looks puzzled. "Seriously?"

"Seriously."

"That's a nice job, only two hours a week."

"No, that's not the whole job. That's just when people call me."

"And how do you spend the rest of your time?" he asks.

"I'm sorry. I'm not trying to be coy. My work is a little complicated. I have a partnership with my younger sister, Jill. She and I write books about getting the most out of your life as a single woman. We have a call-in radio show on Thursdays on satellite radio."

"Aha! From noon to two."

"Exactly."

"So you and your sister write these books and give people advice on the radio and what else?"

"We do some speaking engagements, sometimes we serve as experts on television shows. And there is some merchandising involved."

"Sounds like a booming business."

I'm always nervous talking about our success. I mean, for people who grew up middle class, we're probably considered wealthy.

But we work very hard, and the business is expensive to run. We both take home good salaries, but it isn't millions. We put a lot of money right back into the business, believing that it is far more important to pay great people at the top of the industry scale and know that they are working with us rather than suck out all the profits for our own personal gain.

"We're doing all right," I say.

"Good for you. Is it difficult?"

"What's that?"

"Working with your sister."

"That's the easy part."

"Really? I love my brothers and all, but we'd kill each other if we had to work together."

"I think it's different for me and Jill. After our folks died, we really had to stick together. We grew up relying completely on each other. We've always had each other's back, and we've always been best friends; the company just became the logical offshoot of who we are together."

"It must be nice. So, you lost both your parents, not just your mother."

"Car crash."

"How old were you?"

"I was six; Jill was four."

He reaches over and covers my hand with his hand. It's strong and slightly roughened. He squeezes. "I'm very, very sorry."

For some reason, this moves me. I look him in the eye. "Thank you."

We continue to talk, and several minutes pass before I realize he has not let go of my hand. I catch a glimpse of my watch and realize it's after nine.

"I really should head home to make that casserole," I say.

"I suppose I'd better let you go. But I'd really like to see you again."

"I'd like that," I say.

He takes out his cell phone. "J-O-D-I. What's your number?"

"It's 773-555-5634."

"Your number is 555-Jodi?"

I laugh. "No one ever catches that."

"Well, I'm not a savant. But I did just have to punch in those numbers to get your name loaded into my phone."

"You're a sharp one," I say, and he smiles. His top teeth are straight, but the lower ones are crooked. I've seen the phenomenon before: parents without a lot of money, and with a lot of children in need of braces. Sometimes they have to do everybody's top teeth and leave the bottom ones to nature.

"I'll call you on Friday. See how the casserole worked out."

"Okay. I'll look forward to that."

He leans over and gently kisses my cheek. "It was very nice to meet you. Have a happy Thanksgiving, Jodi Spingold."

"It was nice to meet you, too. Happy Thanksgiving, Connor Duncan."

My head is all swirly. I can tell my cheeks are flushed. I put on my coat and leave the bar. I get to my car, rev her up, and drive off toward home in a blissful fog. I'm pulling into the garage before I realize that I never got the damn marshmallows from him. I smack my forehead on the steering wheel. Just then, my phone rings.

"Hello?"

"You forgot your marshmallows."

I start to laugh. "So I did."

"Tell me where you are. I'll bring them to you."

I pause and think about it. He seems like a great guy. I'm certainly looking forward to talking to him again. And even looking forward to him maybe taking me out. But I'm not quite ready for him to know where I live. I think fast. "You know the Starbucks at Fullerton and California?"

"Sure."

"It's right in the middle between where you are and where I am. I'll meet you there."

"Okay."

I click off the phone, start the car, pull back out of the garage, and head east.

I pick up the phone and dial downstairs to Jill's.

"Hey," she says, "'sup?"

"Marshmallow time."

"Don't start without me. I'll be right there!" she says and hangs up the phone.

Within seconds I can hear her stomping up the stairs. My door opens, and she wails down the hallway, "Don't do it yet, don't do it yet!" She flies into my kitchen, breathless.

"I haven't started. I never start without you. You know that."

"I know, I'm just excited. How come so late? I was expecting your call ages ago."

"I got a little caught up with the marshmallows."

"Why?" she asks.

"I went to four different places before I found them, and once I did find them, they required a little finagling."

"Interesting. Finagling for marshmallows. More details, please."

"I finally found them at Dominick's. In the hands of the sinister gentleman who was attempting to purchase the final bag. I had to use my feminine wiles to get them away from him."

She nods. "I see, did you use whining, crying, or flirting?" she asks.

"Whining and flirting. And the dead mom guilt trip."

"Nice," she says. "Extra points for the combo with the guilt trip. And the gentleman was swayed, clearly."

"Well, I also had to ply him with alcohol."

"Really, a drink?" she asks.

"He was holding the marshmallows hostage."

"You're all smiley. This must've been a nice guy."

"Yeah, actually he was, er, is."

"Where did you go for a drink?"

"Quenchers."

"I've always wondered about the place. Is it any good?"

"It's small but nice. They have like a hundred different types of beer."

"And he was nice. What's his name?"

"Connor. Connor Duncan. Yeah, very nice. Smart, good sense of humor, cute. I liked him."

"You going to see him again?"

"I think so."

"How old is he?

"I think thirty-eight or thirty-nine, forty tops."

"Aha! Right in the middle." She laughs.

"What does that mean?" I ask.

"Well," she says. "You already got the older guy and the younger guy; this one is in the middle." Then she pauses and grins. "The Father, the Son, and the Holy Ghost.

"Are you saying that I'm dating the Holy Trinity?"

"I'm not saying anything. But you have to admit, it kind of works."

"Well, we had one beer. We will have to see if he calls before we add him officially to my roster. Now, let's get these marshmallows done."

It's nearly eleven by the time Jill and I stop messing around in the kitchen. We grab a couple of beers out of my refrigerator and head into my living room.

"I'm glad we didn't lose you for Thanksgiving this year," I say. "I know you and Hunter are probably going to have to do that one year here, one year there thing, but I'm glad it hasn't started yet."

"Actually," she says, "Hunter and I made a deal. Since Thanksgiving is our holiday, I get to always be here. They can always have us for Christmas. Hunter may occasionally need to go to his folks' place for Thanksgiving, but I'm not required to go with."

"Really? That doesn't bother him?"

"Well, think about it, we don't celebrate Christmas, and it's a big deal for his family. So, actually, I think he feels like he's getting away with something, guaranteeing our presence with his family celebrations every year at Christmas."

"Very sneaky. Let me guess. They get Easter, and we get Passover."

She giggles. "You betcha!"

"Very diplomatic of you. How many of these lifestyle negotiations have you guys been through?"

"Not too many," she says. "He agreed to move in with me here for now, provided I'm willing to discuss a bigger place if we end up having more than one child. We got the holiday issue squared away. We agreed to give equal time and energy to both religions and then let the kid or kids decide what they want to be when they grow up. And we agreed that we could both do as much travel and work-related weird hours as necessary for the time being, with the understanding that once we start a family, we both have to make an equal commitment to a more rational lifestyle."

"That sounds like about all of them. I'm glad he's going to move in here, though. I hate to think about you not being right downstairs."

"No more than I hate to think about you not being right upstairs. But Jodi . . ." She gets a very serious look on her face. "You and I are both going to have to be very diligent about making sure that he isn't overwhelmed. He loves you, and he loves the aunts, but I don't think he has a genuine concept of how casual we all are about bopping in and out of each other's houses and lives. One too many three A.M. 'I have to watch *Sixteen Candles* right now' phone calls, and he might kill me."

"Hunter doesn't get the need to watch *Sixteen Candles* at three in the morning? Ever?" Seems suspicious to me.

"*Top Gun*, maybe. But not *Sixteen Candles*."

"I'll try to only do it when he's traveling for business. How's that?"

"Perfect," she says.

"When is he going to move in?"

"We figure, after the first of the year. Too insane right now with all the holidays."

"I think that's great timing," I say.

"I know. And then the wedding on May nineteen, the party out East the following weekend, and if the TV thing goes through, we'll start production next summer. Holy moly. We are in for it this year, huh?" She makes a face.

"The TV thing still scares me. But I know Krista and Paige both really want us to do it." Krista is our agent. She's based in New York, so we rarely see her, but she's worked very hard to ensure that if we move forward on creating a television show, that Jill and I have the protections that we need to maintain the integrity of our message. And to guarantee that we would film in Chicago.

"I know. It scares me, too, but in that good, excited way. I mean, think about it; it could be really cool."

"Or it could be really awful."

"Hey, I'm usually the pessimist; you're the one who thinks we can do anything!" She looks puzzled.

"I know, I just, I know that it's possible that some things will change. Once you're married, I mean. I didn't want to take for granted that you would still want to pursue the television deal."

"I'm just getting married. I'm not moving to Stepford."

"Very funny. I just meant that we might want to push the dates forward a bit. Give you a chance to be a newlywed for a year before we launch such a huge project."

"Okay, what's really bugging you? That was the biggest load of crap I've ever heard."

"Nothing. I just think we should talk realistically about the timing of doing a show." I can't help that my concerns are rising to the surface.

"Jodi, I know when you're bullshitting. Out with it."

"Fine. I think that we should push off the show another year."

"Why?" Jill looks perplexed.

"Because it may very well take that long for the negative publicity to die down, and I don't want to start our television show on the defensive. That is, if they still want to take a chance on even doing a television show with us." So there.

"What the hell are you talking about? What negative publicity?"

I get up and thrust a folder at her. It is filled with almost nine hundred e-mails and letters. "This represents this week's take of angry correspondence. It's been at about that level for the past three weeks. They are pretty evenly split between the 'You bitches are ruining the American family' letters and the 'Why the fuck should I stay single if you're getting married?' letters. The choices you make affect our business, and we can't pretend they don't. This is going to blow big, little sister. We've got Kim working on a press release, and I talked to Mike Thomas over at the *Sun-Times*, and he is going to do a feature. Hopefully, we can get some stuff out before someone else does. But don't sit there all wide-eyed and ready to go on TV when any network exec in his right mind is going to give us a big fat 'Thanks but no thanks' when this hits the fan."

Jill riffles through the pages with a clenched jaw, pausing occasionally to read something. She looks up at me. "Three weeks, you said. Kim's working on the release, you're talking to Mike . . . When exactly were you going to fill me in?" There is venom in her voice.

"When we got all the strategies in place."

"Why. The fuck. Wasn't I. *Informed?*" She is spitting the words at me. "Equal fucking partners, Jodi. *Equal!* We run this business *together*! Major decisions, minor decisions, we make them *together*! Who the hell do you think you are to go running around with our employees making proclamations and keeping me out of the fucking loop? Do you have any idea how much that undermines my authority with them? How impotent that makes me look? How *dare* you take this on without consulting me!"

"Hey. Fuck you. I was just trying to spare you some of the ugliness so you could enjoy the holidays in the flush of your new engagement. So sorry if I didn't want you to have to face the shitty side of this without a plan in place. I wanted to be able to say, 'Here is what is going on, and here is how we are going to protect you and the business,' so you didn't have to worry!"

"You can't protect me from my own business."

"Trust me, I'll never try again. You can have it." I go over to my desk and grab the rest of the files of letters and drop them in her lap. "You send the answers to all these people, then. You talk to Kim about how to fix it. You stay up wondering if the entire business is about to go under, with all the people who work with us at risk. You talk to the fucking security company about how to keep us all safe. I'm fucking done. I'm tired of being the fucking FEMA director of our lives."

"Fine." Jill stands up.

"Fine?"

She nods. "Fine. This is my mess, you seem to think. My fault. My problem. I'll take care of it."

"Fine."

We look at each other.

"It doesn't matter if your intentions were good, Jodi. You had no right."

"Whatever."

"Let's just get through tomorrow and try to have a happy day. We can talk about this on Friday when we've cooled off."

"Yeah, okay." I'm suddenly crushingly exhausted.

"I'll see you in the morning." Jill turns, carrying her armload of poison, and leaves.

I'm too shocked to even cry, at once furious at her for being so angry at my well-intentioned efforts and even more furious with myself for not just keeping my mouth shut.

I head to the kitchen to clean up and then go to check e-mail before bed. There is a message in the website in-box from C. Duncan. I open it.

Jodi—

Imagine my surprise when I Googled your name and got over 10,000 hits! You are quite the cottage industry. I couldn't help

but glance over the website. I don't think I'm your target
demographic, but I was still impressed. Hope the casserole
turned out good. Just wanted to wish you a very happy
Thanksgiving.

Talk to you Friday,
Connor

This makes me a little bit fuzzy. In a good way. In a way that
momentarily makes me forget the recent unpleasantness. I hit
Reply.

Connor—

Imagine my surprise when I opened my mailbox to find your
note. You are a very efficient stalker. The casserole looks
good, but the proof, as they say, is in the pudding. I'll have to
tell you on Friday if it tastes as good as it looks.

Happy Thanksgiving,
Jodi

It appears that this year, whatever shit may be hitting the fan,
I may actually have one extra thing to be thankful for.

❧

"Please pass the mashed potatoes," I say softly, stuffed to the gills
but desperate for one more creamy mouthful of comfort.

Jill picks them up and hands them over without a word.

"Another triumph, Shirley," Aunt Ruth says, patting her mouth
with a napkin. "The turkey was perfect."

"Thanks, Ruthie. It's all in the brining." Shirley is beaming, having truly pulled off an extraordinary meal. "See, the thing is, there's all this flavor in the brine outside the bird and no room inside the bird. So you have to let the bird sort of stew in its own juices overnight to get it to give up some room, so that the flavor can work its way inside."

"Interesting." Ruth takes a sip of wine. "So what you are saying is that in order for the bird to be the best it can be, it has to let some outside influences help."

Sweet Calvin and Hobbes, they're baiting us! "Oh goodness gracious, the two of you are ridiculous," I say.

"And very, very unsubtle," Jill says.

"Well, what do you expect?" Ruth asks. "All that stomping and muffled yelling and slamming of doors and huffing up and down staircases. We're old; we're not deaf or stupid. And the two of you have been polite-ing each other near to death since eight this morning."

"We're having some issues related to work, that's all; we didn't want to make a big deal of it," I say.

"We just want to have a nice Thanksgiving," Jill says, not looking at me.

"The two of you are full of hooey," Shirley says.

"Oh, hellfire, Shirley, they're full of shit," Ruth snaps. "How can we have a nice day when clearly the two of you didn't work through this last night, and now, having slept little, I'm sure, you're working so hard not to say anything that it's making you unbearable company!"

"Maybe we should just . . ." Hunter tries to speak.

"Please," Jill whispers. And she does it in a tone that tells me that he knows everything, and might not have been totally on her side in the matter. Interesting.

"Don't shush the poor boy; he's getting the brunt of it!" Shirley pipes in. "Hunter, darling, would you join Ruth and me for sherry in the parlor while the girls clean up?" She rises, Hunter automatically getting up and offering her his arm.

"Don't forget to soak the roasting pan," Ruth says, and follows her sister and almost-nephew from the dining room.

I look at Jill. She looks at the table and sighs. "We'd better start."

I fork in one more mouthful of potatoes and get up to begin clearing the mess. One wouldn't think five adults could create such an enormous amount of dirty dishes, but there is at least an hour of work ahead of us.

I begin putting leftovers in containers and plastic bags, while Jill starts scraping and stacking plates and dumping silverware into a large bowl. The only noise is the tinkle and clink of china and crystal and a low rumble of talking from the other room. I can't fucking stand it. I won't be the first one to say something here; she's the one who blew up at me instead of acting like a rational person and talking it over.

"Stop thinking so damn loud; this is not all me," Jill says quietly.

"I'm sorry, were you addressing me or those Brussels sprouts?"

"I can hear your determination not to be the first one to talk from a mile away, Jodi. You're pretty predictable." She runs water into the sink and splooshes a bunch of dishwashing liquid over it.

I stick the last of the food in the fridge and open the dishwasher and start loading the silverware. "You know we don't sleep on an argument, and you were the one who bailed last night. I tried to talk to you about this, and you shut me down and yelled at me."

Jill starts rinsing dishes and adding them to the dishwasher. "You stepped way over a line, and I didn't feel like we were going to come to a resolution last night. I was too angry. I'm still angry."

"I appreciate that, and I'm sorry you're angry, but all I was doing was . . ."

"Keeping me out of the loop," Jill spits out.

"Protecting you!" Why can't she see that?

"I said it before: You cannot protect me from my own business. These aren't schoolyard bullies calling me Bill because of a bad haircut!"

I did have to beat up a couple of kids once upon a time when what was supposed to be a Dorothy Hamill ended up more of a Donny Osmond.

"I know. This is worse. This could cause us to lose everything."

"We can't lose everything—we haven't done anything wrong! I'm not doing anything wrong! And what I'm doing has not one fucking thing to do with our business!"

I slam the last fork into the basket. "You have got to be kidding me! You saw the mail, you read the e-mails, how can you think things are separate? It's all there in black and white. People who trusted us feel betrayed. Who are the Spinster Sisters if you aren't a spinster anymore? And who are we if we aren't the Spinster Sisters?" Hot tears begin to fall down my cheeks.

Jill puts down the plate she is holding, dries her hands on a towel, and comes over to me. She opens her arms and we hug tightly. "We are Jodi and Jill, and we will always be sisters and best friends and partners, always. It doesn't matter if I get married or you do, or if the business folds or changes into something else. We are always us; nothing can change that."

I hiccup. "I didn't mean to belittle you or be overbearing."

"I didn't mean to accuse you of ill intentions."

"I'm really happy you're getting married."

"I promise it won't change me or us."

We look at each other and smile.

I tweak her nose. "I love you, Moose Face."

She pinches my cheek. "I love you, too, Butthead."

"Let's get them the hell in here to help dry the damn glasses."

"Indeed."

Jill goes to let Hunter and the aunts know that the storm has passed and that it is safe to come into the kitchen, and I turn to the sink. I hope she is right. I really need her to be right on this one.

Which Way the Wind Blows

Honesty isn't really always the best policy. Whenever you choose to share something potentially hurtful with a friend or lover, you should stop to think about why you are sharing it. Yes, it can be important to talk about issues that are negatively impinging on a relationship. If someone is doing something that hurts your feelings, it is essential to confront them about that. However, some things truly are better left unsaid. If you are jealous of your friend's new job, that isn't about her; it is about you, and telling her will only make her feel self-conscious about talking to you. If the problem rests with you, keep it to yourself, work through your own issues, and try to look at why you are feeling the way you are feeling. I would bet that you are really dissatisfied with your own work situation, and if that is the case, be happy for your friend, and get off your tush and try to do something to alter your own career path.

—Advice given to a caller by Jill Spingold, October 2004

"This is Jodi Spingold," I say into the large microphone in front of me.

"And this is Jill Spingold," she says into her mike.

"And you're having *Lunch with the Spinster Sisters*," I continue. "Today's topic is compromise. How to do it, when to do it, why to do it—"

"And when to avoid it!" Jill jumps in.

"We'll be taking your calls in just a minute or two, so get your questions ready and set your speed dial to 1-800-S-P-I-N-S-T-R, that's 1-800-774-6787. But I want to start with getting some sort of handle on what we mean when we say compromise. Jill, what do you think of when you think of the word *compromise*?"

Jill winks at me. We don't overtly script the show, since we really want it to be spontaneous, but we do go over some scenarios and talk through our ideas. We don't, unlike some radio pairs, try to either always be in agreement or always be at odds. We let our opinions stay organic, letting the chips fall where they may.

"Well, I sort of get two different images in my head when I hear *compromise*," Jill begins. "I mean, the first is sort of the classic, right? Two people who want things that are at odds, coming to an agreement somewhere in the middle. I want Italian for dinner and I want to see the new French movie. He wants Greek for dinner and to see the new action adventure. So we either do a 'You pick the dinner, I pick the movie' thing, or we agree on the French restaurant and the comedy."

I laugh, since last night she and I fought over whether to go to Santorini or Sentimana for dinner, and ended up at Bistro Zinc.

"So, it's either everyone gets part of their way, so that the benefit is split, or you move to a whole different area that you can find some agreement on," I prompt her.

"Exactly."

"But then, what is the other image you get? You said you got two."

"I think, for many women, compromise means giving up something to keep the peace. That it isn't about giving up part of something or changing tracks entirely, but rather about letting something go because they don't believe that they are valued enough to even get a part of what they want or deserve."

"I think we're going to need a less academic description here, sis; you just sort of lost me." Which she didn't, but part of the job is to play the part of the listener, anticipating what they are thinking and would ask if they were in the room.

"Well, I think what I mean is this. Let's say we're looking at that dinner discussion again. She wants Italian. He wants Greek. So in order to not have to have a big discussion, she'll say fine, and they'll have Greek instead of coming to a genuine compromise. Women sometimes see giving in as compromise. As if their wants or desires have less value. And what can happen is that we tell ourselves it isn't a big deal, right? It's just a meal. But those little deals add up, and before we know it there is a major communication breakdown. And it doesn't matter if the situation is professional or personal, romantic or platonic. It can set up an unhealthy pattern of not allowing yourself to get what you want and need."

"I sort of see what you're getting at. I mean, often it seems easier to just acquiesce. Like, when I was married, and I didn't really want to get a second cat, but the minute it started to become a real discussion, and I knew we'd end up in a fight, and I also knew that having the second cat wasn't really going to have any overt negative impact on my life, I just let my husband get the second cat so that we didn't have to argue about it."

"Right, but you didn't want the second cat."

"No, I didn't."

"And the minute the conversation became more than just surface, you backed down so that you wouldn't have to fight."

"Pretty much." True, I did.

"Well, think about the same sort of thing in a professional situation. You have been asked to do something at work that isn't your job. You start to say that it shouldn't be your responsibility, but the person asking you begins to get serious. If you don't stand your ground, then that person knows that they can bulldoze over you." No one bulldozes Jill. Even me. Especially me, as we have recently found out.

"So we are looking to talk about the idea of compromise in

terms of women *really* asking for it, as its core meaning. That you might not get all of what you want or need, but that you shouldn't settle for none."

"Well, don't you think so?"

Our producer, John, points to the phones, which now have enough calls waiting that we are safe to open the lines.

"Well, forget what I think, let's see what Candice thinks. Candice, you're having *Lunch with the Spinster Sisters*. What's on your plate?" It's our signature line. I made it up myself. Isn't it too adorable? We even have T-shirts and memo pads.

"Hi, Jodi! Hi, Jill! I can't believe I got through!" She sounds very excited and potentially Southern. The magic of satellite radio; she could be anywhere.

"Hi, Candice," Jill says. "What do you have for us?"

"Well, my boyfriend and I have been talking about getting engaged, but we have a problem. If we have kids, he really wants to send them to a Catholic school, but I'm not Catholic, and I would want to send them to public school. So I'm not sure what to do."

"Good question, Candice." I pause for a moment. "Does this appear to be about religious upbringing or quality of education?"

"I think it is about religious upbringing. And my feeling is that I'd like my kids to have a more diverse experience than I think they would get in a parochial school setting, and not have such an enormous amount of religion mixed in with the education. It really makes me think about whether we should get married or not."

"How about this," Jill says. "Why don't you agree to find a community that has the sort of diverse representation in the schools that you are looking for but also has a high quality of education, and then agree that your kids can go to Sunday school to reinforce the ideals that are important to your husband. Maybe even agree to find a church you can all attend together, maybe Lutheran or Unitarian, and promise your husband that you can get involved in the church community and attend regularly. Would you be willing to make those efforts in order to keep your future kids in a public school environment?"

"I never thought about getting more involved in a church, but yes, I do think I could do that!"

"Candice," I say. "Talk to your boyfriend about it, and be sure to outline why you are hesitant to commit to parochial education. Be sure that he knows you aren't rejecting him or his beliefs. Let him know the compromises you are willing to make, and see what he says."

"I will! I will tonight. Thank you guys so much; I wait for your show all week long!"

"Thank you, Candice," Jill says. "And call or e-mail us to let us know how the conversation goes!"

"I will! Bye, Jill! Bye, Jodi!"

"You're having *Lunch with the Spinster Sisters*," I say. "And we want to know what's on your plate. We're talking about compromise today. We have to take a quick break so that you can hear a couple of messages from our sponsors, but we'll be right back. And don't forget, this Friday night over on channel 150, the comedy channel, host Sonny Fox will be interviewing Mitch Fatel on *Stand Up, Sit Down*. This is one of our favorite shows, and Mitch is about the most hilarious comic we've ever had the pleasure of seeing. Don't miss it. We'll be right back."

John gives us a thumbs-up from the booth, Jill and I touch fingertips, our version of a high five, and we get ready to take some more calls.

Things have been good today, we're cooking along and the show is almost over. Just time for one more call. John indicates we're coming back from our last break.

"This is Jodi Spingold."

"And this is Jill Spingold, and you're having *Lunch with the Spinster Sisters*. Today we're all about compromise. And we have our last caller on the line."

"Mary Louise, we want to know what's on your plate?"

"Hi, Jill. Hi, Jodi. I was wondering, in all of this conversation about compromise, why don't you talk about compromising the stability of the American family unit by encouraging women to have unrealistic expectations of relationships and by endorsing a single lifestyle?"

Jill and I look at each other. We've had hostiles, as we call them, get through the switchboard before. Jill nods that she'll take the lead.

"Mary Louise, we're glad you called, because it allows us to put to rest some rumors about this very thing. We don't suggest that women should stay single for any longer than makes sense for them and their lives. Nor do we look down on relationships. We do want women to enjoy their lives regardless of their marital or relationship status, and we also want them to know that they shouldn't commit themselves unless it is the right partner for them."

"That is very glib, and clearly rehearsed. You are here, in the public eye, on the air, and in your books, and you are telling women that single is better and that if you decide to pursue a relationship, that it should be perfect in every way! What man can live up to that? Does your fiancé live up to that idea, or do you just say whatever you think people want to hear and live your own life different?"

"My fiancé is a wonderful man, who is perfect for me, which is not the same thing as perfect. And Jodi and I both live our lives by the philosophies we espouse publicly. We are sorry if you have misinterpreted our advice, but we want to assure you and all of our readers and listeners that our only motivation is to be a resource and a support for women, and if you disagree with our pedagogy, you should truly feel free to ignore us!" I can sense Jill getting testy, and decide we'd better end this.

"Mary Louise, we're sorry, but we're getting the signal that we are out of time for today, but we appreciate your call. Thank you all for letting us join you for lunch. We'll look forward to hearing what's on your plates next week, same time, here on XM 187."

"We're out," John says into our headphones.

And so we are.

⋇

"So then Jill says, 'I agree that doggie style isn't much of a compromise; have you thought about getting a copy of the *Kama Sutra* and exploring other positions that might make you more comfortable?' and I had to try not to laugh!" I'm trying to explain the day's best call to the aunts at cocktail hour, since they were both away from the radio today.

"My goodness. What a question!" says Shirley, passing a plate to me. "Have some more spanakopita." Like I need more phyllo triangles in my life. But they are too delicious to pass up. Aunt Shirley finally finished the hors d'oeuvres book and is working on a Greek cookbook, so today's feast is the aforementioned spinach-feta triangles; skordalia, a garlicky potato dip with toasted pita; little spicy meatballs called keftedes; and huge white beans in tomato sauce. We're drinking retsina, the fortified Greek wine.

"Well, really, they should be looking at the *Kama Sutra* anyway," says Ruth. "Any couple that is arguing about missionary or woman on top at this stage of the game is going to be doomed to boredom."

Jill snorts into her wineglass.

"Don't snuffle wine up your nose, darling; it's bad for the sinuses." Shirley never misses a beat.

"Well, compromise is such a big issue for women, I'm glad it's something you girls are really discussing," Ruth says. "In our day, the very idea that a woman would even get a choice was absurd."

"But you guys didn't compromise on the life you wanted to live," I say. "You knew what would be best for you, and you let the world adapt to you."

Shirley laughs. "Hear that, Ruthie? The world just adapted to us!"

"Do you really think it was our ambition to live with our parents our whole lives?" Ruth says, taking a sip of her wine. "We had three choices at the time: get married, live at home, or move out on our own and be thought of as loose women or lesbians, shunned by friends and family. You forget how conservative a time it was. And by the time it became socially acceptable for single women to live their own lives and have their own space, Mama and Papa were elderly and ailing and needed us around to help. So no, we didn't compromise what was most important, our independence, but we did give up plenty in order to protect that."

"Enough of this, too morbid," Shirley says.

Jill turns to me. "Hey, I want to hear your big new merchandising idea." I had tipped off Jill that I had a flash earlier in the day that I wanted to save for cocktail hour. We do this a lot. Sometimes if she and I talk things through, we can talk each other into something, and then when we take it to the aunts, if they don't like it, we gang up and get defensive. This way, everyone gets their initial impulses out on the table without choosing sides. She and I are having a truce at the moment; things are still strained, but we are trying to get back to normal. The day after Thanksgiving we went into the office and really hashed out our issues. We both obviously still think the other was more in the wrong, but at least we got relatively on the same page and have forgiven each other. But it is still hard to forget, so we have both been on our very best behavior, ultrasupportive, ultracommunicative, and ultimately sort of fake. But mending. I hope.

"Okay, here goes." I'm about to be either a genius or an idiot. Jill usually has the merchandising ideas, but every once in a while something comes to me. "So you know how so many of our gals eat lunch at their desks?"

"Terrible for the digestion," Shirley clucks.

"Hush, Shirley, let the girl speak," Ruth scolds.

"So I thought, what about a Spinster Sisters sort of kit that they can use to bring their lunch in a way that allows for a little of that taking-care-of-themselves aspect to even something as basic as having to eat at your desk. So like, we do a fun insulated bag with the logo on it, and inside we can do custom Tupperware in our signature colors, just three or four basic pieces, and matching silverware. But real silverware, not plastic. And then, the pièce de résistance, microwave-safe plate and bowl that they can leave at work so that they can actually eat on a real plate like a human being, and those have What's on Your Plate? printed on them."

The silence is maddening. Then Jill's face breaks into a grin. "I *love* it! It's awesome. We can do different versions, color combinations, maybe a deluxe kit with real porcelain and silver?" Her enthusiasm seems a little over-the-top, but maybe I'm just having some residual trust issues.

"You should do an afternoon tea kit with one of those heating elements that sits right in the glass, with little boxes for loose teas and sugar, maybe a tiny squeeze bottle for honey..." Aunt Shirley always gets lit up thinking about people getting a decent cup of tea during their busy day.

"You could put little recipe books in there, or even pamphlets about ten-minute meditations or at-your-desk stretches or those kinds of things." Ruth gets into the moment.

"So I'm not crazy. It could be cool, right?" I'm really chuffed that they all like it.

"It's so cool! I think we should take it to the team tomorrow and do a huge brainstorming of all the possible kits we could do, and then have the merchandising group start to price it out. We could try to get it done in time to launch with the new book." Jill is already thinking logistics, which is why she is so damned good at her job. And making me think perhaps that she isn't placating me, that she really likes my idea.

"Well, a toast to a new venture. Sounds like you girls are going to have another hit on your hands." Ruth raises her wineglass at us. We all clink and sip and refill plates.

"Now, Jill, we should start to talk details about the wedding. What have you decided so far?" Shirley has been really good about not pushing too hard about wedding details past the date and approximate guest count, but with the date now only five and a half months off, it is definitely time to get going. I myself am sort of ambivalent. On the one hand, usually nothing is more fun than the four of us planning a party. On the other, it brings the whole married thing into very clear relief for me and reinforces all the crap that is going on at work.

"Well," Jill says, "we were thinking that we'd do it at A New Leaf."

"The flower store?" Ruth asks.

"Yeah. They have a space now where you can have private parties, and it is really beautiful." She smiles.

"Oh, dear. It will be like getting married in a garden!" Shirley says.

"I think it's a perfect choice," I say. "It's so you."

"It was Hunter's idea." Jill grins. "He is so into the whole wedding. I swear. He's like one of those girls who keeps a folder of all the things they dream about for their wedding. He has ten ideas for each one of mine."

"Oh Lord," I say. "It's going to be like having two brides!"

The four of us laugh, thinking about sweet Hunter, with his naturally eager and positive nature, getting all worked up about the perfect wedding. If nothing else, I know she isn't making a bad decision about who to marry. Unlike me.

"Well, what other ideas are the two of you bandying about?" Ruth asks.

"We're thinking afternoon with a heavy cocktail hour and a light supper. No idea about caterers yet. Obviously A New Leaf will do the flowers. And if it's not too much trouble, Aunt Shirley, we'd love you to do the cake."

Shirley places her hand on her heart and smiles as her eyes start to shimmer. "I'd be so honored, darling, so honored."

"And of course, you know we'd like to host a shower," Ruth says.

"And I'm in charge of the bachlorette party, of course," I say as brightly as I can. "As long as Hunter knows it's for you and not him! His best man is going to have to plan the bachelor party."

"We're not remotely there yet. Frankly, I wish there were a service where someone could download all your natural preferences out of your head and plan the wedding without you, so you could just show up and get married!"

"Well, honey," Shirley offers, "as much as we want to celebrate with you, you know that we would support an elopement, if the two of you want to avoid a big to-do. We can always have a party afterward."

"Absolutely, kitten," Ruth agrees. "If you don't want the stress or the hassle, no one would fault you for it."

"We know. And truth be told, it is a very tempting thought.

But when we talked about it, Hunter said he really thought it was something he wanted us to do. And I know that when all is said and done, it will be so much more meaningful if we have our friends and family around us."

"Well, then, that's settled. A wedding it will be!" Shirley claps her hands gleefully.

Jill looks at her watch. She drains the last of her wine and gets up. "Speaking of weddings, my esteemed fiancé is arriving at O'Hare in thirty minutes, and I have to go fetch him." She walks over to kiss both aunts on the cheek. "We'll call up when we get home if you want to come down for a bit," she says to me, a white flag.

I smile and nod. "Perfect. Bring home dessert."

"Will do." And she heads out.

"And what is your plan for the evening?" Shirley asks me.

"I have a hot date with the new chapter and some leftover pasta." When Jill and I are working on a book, we will have a big brainstorming meeting, talk through all the key points of the chapter at hand, and then I write the first draft. Then I turn it over to her for what she calls editing, and what I call smoothing over the prose. Then we give it to Ruth and Shirley for approval and proofreading. The new book is due to our editor in the middle of March.

"None of your boys on the docket this evening?" Ruth asks.

"Nope. Abbot is taking me to the opera tomorrow night, and Ben is taking me to the movies on Saturday."

"And the new fellow?" Shirley inquires.

"The new fellow is out of town for a cousin's wedding but has booked me for one week from tonight."

"You and all your boys," Ruth clucks.

"What can I say? I learned from the master," I reply, getting up to help Aunt Shirley clear the plates and glasses.

"She's got you there, Ruthie!" Aunt Shirley giggles.

Aunt Ruth smiles a secret smile, the contented air of a woman who has unapologetically lived her life and enjoyed most every minute of it. "And what about all this wedding business? How does that sit with you?" she asks.

"You have been awfully quiet, dear. Don't you approve?" Shirley is boxing up leftovers in Tupperware.

I think for a moment. "I'm really happy for them, you know? I love Hunter, and I think he's the perfect guy for Jill, and I think he'll be a great husband and father and brother and nephew. And they both seem really clear about what they want in life, and those seem to be all the same things, so I don't worry for them at all."

"But . . ." Ruth prods.

"But I'm trying not to be worried for me and Jill and the business." There, I said it out loud. Now lightning can strike me.

"Oh, honey, do you think your relationship with Jill will suffer once she is married?" Shirley stops loading the dishwasher, wipes her hands on a towel, and comes over to clasp my hands in hers. "You and Jill have the most special relationship. Nothing will change that."

Her sincerity, the comfort, the emotion involved in just being honest about my fears, the wine, my fight with Jill, it's all a little much, and I start to cry. Aunt Shirley pulls me to her in a big hug, and I can feel Ruth's strong hands kneading my shoulders.

"Poor baby, you're really concerned about this, hmmm?" Ruth says.

I hiccup a little and blow my nose on the handkerchief that Shirley hands me. "I just know that when I married Brant, Jill and I didn't spend time together the way we had, and I know we weren't living in the same building then or working together, and this time we will be, but obviously he is going to have to get the lion's share of her time."

"Darling, if I may?" Ruth sits me down at the kitchen table, an antique oak round that belonged to my grandparents. Its worn surface had seen Spingold meals for over a hundred years and seemed ready for a hundred more. I had done homework on it, learned to cut out cookies on it, wept over heartbreaks on it. I knew every line of the wood, and traced the pronounced grain with my fingertip as Aunt Ruth spoke.

"Now, you know that we don't think ill of Brant." She looks to Aunt Shirley for confirmation, who nods vigorously. "Brant is a good man, he has intelligence and a kind heart, and he was always very sweet to you in a lot of ways. However, you also know that he just never fit in with this family. He just wasn't the right match for you, and it was difficult for us to watch that. It was clear from his behavior that he wasn't comfortable with us or with Jill, and we all sensed that and did what we could to not be obtrusive in your relationship with him, because you seemed to be happy, and your happiness is our first hope."

"I know. He can't help it. I tried to fix him, but I couldn't."

"Oh, honey," Aunt Shirley says, "you can't fix someone. You have to take them as they come. Warts and all."

"Brant was pretty warty." I laugh a little, thinking about his weird obsession with Star Trek and his strange conspiracy theories.

"Oh, my, yes. Remember the cappuccino?" Ruth says, shaking her head.

The first time we all went to dinner after the engagement, Brant had a small run-in with a cup of cappuccino. He fancied himself something of a coffee connoisseur, and as he was wont to do, had waxed poetic for a mind-numbing ten minutes about the espresso/cappuccino maker we had received as an engagement gift and the attributes of different coffees from around the globe. So, at the end of the meal, in spite of the fact that none of the rest of us drinks coffee and we were all ready to go home, Brant orders a cappuccino. It arrived, a dash of cinnamon on the top of the foam. Brant puts three sugars in it and stirs noisily while continuing to talk about the joys of a Kenyan blend he had recently purchased. He took a sip. He sighed dramatically. He announced it a perfect cup, as good as his own. He downed it in about three swigs, whereupon the waitress returned to the table with a small espresso cup and said "I'm so sorry, sir, the kitchen forgot to put the coffee in your cappuccino." Poor Brant was mortified; his perfect cup was sugared steamed milk with a little cinnamon. Some expert. The fact that we all stifled laughter didn't help.

"He couldn't help it," I say.

"Of course not, dear. That isn't the point," Shirley says. "The point is that Hunter isn't Brant. Hunter fits in with us perfectly; you said it yourself. And he is moving in here with the rest of the inmates, so while I am sure some things will change, the important things will not. Plus you'll still see each other at work every day!"

This makes me sniffle more.

"What? You're still worried about the business?" Ruth asks.

"How can we be the Spinster Sisters if one of us isn't a spinster anymore?" My vehemence is somewhat surprising, even to me. "I mean, it was one thing that one of us is divorced, right? But still *single*. Still living the single life. And moreover, able to reflect on what she would have done differently, given a chance. But the minute Jill gets married, what is our audience going to think? Now it's one divorcée and one married woman. Some spinsters we are. How is Jill going to spout the single sisterhood stuff if she's all wedded-blissed out? They'll think we're frauds. And the fucking Family First people, who already think we're the spawn of Satan, what a field day they're going to have with it! The whole thing will collapse around our ears. And now the television thing is heating up, but if it goes, we open ourselves up to all kinds of ridicule, because—"

"Hold it right there," Ruth says, covering my hand with hers.

"Drink this." Aunt Shirley hands me a small glass of sherry, which I begin to sip slowly.

"Now, for one thing, your business hasn't become what it has become because you are both single. It has become what it has become because you are smart, kind, thoughtful women with an ability to look at life as a gift, and with a sense of independence that never left you when you were married and won't leave Jill when she is married. The idea that your company will flounder is utter nonsense." Ruth is very stern.

"Not all of your readers and listeners are single, honey," Shirley says. "Some of them are married or in serious relationships and just want to be reminded that they have power on their own merit. Everyone can take what they need from your work, and Jill getting married doesn't negate that."

I sip my sherry. The sweet heat sparks on my tongue and warms me all the way down.

"Have you spoken any more with your sister about your concerns?" Ruth asks, playing with her necklace, a string of red Moroccan amber beads the size of small eggs.

"Some of it." I don't want to hear a lecture on the big brouhaha of last week. "You know Jill, she'll spend the majority of the next five months proving to me that everything is going to be okay, and not enjoying the planning and wedding stuff. I'm going to try to manage my own psychoses for a while, and if I'm still feeling like this after the wedding, I'll talk to her about it then."

"Will you be able to do that, sweetie? Without it ruining the next five months for you?" Shirley asks.

"And do you think Jill would be happy knowing you felt this way and didn't talk to her about it?" Ruth offers.

You have no idea, I think. "I just want her to be joyous and to revel in this special time, and not have to worry about her crazy sister dumping a bucket of water on her happiness."

"You do what you think is best, honey, and it will all work out." Shirley kisses the top of my head.

"And come vent to us anytime." Ruth pats my hand.

"Thanks. I love you guys."

I get up from the table and give them each a big hug. Then I head upstairs to hunker down over the new chapter and try to pretend I feel better.

The Gambler

Don't be reluctant to try new things that are of interest to your partner. So what if you've always thought that golf was a white-elitist waste of land? If your new guy loves it, let him take you to the driving range. So what if the idea of a knitting circle reminds you of your smelly Aunt Melba with the hairy mole? If your new sister-in-law invites you to hers, go with an open mind. Sometimes experiencing something that someone else loves through their eyes can offer a new perspective. Think about how much more fun it is to watch your favorite movie while sitting next to someone who has never seen it. It's about the sharing, and you just might find something you both can enjoy.

—*From* The Thirty Commandments *by Jill and Jodi Spingold*

"No more, Aunt Shirley. I'm stuffed, and I'm meeting Hunter for dinner!" Jill waves off the platter of Turkish manti dumplings and stands up. Aunt Shirley proffers it in my direction.

I get up as well. "And I have to finish getting ready for my date."

"Which one is it tonight, dear?" Ruth asks.

"First official date with Connor," I say, as a little frisson of excitement shivers up my spine. I'm praying it goes well. We've had a great week of e-mail and phone calls, and I continue to be intrigued by him on many levels.

"The great marshmallow bandit of the North Side, hmmm?" Ruth asks. "Very interesting. Good thing we've got a bundle of DVDs to watch, don't you think, Shirley?"

Oy. The dreaded first date oh-dear-we-just-happen-to-still-be-up-how-did-it-go? ambush. "Now, girls, don't keep yourselves awake on my account." I know it won't do any good. And to be honest, I'd be a little disappointed if I didn't see that parlor light burning when I got home. A little tea and sympathy at the end of a bad date, or a nightcap and a giggle at the end of a good one never hurt anyone.

"Call me, too, when you get back, so I can come down!" Jill says on her way out the door.

"Fine, fine, fine. But I have to actually go on the date if I'm going to have anything to report back later." I kiss the aunts and follow Jill out the door.

"Have a good time. I can't wait to hear about it!"

"You, too. Love to Hunter."

Jill heads out the front door, and I head upstairs to get ready. I'm surprised at how quickly this week went. Jill has started planning in earnest, so the wedding discussion is slowly infiltrating the rest of our lives. I'm still equally split between being over-the-moon happy for her and bone-chilling terrified at the possible fallout. Our publicist has recommended that we put out a release on the same day as Mike's article will run in the *Sun-Times*; that way he gets an exclusive, and anyone who starts their research will come across his article. We have to treat this marriage as the most natural thing in the world, which, of course, it is, and play up all the relationship advice we give that is focused on maintaining a commitment.

Abbot thinks that I'm jealous, that Hunter is supplanting me as the most important person in Jill's life. This took me right out of the lovely mood the delicious dinner at Trattoria 10 and beautiful opera at the Lyric Friday night had put me in, and while I am rarely disinterested in his physical affection, I claimed exhaustion and left him chastely at the car. This prompted a particularly large floral arrangement to be delivered the next day, which made me feel worse, since I had asked him for his thoughts and hadn't been fishing for him to tell me *my* opinions, and hated that perhaps he thought I was punishing him with no sex.

Then Ben tried to take me to the movies but got the time wrong, and everything else at the theater one or both of us had already seen. This irritated me, and we got into a sniping match about being attentive to details, which Ben took as my scolding him about his age, and even though we made up over ice cream at Cold Stone, the date left me more annoyed than not, and questioning how much longer I'd be interested in hanging out with him.

Jill, of course, thinks that I'm so excited about Connor that it is making me pick fights with the Father and the Son, so that I'll feel mentally free to focus on the Holy Ghost. Jill never lets go of a metaphor if she can help it. And she is right about one thing; I am really sort of excited about this date. He's coming in about a half hour, and I just need to perk up my makeup and change clothes. He wouldn't tell me where we're going, so I'm trying to be strategic about the wardrobe. Skirt, in case it's a little fancier, but flats in case it's more casual. Light shimmer on the eyes, and a simple gloss on the lips, but a serious red lipstick in the purse just in case.

I'm just finishing the last coat of mascara when the doorbell rings. I skitter down the long hall to the buzzer and press it. "Hey, hang out in the foyer. I'll be right down." I grab my coat and purse, take a deep breath, and head out the door. By the time I get down to the second landing, I can hear the hum of voices. Oh crap. I pick up the pace. But turning the last curve of the stairs, I realize it's no use. Ruth and Shirley have cornered Connor in the foyer. Sneaky bitches.

"Really? Five brothers?" Shirley is saying.

"That must have been exciting," Ruth flirts.

"Yes, ma'am. Never dull at the Duncan house." Connor looks up to see me coming down the stairs and catches me off guard with his bemused air. "Well, there she is."

"Well, dears, you run off and have fun, now," Shirley says, pulling on Ruth's elbow.

"Stop tugging at me, Shirley, I know we can't keep them." She snatches her arm back. "Have a lovely evening, chickens." She leans over and kisses me. "Dishy," she whispers in my ear. I feel my cheeks flush.

"Good night, you old biddies." I shoo them into their apartment. I turn to Connor. "Shall we?" He still has his little smirk on.

"I don't know, I have half a mind to ask them to join us." We head out the door and down the front steps.

"Oh no, you don't have dinner with the aunts until you have proven yourself worthy."

"And what, pray tell, would make me worthy?"

"Not that easy. Trust me, when you get there, I'll let you know."

"So coy." He walks up to an old Chevy pickup truck and unlocks the door. "Your chariot, m'lady."

"Thank you, sir." I hoist myself into the cab of the truck and settle in as Connor closes the door. I like the car. It's a nice contrast to Abbot's sort of stuffy Mercedes and Ben's more and more irritating lack of one. Unpretentious, but clean and obviously well-loved. The sort of car Jill and I refer to as noncompensatory, as in, the opposite of sports car.

"So, you up for an adventure?" he asks.

"Always."

"Glad to hear it. Settle in, we have a little drive ahead of us."

The conversation is as easy as it has been all week. He admits to listening to the show earlier today and praises our style. He also admits to having ordered the books on Amazon.

"I'm very flattered." Usually guys don't feel obligated to read the books, figuring they're just fluffy girlie things anyway. Or they run out and read them right away and start to quote them back at me. But this is nice. He appears to be genuinely interested but not feel the need to put any pressure on it.

"I believe in research," he says simply.

"Well, you aren't our target demographic, but I hope you enjoy them."

"I think the idea of being strong and independent and not needing a man to define your life is a great message," he says. "I knew a lot of girls growing up who could have used your advice."

"We do what we can," I say as I look out the window at the passing scenery.

"So, where does that leave you on the relationship front?"

This is a bold move, considering it's a first date, but I'm inclined to approve of his forthrightness. "Well, I suppose you would define me as currently out in the world. I'm not dating anyone exclusively, but I am dating and interested in new people. If someone comes along with whom I am compatible, and it organically develops into something serious, I'm not a commitment-phobe, and I will take steps to explore that potential with someone. But I'm not really looking for that sort of relationship; I'll just be open to it if it happens to arrive."

"Good to know."

I can't read him at all. He doesn't seem angry or disappointed like some guys. "How about you?"

Connor pauses. "I suppose I am most focused on my work these days. It has been a long time since my last serious relationship, and like yourself, I haven't been terribly inclined to pursue another commitment, but I'm not averse to the idea either."

"Sounds like you and I are very much on the same page," I say and decide a change of subject is in order. "So, where are you taking me?"

"You really want to know?"

"Please."

"Hammond."

"Hammond? As in, Indiana?"

"Yep."

"And what, if I may be so bold, is in Hammond, Indiana?"

"Riverboat."

"Gambling?"

"Is that okay? I just thought it might be fun. Bad idea?"

"No, great idea. Very great. It's just, well . . ."

"What?"

"I don't know how to gamble. I've never done it before. Is it hard?"

"Of course not. You stick with me. I'll teach you all the tricks."

And bless him, he did just that. After a quiet drive, which flew by in light conversation about work and family and friends, we boarded the floating casino, and I began to feel the buzz that everyone always talks about. We started at the blackjack tables, where he handed me a stack of chips and gave me the simplest of instruction. You always assume that the dealer has a ten under the card they show. If your hand can't beat your assumption of their hand, you take a hit until seventeen. If you can beat it, you stay. Apparently, I learned this lesson reasonably well, because after a while, I have a pretty big stack of chips in front of me, and a small crowd has gathered. Connor's luck has been up and down; he's probably about even from when we first sat down, but he seems to be taking personal pride in how well I am doing.

"Okay, then. Feeling ready for another challenge?" he asks.

"Sure!" I love the giddy feeling I have, like I'm getting away with something.

He turns to the dealer. "Color us up, please." The dealer leans over and counts up my pile of chips, over $700. He hands me several black chips, a couple of green, and a couple of red. "Give him the red ones," Connor whispers in my ear, "as a tip."

I smile at the dealer and push the two red chips toward him. "Thank you very much!"

He smiles at me. "Thank you, ma'am." Then he knocks the chips loudly on a small metal box next to him and drops the chips inside.

Connor receives his chips, just slightly over the $200 he started with. I hand him two of my black chips.

"What's this for?"

"That's the money you gave me to start with. I thought I should give it back." He looks puzzled.

"I didn't mean . . ." he says. "I wanted you to play, you know, it isn't about the money."

"I know, but it is actual money, and now I've won a bunch to keep playing with, so I thought you should get your stake back."

"Tell you what, you keep it for now. We'll settle up at the end of the night."

"Okay. Where are we going now?"

"You hungry?"

"Actually, not really. It's weird, I should be, but I'm not." I should be starving. But I'm so excited about the evening that I just don't feel like eating. Plus I did go pretty heavy on the hors d'oeuvres at cocktail hour. "But if you're hungry . . ."

"Nope, the adrenaline gets me, too. Makes my stomach shut itself off for a bit."

"We've invented a new diet!" I say. "Trade your food addiction for a gambling addiction, and you'll be skinny!"

"But broke." He laughs.

"Only if you lose."

"Which, eventually, you will. But hopefully not tonight. And besides, skinny never really appealed to me."

Which is exactly the thing a curvier gal like myself wants and needs to hear, especially early on in a new relationship. I get a teeny shiver up my spine the way he says it, not with pointed eye contact or anything lascivious, just a simple statement of fact. Skinny never appealed to him. He just went up fifteen points on the yummy scale.

He scans the casino while I silently preen. "Wanna try your hand at shooting craps?"

I've always loved the idea of craps. It seems like the sexiest of the games. Very Rat Pack, which I'm a sucker for. I have long fancied myself the gamine companion of a Frank Sinatra type, the kind of guy who would call me "doll," and have me kiss his dice for luck, and buy me diamonds and furs just for the hell of it. You know, minus the mob ties and the alcoholism and smacking around.

"Absolutely," I say.

We wind our way through the crowd and get to a craps table. We settle in at one end, and Connor asks the croupier to exchange our chips for smaller denominations. Actually, what he says is, "Can we get color?" which makes no sense to me until the guy hands us our chips. I must look confused, because Connor says, "*Color up* means take the chips and give the smallest number of chips in return, and *get color* means to break a larger chip down into smaller ones."

"Thanks. I don't seem to know any of the lingo!"

"Stick with me, doll. I've got your back." Oh. My. Goodness. I'm suddenly all squishy. Funny what one little endearment can do. "Now, just bet exactly how I bet. Same number of chips and everything. We're going to start small to get your feet wet. Craps moves really fast, so you can lose a lot pretty quickly. Just remember, you're paying for entertainment; don't think about winning—just have fun. If the money is all gone in ten minutes, we can still make a movie." He makes me feel very at ease. He places a single chip on the table in front of him, on something called the pass line. I do the same in front of me. The guy with the dice rolls.

"Yo, eleven," the croupier shouts. "Pay the line!" One of the other guys hands chips all around.

"We won?" I ask Connor.

"We won. Pick up your chip."

The guy rolls again.

"Four, the point is four," the croupier yells. The guy who paid me my chip takes a huge hockey puck that says On and places it on the box marked four.

Connor puts two chips behind his pass line bet, and I follow suit. Then he puts one chip in the middle of the table, in a section marked Come, which, twelve-year-old that I am, makes me smile. I put my chip next to his.

The guy rolls the dice for about ten minutes, the croupier calls numbers, I keep following Connor's bets, and periodically pick up the chips the croupier hands me, which I assume are winnings. It does move very quickly, but I'm starting to understand the game a tiny bit, not enough to play on my own, but enough to anticipate some of Connor's moves. We are like synchronized swimmers. Suddenly something happens, and the whole table sighs. Then all of our chips on the table get swept away.

"What happened?" I ask.

"He rolled a seven, crapped out."

"New shooter, new shooter coming out, place your bets!" The croupier does a weird shuffle of five dice and then pushes them toward me with a long stick.

"You ready?" Connor asks me.

"I'm going to roll?"

"Yep. No problem. Just pick the two dice that look lucky to you."

There are two dice right next to each other, a four and a two. Well, I'm thirty-four, and Jill is thirty-two, so they seem a good pair, even if we aren't so much these days. I pick them up. They are heavier than I would have thought, and sharply pointed on the corners.

"Now just throw them so that they hit the bunkers at the other end of the table, and keep betting the way I bet." Connor looks deep into my eyes. I nod. And throw the dice.

We're sitting at a small table in the casino, and I'm drinking my third glass of water. Gambling is thirsty, dehydrating work.

"I know, it's all the extra oxygen," Connor says, draining his own glass.

"What extra oxygen?"

"They pump extra oxygen into the casinos. Helps keep the crowd awake and euphoric and gambling."

"Is that legal?" I ask.

"What are you going to do, sue them for making you breathe oxygen?"

We laugh. "Connor, this is the most fun I have had in a long time. Thank you."

"Well, nothing like winning a few grand to make a girl perky, huh?"

Yep. Six thousand four hundred and twenty-four dollars to be precise. Apparently, I am the best craps shooter *ever*! The croupier said he'd never seen six hard eights in a row. Connor won just over four grand, because he never plays the "hard way" bets, but those paid off really well for me.

"Well, it doesn't hurt, that's for sure!"

"What do you say we get out of here before they realize you have telekinesis and are controlling the dice with your mind?"

I drain my water glass and get up. "I think we've done enough damage for one night."

We start to walk out, and I turn to him. "You said we could settle up," I say, handing him two crisp Ben Franklins.

He looks at the proffered money and smiles. "Tell you what. Go put it on a roulette number, Lady Luck. If it wins, I'll split it with you, if it loses, we're even."

We walk to the nearest table. I look at the numbers.

"What do you think?" he asks me.

"I think twenty-two, since that was the date we met."

"And the lucky number from *Lost in America*," he adds.

"That, too."

"Go for it."

I put the two hundred-dollar bills on number twenty-two. The wheel spins. Double zero.

"Oh well, guess we can't win all the time."

"That's why the casinos stay in business. Eventually they always get their money back. C'mon. Let's take their money and run!"

We head out and find Connor's truck in the lot. Once we find the highway, in a very quiet moment, my stomach decides to make itself known.

Bbbbbrrrrrrooooooowwwwwwwllllllllggggggggggg.

Oh Lord.

Connor starts laughing. "Guess I'd better feed you, huh?"

"Guess you'd better."

"Can you wait till we get back into the city?"

"Absolutely. On one condition."

"What's that?"

"Wherever we go, I need steak. My blood is feeling thin."

"Steak it is. Settle back; I'll go as quick as I can get away with."

I lean back on the seat, my newly flush purse in my lap, and breathe deep.

It's just after one by the time he walks me to my door.

"Connor, this was probably the best date I have ever had. Thank you."

"I had a good time, too. I'd like to get together again."

"I'd love that."

He leans in and kisses me. Strong mouth, soft tongue, just heavenly.

He pulls back and smiles at me. "Well, the next week is pretty crazy for me. I'll call you Mondayish and see if we can't set something up for early the week after."

"Okay." This is perfect, since I'm supposed to be seeing both Abbot and Ben this weekend, and I can feel free to put them in my calendar without worrying about saving time for Connor.

"Okay then, you have a great weekend, and I'll talk to you on Monday."

"Okay. Good night, Connor."

He kisses me again. "Good night. And tell your aunts I said good night as well." He gestures at the parlor window, where two forms are silhouetted behind the drapes.

"They're incorrigible."

"They're sweet."

He kisses me one more time, dipping me for effect.

"Go inside and explain that one!"

I laugh and watch him retreat down the stairs. Then I go inside to face the music.

❦

"You four are impossible!" A sleepy Hunter appears in the aunts' parlor. It is nearly two in the morning, and we are all a little soused. I got home after my date and knocked on the door to find that not only had Ruth and Shirley waited up, they had champagne chilling. Pink champagne, no less.

"We figured if it was great, we'd celebrate, and if it was awful, pink champagne would perk you up!" Shirley said.

"It's hard to argue with logic like that," I say, gesturing for Aunt Ruth to pop the cork. Aunt Shirley goes to the phone and dials. "She's home; come down," Shirley says. Within moments, it seemed, Jill joined us, wearing her pajamas and a bathrobe and clearly half asleep.

"Did I miss anything?" she said, accepting a glass of champagne.

"Nope, she hasn't begun yet."

Once we all had our drinks, I raised my glass. They all looked at me expectantly.

"To Mr. Connor Duncan, the best first date in the history of the world!"

They all started buzzing at once, asking questions, and I took them through the date, but leaving out the most important detail.

"It sounds lovely, sweetheart. We liked him immediately, didn't we, Ruthie?" Aunt Shirley said.

"Yes, of course, as much as you can like someone based on two minutes of superficial conversation in the foyer."

"But, wait," Jill says. "How'd you make out? With the gambling, I mean. Did you win anything?"

This was the cue I'd been waiting for. I grabbed my purse, reached inside, and pulled out the wad of cash and tossed it into the air.

"I won a little," I said.

We all giggled, and Jill and I rolled around in the money on the floor, and it must have been this ruckus that woke Hunter.

Aunt Ruth fetches him a glass, and Jill tells him about my date. I love this about Jill. She takes your story and tells it with total joy and abandon, as if it is as meaningful to her as it is to you. Listening to her, and watching Hunter react, I'm filled with love. He isn't angry that we woke him at two A.M. on a work night, tipsy on pink champagne and laughing loudly for no other reason than that I had a good date. He seems to really like our personal Spingold brand of crazy. Bless his heart. Jill catches me looking at them and smiles the most genuine smile I've seen from her since Thanksgiving. Something in my chest loosens the littlest bit.

I raise my glass again. "To Hunter, for putting up with four insane women!"

"To Hunter!" we all say.

"Aw, shucks, ladies. I'm a lucky, lucky man!" We all laugh again and start to gather up my winnings off the floor.

I count out four stacks of $500 each and hand them around. "I want each of you to buy yourself something totally frivolous and wonderful!"

"Oh no, sweetie, we couldn't possibly. That's your money!" Shirley says, waving me off.

"Like hell we can't, sis." Ruth snickers. "I've had my eye on a new purse that I've been hesitant to splurge on, and this is just the ticket. Thank you, honey." She takes the money and kisses me.

"Well," Aunt Shirley says, a little puzzled.

"Oh go on, Aunt Shirley!" says Jill, taking hers. "I'm buying my first pair of Jimmy Choos!" She nudges Hunter. "And Hunter really wants one of those new Xbox things . . ." Hunter shrugs and takes the cash.

"Thanks, Jodi. I'll let you play with it whenever you want!"

"You're very welcome."

"I have wanted to get one of those new home ice-cream makers . . ." Aunt Shirley is struggling.

"Please take it, Aunt Shirley. I had so much fun winning it, and I still have plenty left. It would make me so happy to know you were able to buy something fun for yourself!"

"Well, dear, if you insist!" She grins.

"I do." I drain the last of my pink bubbles. "And on that note, I think we should all get to bed."

"Indeed." Shirley yawns delicately. "I'm glad you had such a nice time, dear."

"Me, too, darling." Ruth pinches my cheek.

"C'mon, let me escort you ladies upstairs." Hunter offers his arms to Jill and me.

We head up the stairs, and on the second landing, I kiss my sister and brother-to-be good night.

"G'night, Butthead. Glad it was a good date," Jill says.

"G'night, Moose Face. Thanks for coming down to celebrate. You, too, Rusty." I sometimes call Hunter Rusty because his hair gets reddish in the sun.

"I'm glad you had fun. Hopefully this one will stick. I could use some more testosterone around here! Good night, Kangaroo Arms!"

Jill shakes her head at him.

"No?" he asks.

"Keep working," I say. I smack him lightly on the arm and head up to my apartment. I check my voice mail.

"Hey, Jodi, it's Connor. I figure you're downstairs telling those great aunts of yours all about tonight. I hope I come off okay . . . Have a great weekend, and I'll call you early next week. I want a full report on everything you plan on buying with your loot, and no charitable donations! Good night, Jodi. Thanks for a great evening."

Hmmm. I have to say, I really do like this guy. If his second dates are anything as good as the first, I might have to reconsider my current dating roster.

I get ready for bed in a pleasurable haze, climb into bed, and fall asleep with the taste of Connor's kisses and pink champagne on my tongue.

Gotta Getta Get

❦

Religion is always a touchy issue, especially in an age where interfaith relationships are far more common than same-faith ones. Keeping a clear head and finding common ground is essential to merging your feelings about a person and your spirituality. It is closely interwoven in more aspects of your life than you can imagine, and if you are considering a serious commitment, having a very honest dialogue about religion and expectations will be as important as the dialogues you will have about money and family. This is particularly true for Jews, where the differences in types of practice can make the chasm between two people of different sects as divergent as if they were from two different faiths altogether. While Judaism embraces many ways of practice, when two Jews get together, it cannot be assumed that they both have the same relation to the faith as the other.

—From an article about inter-interfaith marriage for the JUF News,
Jodi Spingold, May 2003

"Jodi?" The intercom squawks at me.

"Yes, Benna?"

"Mr. Summit is here to see you."

"Tell him I'll be right out."

I look up at Jill across the office. "Were you expecting Brant today?" she asks.

"Nope. The king of the drop-in strikes again."

"Want me to vacate so you can have the office?"

"Nah. If it's more than just hello, I'll take him to the conference room." Brant and I are going to have to have a little discussion about his new habit of popping in on me without calling.

"Okay," Jill says, turning back to the budget she's going over. "Tell him I said hi."

I head out to the reception area and accept the kiss on my cheek from Brant. He has a new haircut, courtesy, I assume, of Mallory.

"Hey, Jodi, hope this isn't a bad time," he says.

"Not at all. Just in the neighborhood?"

"Yep. And I had something I sort of wanted to talk to you about. Do you have a few minutes?"

"Sure." *Interesting.* "Come on back." I lead him to the conference room and shut the door behind us. "Want something to drink?"

"Nope, I'm fine, thanks."

"So, what's up?"

"Okay, this may be a little weird, but I wanted to talk to you about us getting a get."

Fantastic. A get. A get is a Jewish divorce. Civil divorces aren't recognized by the faithful, if you had a Jewish ceremony. If you split up, you need to get a Jewish divorce, which, according to custom, can only be sought or granted by the husband. This is an ancient exercise that, frankly, can be pretty misogynistic. The woman has to come before a tribunal of rabbis, and in some cases, announce her failure as a Jewish wife, circle the husband seven times in the opposite direction of the seven times she circled him when they married, face the wall . . . a horrible and humiliating exercise. Which is why Brant and I had agreed, despite having signed a Jewish marriage contract and having had a fairly traditional ceremony, not to seek a get. In fact, at the time, we laughed about how archaic it was and that our Judaism was so nontraditional anyway, what did it matter?

I take a deep breath. "A get? I thought we agreed not to pursue that."

"I know," he says sort of sheepishly. "And I wouldn't ask, but Mallory says she feels uncomfortable dating someone who is still married in the eyes of Jewish law."

Mallory. That self-important, manipulative twat. "Well, that seems incongruous."

"In what way?"

"Well, she clearly isn't so Orthodox as to pay attention to the no sex before marriage edict." Brant had shared the fact that the relationship had indeed moved into the realm of the intimate shortly after he brought her over to my place. I had finally gotten up the nerve to suggest that I did not need to be introduced to all his women friends unless something was getting serious, and he replied that things were serious with Mallory, a fact that seems to be horribly reinforced by this latest development.

"She isn't Orthodox, more sort of conserva-dox. But she's getting me in touch with my Judaism, and she seems really adamant about the get thing. I know it's a pain, but it would mean a lot to me if you would do this with me."

"Brant, I'm going to be honest. I'm not thrilled. You and I are the ones directly involved, and we agreed when we split up that this was not something either one of us needed to do."

He looks crestfallen.

"I'm not saying no; I'm just saying I'm not happy about it, okay? I'm allowed to have an issue with your new girlfriend dictating something this personal to me."

"Mallory isn't trying to make things tough for you; she just has her own beliefs, and they include this area of Jewish law."

Yeah, right. I'm sure that's it. "Okay, look. If you can do the research, find a rabbi to make it reasonably painless, I'll do it." *Good grief. What am I getting into?*

"That's great, Jodi, really. I appreciate it. Mallory's rabbi is—"

"No."

"No?"

"Brant, Mallory isn't a part of this. Mallory's rabbi is *really* not a part of this. I'm not doing this for Mallory. I'm doing it in good faith for you, so *you* find a rabbi, *you* make the arrangements. Mallory has no place in this endeavor, all right?" I know I probably sound a little harsh, but the idea of Mallory hanging out while Brant and I go through this farce is more than I am willing to deal with.

"Fine. No problem. I'll figure it out. Thanks, Jodi, really, it means a whole lot to me."

"Well, I know you'd do it for me, so what the hell. But you owe me *huge* for this, you do know that . . ."

He laughs. "Of course. Anytime, just call in your favor."

"Oh, I'll think of some appropriate punishment for you." We are back to our old, comfortable banter. The tense moment seems to have passed.

"I know you will. I'm going to head back to work, and I know you're busy. I'll get some research done and be back in touch about things." Brant gets up and gathers his coat and briefcase.

"Okay, I'll talk to you later." I walk him out to the front, accept the kiss good-bye, and go back to my office.

Jill looks up when I push open the frosted glass door. "How's Brant?" she asks, putting down her highlighter.

"Oh, fine. Work is busy, the cats are getting fatter . . . oh, and Mallory needs us to get a get."

"A get?" Jill looks flabbergasted.

"Yep. Ye olde gette of yore."

"The whole flagellating yourself in front of all the old rabbis sort of get?"

"Apparently."

"*Mallory* needs this." Jill is shaking her head.

"She, and I quote, 'doesn't feel comfortable dating a man who is still married in the eyes of Jewish law.'"

"But the premarital fucking is pretty much no problem?"

In case it has been remotely unclear up until now, this is concrete proof that Jill and I share a brain.

"That's what I said!" We chuckle together. "But what can I do? I can't speak out against her; it makes me the bitchy ex if I do."

"Which is clearly what she wants."

"Do you think? I mean, far be it from me to denigrate the way that someone practices their faith. But it does feel really weird and kind of manipulative, doesn't it? Especially so early in their relationship. I mean, they've only known each other like three months!"

"Oh, come on, Jodi! Wake up and smell the insecurity. She obviously is trying to take some sort of control over Brant, and she's scared that he's still hung up on you."

"Brant is so over me. C'mon, we broke up almost five years ago!"

"Yeah, but you wanted the divorce, not him, and you know he doesn't have that many other friends. I'm sure he talks a blue streak about you and how awesome you are. And you know she's Googled you to death. She's intimidated by you, and has set her mind on Brant, and she's going to do whatever she can to drive a wedge between you guys."

"Do you really think so? I'm hoping that this will be the end of it, you know, if I get the stupid get, she can feel like I'm not a threat."

"Well, think about it. She waits until he's all smitten and in a sex haze, and then springs this on him. What is she, the second woman he's ever slept with?"

"Third. Don't forget the twenty-two-year-old right after the divorce."

"Okay, third. He's thirty-five. He's had sex with three women in his life. And the current one is making demands. He's going to say no? It's a test. She's fucking testing him. If he asks you for the get instead of honoring his original agreement with you, it shows that she has power over him. Then if you refuse, you're the shrew."

"Oh, I fucking hate this!"

Paige knocks on the door, and Jill waves her in.

"Hey, I just saw Brant leaving. What's up?"

"He had a very important thing he needed to discuss with Jodi," Jill says, affecting a serious manner.

"Is everything okay?" Paige asks.

"Just fine. Except we need to get a get. A Jewish divorce," I say.

"Why?" Paige asks.

"Jewish law doesn't recognize civil divorce." I shrug.

"Oh come *on!*" Jill explodes. "Stop being so calm. You know you're seething." She turns to Paige. "Mallory suddenly doesn't feel comfortable dating someone who is still married in the eyes of the temple."

Paige barks out one of her deep-throated laughs. "How did I just sense that Malevolent was behind this? What a cow."

"I'm trying to be calm about this, guys," I say, attempting to explain myself. "I mean, everyone is entitled to their own level of faith. It's what we always say we love so much about being Jewish, that you can find whatever way of practice is meaningful for you as an individual. So, Mallory is entitled to believe what she believes. I can't argue with it."

"You are so full of shit." Paige snorts.

"Give it up. You aren't that Zen about this, and you know it!" Jill says, pointing a manicured nail in my direction. "What is with you and the need to be the perfect ex-wife? Why do you have to prove that you are all twenty-first-century sensitive about everything with Brant? The man is a very nice, reasonably benign *idiot*! He wasn't worth your time when you were married to him and is worth even less now that the relationship is over. Go ahead. Be angry. Be irritated. But stop being so fucking *accommodating* and *understanding*. It is seriously working on my nerves!"

Paige and I look at each other when this explosion is over and then burst into hysterical laughter. Benna peeks around the corner and enters the office gingerly. She is a teensy-tiny girl, no taller than four ten or eleven, built like a ten-year-old boy. She is half Japanese and half Portuguese, and this unusual combination has resulted in a delicate beauty that is pretty breathtaking. She keeps her black hair in a simple and sleek pageboy, her skin is the color of caramel, her wide eyes are only slightly almond-shaped, a sparkling golden hazel, and she has the most perfect pink rosebud mouth anyone has ever seen. She is thirty-two, looks sixteen even on a bad day, and has been with us for just over a year. She, like Paige, came to us organically, calling in to the show. Then calling back. Then making an appointment to see us privately. She had always fancied herself as an old-school executive assistant, wanting to be the foil for the right CEO, and her skills are staggering. But after a series of staid corporate gigs, none of which were the right fit, she offered to take a 20 percent pay cut to come work with us. She is a godsend, and we all love her.

Unfortunately for her, men seem to take her petite frame and delicate features to mean that the girl herself is a withering flower, when in fact she is badass to the bone. So she's forever in the midst of a guy crisis, because the guys who want her all have a need to protect and coddle, and the guy she really wants is the one who would treat her like the hellcat she actually is. Benna drives a sixty-three Mustang she restored and maintains herself.

Benna was an undefeated amateur featherweight boxer with twenty-three fights to her career. Benna is hiding two full sleeves of intricate tattoos under her Donna Karan suit. Benna skis the double black diamonds metaphorically and literally, and she is desperately in need of a like-minded fellow to sweep her off her size-five feet.

"No fair you all having fun in here while I am wrestling with the fucking copier." She has a smudge of toner on the tip of her button nose. Jill hands her a tissue and gestures for her to clean herself up. Kim rounds the corner, all slim efficiency.

"Please tell me there is something in here related to anything except PR. I'm cashed."

Benna wipes her nose and plops onto the couch next to Paige. "What's up?"

Kim perches on the arm of the couch, and Jill fills them in on the Brant situation, Paige fills them in on the Mallory situation, and pretty soon they are laughing along with the rest of us.

"Just when I think my husband is the biggest idiot and that I should leave him, you make me think he's a godsend!" Kim says.

"What a mess. Makes my guy crap look like nothing!" Benna shakes her head.

"Come on, dish. What's the latest?" Paige says. "I thought the new guy was sort of great?"

"Gino? He is great. Almost too great. Smart, fun, not soppy, and so far doesn't seem to want to paint me as some sort of damsel in distress."

"So?" Kim says. "What's the catch?"

"Well, the ink is barely dry on his divorce, and so I think he isn't in a place to be thinking seriously about anyone, which is fine for the moment, but you know, I can't hang too long if he isn't ever going to get serious. I mean, tick tock and all that." Benna is very certain about her desire to have kids, and while she isn't exactly testing the DNA of the gents she dates, she does have a strict four-month rule. If by the fourth month they don't have daddy potential, she kicks them to the curb, even if she is having fun. Which, usually, she isn't.

"Well, it hasn't been four months yet, right?" Kim asks.

"Not yet. But I really do like him, so that always makes me nervous."

"Just let it flow, kiddo. It seems like it has potential," Jill says soothingly.

"Ditto," I say.

"Me, too. Follow your bliss," Paige says. "Enough girl talk for me. I have to go return some calls." Paige gets up, and Benna and Kim follow her out of the office.

Jill and I turn back to our computers.

"Do you really think I'm that bad about the Brant thing?" I ask.

Jill looks up from her monitor. "I think sometimes you act like you can pretend that the marriage wasn't a mistake by keeping up appearances. But you know and I know that if you met Brant at some function tomorrow, you'd never choose to be friends with him. You guys have nothing in common except your history together. And you know that you're still doing this whole friendship thing for his sake, not your own. You don't need him in your life; you never really did."

"But I did genuinely love him, once. I mean, I was really happy with him." Which I was.

Jill pauses. "Here's what I think, for what it's worth. I think that you tended to be more involved with your boys than they were with you. When Brant came along, you were full of your own power, you got to play teacher, which you love, and you got to have everything the way you wanted it, which you also love. I think there was a huge rush in being the one who was loved more than the one who was *in* love for a change. And I think his eventual inability to be anyone other than himself was a disappointment not only in him but in yourself. You couldn't make him what you needed, and that made you something of a failure. But you're just human, and you can't change anyone. Your marriage ended because you married the wrong guy. Period. Perpetuating this friendship, worrying about what he thinks of you, worrying about what his new girlfriend thinks of you, that is just stupid."

"So you really haven't thought about it at all," I say. I know she's right. I have a pathological need to be a good person. Or rather, for people to think I am a good person, which isn't exactly the same thing. I don't know why.

"You know me. I never really think about anything for any length of time; I just say whatever comes to my head!" Jill laughs. "Look, don't get me wrong. I think it's commendable that you are so concerned about the whole thing. Just know that you'll never win in this Mallory situation, so don't do anything that goes too far out of your way or too far beyond your comfort zone. Fuck her. She's gonna hate you regardless, and the sooner you get over that, the easier it is going to be for you to make decisions. And if you end up losing Brant as a friend because of his need to submit to her will, that isn't ultimately much of a loss. That's all I'm saying."

"I hear you. I do. Onward and upward."

"Good girl. In the meantime, I can't wait to hear how this get thing plays out. Should be a hoot!"

"Oh, yeah, I can't wait."

"Hey, speaking of marriage stuff . . ." Jill says.

"Yeah?"

"Will you come with me to look at dresses this weekend? Maybe Saturday afternoon?"

Oy. So it begins. So far, since Hunter is the most excited groom ever, I have been off the hook on decision making. But obviously, the dress is key, and he can't be a part of it.

"Of course I will! Do you have an idea of what you want?"

"Mostly what I want is a different, more dress-friendly body, but all I know for sure is that I want it to be simple, elegant, and not require foundation garments made of steel."

"Shut up. You'll be the most gorgeous bride ever." Which she will.

"You shut up. You were a pretty stunning bride yourself once upon a time."

"I was young. My boobs were up where they belong, my skin was flawless, and I had fourteen ounces of shellac keeping my hair in place."

"You were gorgeous. Even if you were marrying an idiot."

We both crack up.

"Okay, okay, Saturday afternoon. Now really, shut up. I'm working now." Which I really should be.

"Shhh. I'm working. Stop talking to me." Jill tries to be serious.

We laugh and then settle back down to work. While Jill edits the latest chapter and I draft new copy for the blog, I try not to think about how right she may be about my marriage simply having been an error in judgment. A pure and simple mistake. And I take a minute to send a little prayer to the universe that I am the only one of us who will ever make that particular mistake.

Good Tidings We Bring

The first rule of dating more than one person is to be sure that none of the people you are dating think they are the only one in your life. It isn't necessary to announce that you are going on a date when they ask you for plans on a day you have committed to someone else, but don't treat any of your relationships as illicit or secret. There is nothing wrong with not being in a place to engage in a serious and exclusive relationship, and it only becomes shameful if you are ashamed.

—From Living Twenty-five *by Jill and Jodi Spingold*

"So, I think the good news is that the engagement backlash is settling down a little bit," Kim says. "The e-mails have decreased by about twenty-two percent, and the phone traffic by about thirty-four percent."

"That's great news," I say, relieved that some of the hoopla is dying down.

"Not necessarily," Kim says. "I think it's a lull connected to the holidays. We should be prepared for a flurry of activity mid-January when people are stuck inside and bored."

"Great," Jill says.

"And *People* wants to cover the wedding," Kim throws in.

"Not in ten million fucking years or for a hundred million fucking dollars," Jill says.

"Duly noted," Kim says. "That's all I have."

"Benna?" I turn to her.

"Okay, holiday calendars." Benna looks at her notes. "I have Jill leaving the twenty-third and returning the twenty-eighth. Jodi, I have you out of the office on the twenty-fourth and twenty-fifth, but not out of town. Paige, I have you leaving the twenty-second and returning the second of January. I leave the twenty-third and return the twenty-sixth. The office is closed Christmas Eve and Day and New Year's Eve and Day. Kim, you'll get me the marketing team's dates?"

Kim nods.

"Great. That's all I have." Benna checks something off on her notepad.

"Sounds good. Everyone, don't forget to remind your staff that the reason we don't roll over vacation days is that we want you all to take a break now and again. So if they haven't used up all their days, be sure that they make plans to do so before the grace period is up at the end of February, okay?" I look around the table at a circle of nodding heads. Jill and I fought about the issue when we started hiring employees; she wanted to let people accumulate days indefinitely, and I thought it set a bad precedent. The compromise was to allow a two-month grace period into the new fiscal year for people to use up any days they might have missed.

"Okay, everything sounds like it's falling into place for holiday craziness," Jill jumps in. She rubs her eyes and yawns. "Is anyone else ridiculously hungover today?" She reaches for a Krispy Kreme, courtesy of darling Benna, who knew that after the office holiday bash last night, we'd all need the sugar and grease.

"I'm not too bad, actually," Kim says. "But Eileen, Maddy, and Cleo all look green around the gills." Poor Kim manages a trio of twenty-somethings: Eileen the press assistant, Maddy the graphic designer slash website manager, and Cleo, who is the assistant marketing director. All three got way into the wine at the party last night, making them vivacious and entertaining company, but I'm not surprised they're slightly under the weather today.

"Poor things." I can't help chuckling. "Benna, let's order in pizzas for lunch for everyone . . . and get Bill over at the White Hen to send up a case of that Glaceau Vitamin Water stuff. I think they have a hangover cure version."

"Good idea," Paige says. "A little recovery won't hurt me either."

"At the risk of being insensitive to everyone's day-after pain, what are you guys doing tonight?" Benna asks with a tone in her voice that tells us it doesn't matter what was on the agenda, she needs our support.

"Hunter is out of town, so I don't have plans," Jill says.

"I'm supposed to hang out with Ben, but nothing serious," I say.

"I'm having a quiet night at home with my long-suffering husband," says Kim.

"I got nothing," Paige says. "Why, what's up?"

"It's Gino's birthday. He has a busy day, so we are technically celebrating this weekend, but I talked to his neighbor yesterday, and he agreed to help me surprise him with a wee cake and champagne party when he gets home. Can you guys come? Around nine? You can bring Ben, no problem." Benna looks at us hopefully.

"Of course, just give us the address," Jill says.

"We'll be there," I say. Ben has been clamoring to meet my friends, and I suppose I should oblige him. Although I'm nervous to hear their opinions about him.

"Sorry, kiddo, no can do," says Kim. "Marc will kill me if I bail on our date night."

"Will there be any single guys there?" Paige asks.

"I've invited a few of his friends, some nice guys he works with, but I can't really vouch for them!" Benna laughs. "You guys are the best. I'll e-mail everyone directions."

We all file out of the conference room, and Jill and I head back to our office.

"Do you want to come to this thing tonight with me and Ben, or do you want to meet there?" I ask.

"I'll meet you there. Paige and I can grab dinner or something before. You really are going to bring him?"

"Might as well. He'll be good in a party situation; he's very personable." I hope.

"Isn't it past his curfew?" Jill loves to tease me about the age difference.

"Ha-ha."

"Has he ever been to a birthday party that wasn't at Chuck E. Cheese?"

"Fuck you."

"Gesundheit."

"Very funny." She cracks me up.

"Well, I'm looking forward to meeting him." She has an evil twinkle in her eye.

"You have to promise to be nice. He's a sweet guy, and it isn't his fault he happens to be slightly less aged than myself. No teasing him."

"I promise," she says in a tone that makes me very skeptical indeed. "Do you think we should have told Benna this party wasn't a good idea?"

"I was just thinking that," I say. "I mean, three months, way too early to do this sort of thing. She's going to come off desperate."

"Maybe not," Jill says, chewing on the end of a pen. "Maybe he'll think she's just really sweet."

"Come on, let's be real. He's a guy. None of us have met him, and she doesn't appear to have met many of his friends. A party is a really shitty idea."

"Yeah, I know. You're right. But she's so excited, we can't tell her. And maybe it will be okay." She turns to her computer. "So what are you going to do with me gone over Christmas?" she asks, scanning her e-mails.

"Well, the aunts and I are going to keep the movie/Chinese food/movie tradition alive in your absence on Christmas Day. Abbot leaves the same day you do to go home but is coming back on the twenty-ninth and has requested that he be able to come straight to my place when he lands, which means I'm getting an airport holiday gift for sure. Ben's folks are taking the annual family vacation to Hawaii, so he will be out of my hair from the twenty-first to the thirtieth. And Connor has put in a request that I join him, his brothers, and their assorted wives and girlfriends for their annual Christmas Eve party." I tell you, anyone who thinks it might be fun to have three beaus never tried to juggle them over the holidays.

"Sounds like you have plenty on your plate without me! More important, what are we going to do for New Year's?"

Jill and I always spend New Year's Eve together, and in the last few years have eschewed big parties in favor of quiet get-togethers with small groups of friends.

"I dunno." I think for a minute. "What about a retro thing? Like Mom and Dad used to do. Do you remember their New Year's parties at all?"

"You mean like with the cheese fondue and sweet and sour meatballs and stuff?"

"Totally. And then a standing rib roast with the double-baked potatoes and steamed asparagus with hollandaise! We can party like it's 1979!"

Jill gets a serious look on her face. "No rumaki! I always hated the smell of the chicken livers."

"Deal. Who should we have?"

"Well, the aunts, of course. Me and Hunter. You and . . ." She trails off expectantly.

"Me and someone."

"Which someone will draw the short straw on this one?"

"Well, Ben and Abbot have both asked, and I've put them off, blaming you for not deciding yet. Connor hasn't asked, but I think he will."

"And clearly Connor is the one you'd like to come; otherwise you would have said yes to one of the others already."

"I guess. Frankly, I'm nervous about either Ben or Abbot meeting the family. Ben will get all hyper trying to impress everyone, and Abbot will get smug like it means I'm making some sort of commitment to him. At least Connor would just be normal. But it's early to be thinking New Year's. I mean, we've only had two dates, we haven't slept together yet, and New Year's is a big deal. He might not want to go there."

"Except it isn't a big deal to bring you home on Christmas Eve to meet all his brothers? Come on. And sex or no sex, you do have obvious chemistry."

Last weekend he took me to dinner at the Eleven City Diner, loads of amazing comfort food, one malted with two straws, and then we drove up Michigan Avenue to look at the holiday lights. Then we came back to my place and made out on the couch like a couple of teenagers for about two hours. Totally delicious. He's the best kisser and never tried to push things too far or pressure me to take him to bed. Just seemed to really enjoy necking. Which of course made me want to tear his clothes off.

"Yes, it's pretty clear that there is some chemistry, but I'm not sure what to do. I mean, my relationship with Ben isn't passionate,

but things with Abbot are pretty great in that department, so I'm
not totally inclined to give him up quite yet. But I do really like
Connor, and I am very physically attracted to him."

"Well, maybe you'll find that the more you want him, the less
you'll want Abbot."

"Yeah, that is sort of what I'm thinking." Actually, what I'm
thinking is that Friday night I may take things the teensiest bit
further, just to test the waters. We're going to see *The Santaland
Diaries*, which is supposed to be one of the funniest nonsectarian
holiday events around. Anything written by David Sedaris has got
to be good. I might let him get to third base.

"And he's the one you'd rather be with," she clucks.

"Stop analyzing it, sister dearest. Just put me down as a plus-
one, and it will be determined soonish." Yeesh.

"All right. If you insist. Who else?"

"Paige is out of town. How about Hunter's friend Matt and
his girlfriend? They're fun." Matt, a friend of Hunter's from architect school, is going to be the best man at the wedding, and his
girlfriend Shelly is really sweet. "It would be good to get to know
them better before the wedding, don't you think?"

"That's a great idea. And then what about Raj and Tim to fill
out the party?" Raj is a friend of ours from college. He worked
on the newspaper with me. Now he works for *Chicago* magazine
writing features. His partner Tim is a personal stylist, and the two
of them are hilariously funny.

"Perfect. Ten's a party, twelve's a nightmare." One of Aunt
Shirley's sayings. She thinks the ideal dinner party is between six
and ten people, no more.

"We can tell them about it at cocktail hour tomorrow." Jill
stands, heads over to the coat rack in the corner, and slips on her
coat. "You ready?"

We have a meeting with a designer to see a couple of proto-types of the new lunch kits. I get up and get my coat on. "Let's go."

We stop by Benna's desk to tell her to order the pizza for twelve thirty, since we should be back by then, and head out into the snow to see if my little kit vision has become a marketable reality.

※

"So then the guy says that he thinks we should have known what he meant and ignored what he said! Can you fucking believe it?" Ben is railing about work, in between bites of his burger. We are having dinner, before Gino's surprise party, at the Athenian Room. Ben seems to survive almost entirely on hummus and burgers. He is the least adventurous eater I've ever met, and while he reluctantly accepted a bite of my delicious skirt steak and grudgingly pronounced it tasty, I know that he will still order a burger the next time he is here. I also know that I may not be with him the next time he is here. Ben is beginning to bore me a weensy bit. Even if he does look like Zach Braff and makes me laugh a lot.

"Well, isn't some of what you do intuiting what your clients really want and need?" I ask, nibbling on a vinegary steak fry.

"Okay, yeah, some of it. I mean, when they say they want their website to be sexy, I have to figure out what they mean by sexy. Is their sexy Pamela Anderson or is their sexy Maggie Gyllenhaal?"

I laugh. "Sophia Loren or Audrey Hepburn."

His face is a blank.

"You know, the actresses. One was earthy and voluptuous, and the other was gamine and elegant. Both sexy, but different. Pam and Maggie of their time. Actually, Sophia still has the juice—"

"You and your black-and-white babes."

"Yes, honey. But some color stuff, too."

Ben refuses to watch black-and-white movies. They bother

him. He likes bright colors. And car chases. I like William Powell. He likes Will Ferrell. I like Cary Grant. He likes Carey Hart. 'Nough said.

"Anyway. Enough of my whining about work. How was your week?" One thing about Ben, he is always genuinely interested in me, which is enormously flattering.

I look across the table into his liquid brown eyes. They look back, full of hope and longing. What a muffin.

"Good, really. We met with the product development designers today and saw some good mock-ups for the new lunch kit, so looks like we may move forward on that. The merchandising folks seem pleased, so they are crunching the numbers as we speak."

"That is so cool. What a great idea. You'll sell a bundle."

"Well, I hope so."

"You're such a genius."

Sigh. Whenever I wonder what the hell I am doing hanging out with this guy, he looks at me like that, and then I remember.

"Thank you. I do try."

He kisses my hand. There is a giggle behind us. Ben turns around to see a little girl of four or five, who is watching us and laughing.

"Hello, there," Ben says to her.

"Hi," she replies.

"Carly, don't bother the nice people," her mother admonishes. "Let them eat in peace."

"She's no bother," I say.

"Carly, that's a nice name," Ben says. He is amazing with kids. Probably because he still is one.

The two of them talk very seriously for a few minutes. I watch Carly develop her first crush. Ben is a very charming fellow. But they are interrupted when Carly's parents receive the check and get up to leave.

"Say good-bye, sweetheart."

"Good-bye, sweetheart," Carly says to Ben solemnly, clearly sad to be leaving.

"Good-bye, princess." Ben kisses her hand dramatically. They leave, Carly looking back over her shoulder all the way out the door.

"Careful, tiger, I'm liable to get jealous, you fawning all over that younger woman right in front of me!"

"Wasn't she a doll? I can't wait to have a couple of my own!"

"You'll make a wonderful father." Which he will.

"And you'll make a wonderful mother." He leans in to kiss me again. I stop him.

"I'll make a wonderful godmother. A helluva aunt. But not a mother, not me."

"Stop that, you'll be fantastic."

"Ben, I didn't mean that I questioned my own ability to be a good mother; I meant that I have no intention of being one. I don't want kids."

"Sure you do."

"No, darlin', I don't."

"But you're a woman." For Ben, this is all the logic he needs.

"Yes, I am."

Ben pauses, obviously confused. Then a strange look comes over his face, and he tilts his head at me. "You know, there's always adoption."

Oy vey. "Ben, don't look at me like that. I'm not barren. At least I don't think I am. I just don't want to have kids. I like my life, I like my vision for my future. And it doesn't include children of my own, natural or adopted."

"I don't know what to say." He is looking at me like I'm an alien life-form.

"You don't have to say anything; it is just who I am."

"But what if your husband wants children?"

"Ben, if I get married again, and that is a *big* if, I would never marry someone who wanted kids. I would marry someone who already had kids. Frankly, I think I'd make an adorable stepmother. But this is sort of a deal-breaker for me."

"So you're saying I have to choose between you and my desire to be a dad or I have to get married to someone else, have kids, get divorced, and then come back to you."

"Oh, Benji. I'm flattered that you would even think of me as the possible mother of your future children, but we have only known each other for a couple of months . . ."

And a dark cloud moves across his features. "Are you seeing other people?" He looks wounded.

"Well, yes. I mean, I told you when we first started going out that I wasn't looking for a serious relationship. Aren't you dating other women?"

"No. I'm not. I thought, I mean, it was one thing in the very beginning, but I can't, I mean, splitting focus and all, and . . ." He can't seem to get a coherent sentence out.

I reach over and squeeze his arm. "Ben, I think you're wonderful, but I'm not in a serious relationship place right now. And I enjoy your company, but I have to be free to live my life my way. I don't mean that to be hurtful; I just want to be honest."

"Well, do you think you might get into a more serious place sometime in the foreseeable future?"

How do you tell someone that he just isn't ever going to be that guy? You don't. You chicken out. "I honestly don't know, Ben." Always use the word *honestly* when you're lying. No one will suspect you. I'm a cow. "I'm not ruling it out. But I'm not making promises."

I hate this. I really do like him, I like hanging out with him. Why I can't just say that we should be friends is beyond my own comprehension. We aren't compatible physically, so the relationship is pretty chaste, with the exception of some decent goodnight kissing. But I know he thinks he is giving me space to get back to a place of intimacy, and it just isn't going to happen. So why can't I tell him that? What is it about me that I like having him pursuing me romantically and not just being friends?

Ben smiles. "No, it's fine. I'm glad we both are on the same page. I definitely want us to keep hanging out. No worries. Nonexclusive. It's fine."

This is where I get nervous. Ben looks like I just handed him a challenge. But I have to take him at his word.

"Okay then, shall we go to this party?" I say, getting up out of my chair.

"Absolutely," he says, his voice filled with brave enthusiasm. I can hear his gears turning. I'm starting to dread the evening. Mostly because I feel like sort of a bitch, and I hate that.

"Off we go." He offers me his arm, I take it, and we head out to surprise Benna's new boyfriend.

*

"Okay, everyone, quiet! He'll be here any minute!" Benna says in an exaggerated stage whisper.

There are maybe fifteen of us crowded into Gino's spare living room, waiting for the door to open. It is almost nine thirty, and so far, so good. Ben has been charming and funny, Jill has given her stamp of approval, and Paige has winked at me so many times she looks as if she has a tic. He has fetched drinks, made friends with all of Gino's pals, and been generally adorable. He's bounced back remarkably from our uncomfortable earlier exchange and seems bound and determined to be a jovial and attentive companion, which is part of why I do like him so much.

"*Shhhhhhhh!* He's here!" Gino's helpful neighbor yelps from the window where he has spotted Gino's car turn the corner. We all hunker down, and I wonder how it is that the sound of fifteen people breathing can be so loud. After several long moments, there is a key in the lock and the door swings open.

"*Surprise!!!*" we all yell as someone throws the lights on. And then, silence.

Gino is standing in his open doorway with an attractive blonde, one hand still inside her blouse, the other holding his keys, mouth agape.

"Who the fuck is *that*?" Benna says with venom in her voice.

"Who the fuck are *you*?" the blonde snaps.

"What the fuck is going on?" Gino says, releasing the blonde's left breast and letting his hand drop to his side.

One by one we all replace our drinks on the nearest surface and begin to sidle out, no one making eye contact, sheepish and embarrassed.

❧

"Poor baby, what a mess!" Paige says to Benna, handing her the umpteenth tissue.

"He doesn't deserve you," Jill adds, squeezing her arm.

"He's a total tool," Ben says, which makes the rest of us laugh. We all waited downstairs for Benna and then whisked her back to Jill's, where the four of us are commiserating with a bottle of Glenlivet.

"I mean, three months we've been dating! Three months! Shouldn't I have been able to expect that he wasn't still seeing other people?"

"Well . . ." I begin, then I think better of it.

"Well, what?" she asks.

"Nothing. Never mind." This is not the right time to explain my views on dating protocols.

"No, really, I'd like to hear." Benna blows her nose loudly and takes another swig of her whiskey.

"Well, did you and he ever have a conversation about making the relationship exclusive?"

"No, not specifically, but I just thought, I mean, once you start seeing someone regularly . . ."

"Look, Benna, tonight was awful for you, and I'm so sorry. I know your feelings are hurt. But it has only been three months you and he have been together, and if you never had a conversation about not seeing other people, then he wasn't doing anything wrong. And since you didn't have plans with him tonight, it's sort of hard to fault him."

Three pairs of eyes turn to glare at me.

"What? I'm just being honest." *Yeesh.*

"Jodi, I think it's easy to believe that in a dating situation, after several months and a certain level of intimacy, one might be able to assume exclusivity without having to make a federal case of it," Paige says.

"You can see how she would believe that," Ben pipes in, making pointed eye contact as he does.

"Now wait, don't everyone jump on Jodi." Thank God Jill will be on my side. "We have always recommended that women should be more direct about periodically addressing the boundaries of their relationships and ensuring that they are on the same page as their partners."

"In order to avoid these sorts of misunderstandings," I say.

"That's all well and good," Benna says. "But can we just not talk about it right now? Right now I want to just focus on the continuing proof that I only pick the wrong guys."

"You got it," I say. "How about we leave you to it?"

"Thanks, Jodi," she says.

"Good night, Benna," Ben says, walking over and kissing her

hand, much as he did earlier with little Carly. "I'm sorry about that idiot. But it was nice to meet you anyway."

"Good night guys," I say, and Ben and I leave Jill's.

"Can I come upstairs?" he asks.

I think it over. On the one hand, I'm tired. On the other, I don't want Ben to feel like I'm punishing him for our earlier conversation.

"It's fine if you want to come up, but I'm kind of tired, so I'm not up for much. Is that okay?"

"Of course. You know, Jodi, I just like being with you. It isn't always about sex."

"Well, I like being with you, too."

He leans over and kisses me gently, and we walk upstairs.

A nice, quiet snuggle and a good-night kiss turn into talking, laughing, more kissing, and a witness to the sunrise. And this is why I am so reluctant to let go of Ben. Because not once did he try to push the advantage. Not once did he try and go further than I wanted. He just kissed me and talked to me and listened to me and held me close. And when he left early this morning, he told me how much he adores me. Which makes me adore him back, even if it doesn't make me want anything more than what we already have. I hate that I know I'd miss him; it makes me really embarrassingly selfish. And what is worse, times like this really do make me feel like a fraud, since I'd read the riot act to any caller who behaved the same. Ugh.

Silly Rabbi, Trix Are for Kids!

You cannot blame someone else for something you allow them to do to you. If you have an opinion, assert it. If you don't want something, don't accept it. There is a difference between strong and bitchy, and you will have very little control over which label someone else places on you. But you should never be afraid to express your feelings, even if they are potentially offensive to someone else. You can't live your life doing things you don't want to do just because you don't want someone to call you a bitch.

—*Advice given to a caller by Jodi Spingold, March 2005*

Riiiiiiiiiiinnnnnng.

Fuck. Phone. I hate when the phone rings early in the morning. I peek at the clock, seven-fucking-thirty for Lord's sake. My alarm isn't set to go off till eight.

Riiiiiiiiiiinnnnnng.

"H'lo?" I mumble.

"Yes, is Jodi Spingold there?" The thick Jewish accent on the other end of the phone is completely unfamiliar to me. Probably trying to get money for JUF or something.

"I'm sorry, I don't take solicitations over the phone. You can send me your materials, and I'll review them."

"No, miss, I'm not calling to ask you for money. I'm Rabbi Silverman. I'm calling about your get."

Great, Brant. Just give some random rabbi my number, and don't bother to tell me. I take a deep breath.

"I'm sorry, Rabbi, I wasn't expecting your call."

"I just wanted to tell you that you need to come pick up your get; I have it."

"It's all set?" Well, maybe Brant isn't a complete idiot, if he found a way to get it done so easily.

"Well, if you can come by maybe Sunday morning, we can take care of everything."

"Christmas Eve day?" Seems an odd choice.

"You have big Christmas plans, *nu*? Going to Mass?" he says with a healthy dose of sarcasm.

I laugh. "No, of course not. But I thought Brant was out of town?"

"Brant doesn't need to be here; he has already taken care of his part."

I take back all my bad thoughts about this get business; Brant clearly really has organized this in the least painful way possible for me.

"Fine, Sunday morning it is."

The rabbi gives me his West Rogers Park address, and I agree to meet him at ten in the morning on Sunday. Then I hang up and roll back over, bound and determined to sleep till the alarm goes off if I can possibly manage it.

<hr>

"Can I have extra cherries, please?" Jill asks Aunt Ruth, who is pouring Manhattans.

"Will three suffice, dear?"

"Ample. Thanks."

Aunt Shirley appears from the kitchen with a tray. She sets it down on the coffee table in front of Jill and me and begins to point things out. "Crostini with goat cheese and fig preserve, marinated olives, pâté-stuffed cremini mushroom caps, and snow peas filled with Boursin."

"Yum," I say, grabbing a small plate. "I'm starved."

Aunt Ruth brings over the drinks, we all settle in, and for a few minutes there is only the sound of contented chewing and sipping and compliments to the barmaid and chef.

"So, darling, are you and Hunter ready for your trip?" Aunt Shirley asks Jill.

"Not remotely. I mean, he is. You know Hunter, always ready. Plus it's his family, so he has nothing to be nervous about." She fishes a cherry out of her drink and chews it thoughtfully.

"What do you have to be nervous about? They're lovely people," Ruth says. "In spite of themselves."

"Yes, of course they are, but I'm going to meet Hunter's grandmother for the first time, the grande dame matriarch, and apparently hell on wheels, which, considering who we've already met, is quite a statement. Plus all the aunts and uncles and cousins. And there I am, the heathen Jew at midnight Mass!"

We giggle. "I hope the church doesn't burst into flame when you cross the threshold," I say.

"Of course not, Jodi," Ruth says. "Lightning will strike her in the parking lot first."

"Ruthie, that's terrible!" Shirley says. "You know the one true God will smite her before she enters the sacred parking lot!" One forgets how wicked Aunt Shirley can be, and how quick-witted, just because she has a soft, comforting presence and angelic hair and usually smells like cookies.

We all laugh.

"Then again, at least I don't have to go see Rabbi Silverman and get spanked with the fourth book of the Talmud for marrying a nincompoop!" Jill says, reaching for a mushroom.

"Still with the get business?" Aunt Shirley asks.

"The rabbi called this morning. I have to go pick up my get on Sunday at ten."

"Well, at least you'll have it over and done with," Ruth says, freshening my drink the tiniest bit.

"Maybe it will be a cleansing sort of thing," Aunt Shirley offers hopefully.

"Like a colonic," mutters Ruth.

"I highly doubt it. But I will give my nincompoop ex some credit; he seems to have set it up to be as simple as possible for me."

"I still think old Malicious is up to something sinister," Jill says. "And frankly, her power over him is entirely your fault, missy!"

"My fault? How is it my fault?"

"You trained him to completely subvert his will to the influence of a strong woman! And Lord knows he needed the guidance; the man couldn't dress himself without you. But when you released him into the wild, he found another strong woman and has put all the decision making into her hands. You reap what you sow."

I punch her in the arm. "You make me sound like such a manipulative bitch! I never asked him to subvert his will. I just, well I, I mean he needed . . ."

"You were a benevolent dictator, dear," Aunt Shirley says.

"And you did dress him very nicely," Aunt Ruth offers.

"I can't take it when you all gang up on me like this. It isn't fair! Was I really so awful?"

Jill pats my arm. "Not awful. Young and determined and with the wrong fellow. Who is now, sadly, allowing his new gal pal to wreak havoc with your life."

"I hate that you are going to be out of town. I wanted you to come with me." Somehow, facing the whole business would become an adventure if Jill were there.

"Well, I wish I were going to be here as well. But I will be in the wilds of Pennsylvania eating oyster stuffing and creamed onions and drinking eggnog."

I sigh. "Will there be ham? God bless the goyim and their Christmas hams, so succulent and pink . . ." Say what you will, but nothing really beats great ham.

"Yes, I believe there will be refreshment of a porcine nature at the groaning board." Jill reaches for an olive.

"Well, we will be missing you," Aunt Ruth says. "Emperor's Choice won't be the same without you."

Emperor's Choice, the family favorite of all the Chinatown haunts, with its unobtrusive green awning and the most delectable treats, has been the site of all of our Christmas Day dinners since time immemorial. When my folks were alive, we all went together, usually in between the two movies we were likely to see.

"And I shall miss the Emperor." Jill places the back of her hand on her forehead in a melodramatic fashion, which makes the rest of us crack up.

"Well, if I survive Sunday, I'll need all the dumplings they can fry up!" I say.

"It'll be fine. No problem. A quick trip to West Rogers Park and home in time for lunch," Jill says.

"Sure, home in time for lunch and to obsess about what to wear to the party Sunday night."

"Ah, yes. The Duncan clan Christmas Eve. Are you nervous?" asks Shirley.

"Well, of course she's nervous," Ruth snaps. "Meeting the brothers is a big deal, probably more important than meeting his parents."

"I do really like him, and his family is important to him, so in terms of our continuing to see each other, yes, it is important to me that I not make an idiot of myself."

"You'll be great. He wouldn't be bringing you if he had any doubts, so just be yourself," Jill says.

"And just think, at least you'll be freshly divorced! The new primping, manicure, pedicure, blow out, ritual religious act . . ." Ruth says, raising her glass to me. "To a Sunday night that makes Sunday morning worth the trouble!"

"Hear, hear," Aunt Shirley says.

"I'll drink to that!" Jill picks up her glass.

"*L'chaim!*" I say, and we all clink and drink.

At ten sharp I pull up in front of the small bungalow in West Rogers Park. I take a deep breath and steel myself to go inside. Piece of cake. Meet the rabbi, grab the get, and go.

As I climb the front stairs, I think about how strange it is to be focused again on my divorce after so many years. Jill's words are still ringing in my ears. My marriage was a failure, a mistake from the beginning. The kind of mistake smart girls aren't supposed to make. The kind of mistake girls like me counsel the less fortunate girls against. This strange exercise brings that into clear relief for me all over again. And what is worse, it makes me deeply embarrassed. I married a man who was the totally wrong guy. I married a man to whom I was only peripherally attracted, because he was nice to me, and in love with me, and made me laugh, and didn't cheat on me or make me feel like shit. I married a man who was socially inept and boring in bed because I was so full of my own ego that I thought I could change both those things and make him into the perfect husband. A rookie mistake if ever there was one, and I am mortified. And Jill is right. If there wasn't ever going to be public opinion about my actions, I'd never remotely put any effort into maintaining even a semblance of a relationship with him.

I climb the front stairs and ring the bell, which makes a tinny noise inside the house. After a few moments, a tiny woman opens the door. She is wearing a faded calico housedress and dirty slippers, and the curly gray wig atop her head is slightly unkempt and in a very old-fashioned style.

"Can I help you?" she asks.

"Yes, ma'am," I say. "I'm here to see Rabbi Silverman."

"Oh, I'm sorry," she says, shaking her head. "The rabbi isn't in at the moment."

I look down at my watch: 10:03. "I'm sorry," I say. "There must be a misunderstanding. I have at ten o'clock appointment with the rabbi. He said I should meet him here."

"Oh my. He didn't mention anything to me before he left. May I ask, what is it regarding?"

I close my eyes for a moment. "I'm here to pick up my get," I say, and a look of deep consternation crosses over her features.

"Oh, I am so sorry, dear. Let me see if I can get him on the cell phone."

I can hear her mumbling into the phone in the other room. She seems somewhat put out. Soon the mumbling stops, and she returns to the foyer.

"He's on his way back, dear. It will take probably fifteen minutes or so. Won't you please come sit down?" She leads me into the dining room and offers me a chair. "You're welcome to read the paper if you like," she says, gesturing at the *New York Times*, which is strewn about the dining room table. "Can I get you something, a cup of coffee, perhaps some tea?" she asks.

"No, thank you," I reply, thinking I'd really like a cold martini. "I'm fine. Please don't go to any trouble."

"Well, then, I'm sure the rabbi will be back shortly." She leaves me alone in the room as if somehow uncomfortable to be in my presence. I suppose that makes sense. My being a living representation of a failed marriage, a Jewish wife who couldn't cut it. Wouldn't want it to rub off.

I sit at the dining room table, reading sections of the *New York Times* and waiting for the rabbi to arrive. I'm trying to control the anger that is building in me. The waste of my time. How rude it is for him to not have even remembered that we have an appointment. After nearly twenty-five minutes, finally, the door opens. I rise and turn to meet a slightly stooped man, probably in his late sixties to early seventies.

"Rabbi Silverman?" I ask, and he extends his hand.

"Yes, Jodi dear, I am so sorry. I must have forgotten to call you."

"Forgot to call me about what?

"To cancel, of course. I was unable to get two other rabbis to join us for our meeting this morning."

"I'm not sure I understand. I thought I was just here to pick up my get."

"You are," he says, "but there have to be two other rabbis here to witness it."

"I was under the impression from our phone call that the get was completed, and I simply needed to come and pick it up." I feel ambushed, though probably not as ambushed as I would have felt if there had been a roomful of rabbis here when I arrived.

"Well, not quite, dear. After all, there needs to be some discussion, there are some prayers . . ." He trails off.

"But you said on the phone that Brant didn't need to be here, that everything was taken care of."

"That's true, Brant already has his get."

I think about this for moment. Brant already has his get. I turn back to the rabbi. "If Brant already has his get, does what we do here somehow validate it or make it legal?"

"No, of course not," the rabbi says. "Brant's get is complete and final and cannot be altered. What we do here is for you."

Thank goodness. I breathe a sigh of relief. "Well then, Rabbi, it doesn't matter; we don't need to reschedule. I don't need a get."

He looks puzzled. "I don't think I understand you, Miss Spingold."

"I don't need a get," I explain. "Brant wanted the get, and you've just told me that Brant has his get; he's finished. Therefore you and I don't need to worry about anything."

"But you don't have a get," the rabbi says.

"But I don't need one," I say.

"I'm confused. Have you remarried?"

"No."

"Well, what if you want to get married again someday?"

"I may."

"Well, then you need a get."

I hate the assumption. "No," I reply, trying to stay calm, "I don't."

"What kind of man would have you without a get?"

Something in my head snaps. "Well, for starters," I say with a coy smile, "a Gentile man."

He blanches. "Are you engaged to be married to a Gentile man?"

"No," I reply. He looks relieved.

"Well, what if you wanted to marry a Jewish man?"

"I may very well."

"Well, what if he requires it of you?"

"I can guarantee you that I would never marry a man who would require this of me."

"It's an important step that you should take."

"That is your opinion, Rabbi, one you and I do not share. My

Judaism is different from yours. I thank you for your time and your effort."

I turn to leave.

"You're making a mistake," he says.

"I made a mistake. The civil courts have undone that mistake."

"You cannot be whole and free without your get."

"I have been whole and free for my entire life. I don't need you, a team of rabbis, or some religious document to tell me that. Good day, sir."

I open the door and step outside into the crisp air. Feeling lighter than I have felt in a long time, that strange giddiness that comes with being slightly disrespectful to an authority figure, I hear the screen door creak open behind me.

"I'll keep the paperwork on file," he calls after me. "You come back any time to complete this process."

I turn back over my shoulder. "Don't waste the file space."

I get into my car and head back toward the city.

Now, what the hell am I going to wear tonight?

Six Geese A-Laying

Meeting the family is a big step in a new relationship. Don't try too hard to be either accommodating or entertaining. Sit back and observe a little. Watch the interactions. There is much to learn about your partner from the way they behave with their family members. Don't try too hard to make an ally of any particular family member. Allow them to get to know you organically, ask questions to get them talking about themselves, and be politic about what you share about yourself. And most important, don't let your nerves lead you to drink too much or talk too much; you really never do have a second chance to make that first impression, and drunk-girl-talking-about-sex is not the impression you want them to remember.

—*Quoted in an article in* Chicago Tribune Sunday Magazine,
Jill Spingold, February 2004

I'm helping Connor organize the buffet in his dining room in preparation for the Christmas Eve festivities. We are laying out plates, flatware, and napkins, as well as serving platters. His family will be bringing all the food. We already set up the bar, made the family recipe eggnog, and decorated with pine boughs and twinkle lights. Bowls of Aunt Shirley's praline pecans are on every occasional table, and my own contribution, a layered café au lait and chocolate cheesecake, is in the fridge.

"Okay," I say to Connor as I roll green napkins into cylinders and slide them into holly napkin rings, "tell me if I have them all straight."

"Will do."

"Michael is the oldest, and his wife is Peg, and they have three boys," I start.

"Right," says Connor.

"Then you, with your delightfully charming companion, me."

"Indeed." He smirks.

"Then Patrick, and his second wife, Ashley, who nobody likes. And he has one girl and one boy from his first wife, Patti, who everyone loves."

"Perfect."

"Then Darren, with his girlfriend Jeanette, and she's pregnant, and your folks are freaking out that they have no plans to get married." I'm totally on a roll.

"Nope."

Shit. "Wait, wait, don't tell me . . . Liam and his fiancée Ana Maria, and then Darren."

"Right."

"And then Jack is the oops baby, ten years younger than Darren, and his girlfriend of the week is Andrea."

"You know it better than any of us!" Connor laughs. "Don't worry, it's a fun evening. Mom and Dad take all the grandkids for a sleepover at their house, so we can all have a nice adult evening. Every year we take turns hosting. Which is the easy part, since all you have to do is provide the location and beverages; everyone else brings the food and cleans up before they go." Connor comes over and slips his arms around my waist. "I'm glad you're here." He kisses me softly.

"I'm glad you invited me."

He kisses me again. The doorbell rings.

"You ready?" he asks.

"Absolutely."

He kisses me one more time and then goes to answer the door.

We are all sitting in Connor's living room having coffee and more eggnog, stuffed to the gills. Minus Jack and his girlfriend Andrea, who left right after dinner, claiming another obligation.

Peg, a porcelain strawberry blonde with delicate freckles, points at Jeanette's gently rounded belly. "You'd better hope that one's a girl, because these Duncan men are exhausting. Little Sean pitched a fit in the middle of the cereal aisle the other day. I thought I was going to get arrested for child abuse. Just shrieking and wailing because I wouldn't get him some sugary mess, and everyone looking at me like I'm the worst mother in the world."

"Kids are guaranteed to embarrass you at every opportunity," Patrick says. "Remember our wedding?" Everyone giggles again. Patrick turns to me to explain. "When Ashley and I got married, my kids were five and three. Joe was the ring bearer and Bridget was the flower girl. They were walking in together."

"Looked like little angels," Ashley says.

"Until they got halfway down the aisle," Liam jumps in.

"Then Joe grabs Bridget's little basket of rose petals and starts hitting her with it!" Peg says.

"Bridget hunkers down in the middle of the aisle like a miniature sumo wrestler and begins to shriek at the top of her lungs," Patrick continues.

"Peg bolts down the aisle, throws a kid over each shoulder, and scoots out the side door," Michael pipes in.

"So we get everything back on track, we all do the processional, and then, in the middle of the vows, Joe gets away from Peg, runs back out into the ceremony, and starts yelling at the justice of the peace, 'That's not my mommy!' It was one hell of a fiasco," Patrick finishes.

"The wedding every girl dreams of," Ashley says.

"Wow. You all have just completely reinforced my decision to not have children," I say.

"Oh, honey, kids are great. Just because you and your first husband didn't have them, it isn't too late," Peg says. "You're plenty young."

"And Lord knows the Duncans are a fertile bunch of boys!" Jeanette offers.

"I appreciate the encouragement, but I think I'm going to leave the child rearing up to the rest of you." What is it about December? Suddenly everyone thinks I should be a mom.

"Leave her alone, guys. Not everyone feels the need to populate the city." Connor comes to my rescue. His own admittance to a lack of the parenting gene was one of our earliest bonding moments.

"Well, considering some of the behavior of our bunch of monsters, I can certainly see why you would opt out!" Darren says. "What do you think, honey, should we put this one up for adoption when it arrives?" He rubs Jeanette's bump affectionately.

"This bastard spawn of sin that you've saddled me with? Absolutely," Jeanette says, laughing.

"We're getting her a scarlet letter for Christmas," Liam says.

"I still don't know why you guys don't just get married. Save yourselves the hassle," Darren says.

"I've been married twice, thank you," says Jeanette. "I think the Goldie/Kurt model is the way to go."

"Twice?" I ask. "But you're so young!"

"I know! First time to my high school boyfriend. We eloped just after my eighteenth birthday, annulled after three months. And the second time to my college sweetheart, which lasted two years," Jeanette says. "I'm done with the marrying. We're going to live in sin forever."

"Works for me," Darren says. "I know where home is. I don't need a ceremony to tell me anything."

Connor offers around more coffee, and I retreat to the kitchen with Peg, Ana Maria, and Jeanette to begin cleaning up a bit.

"You're a brave girl, to suffer through tonight," Peg says, beginning to rinse plates and load Connor's dishwasher. "But I'm glad you did."

"Connor never brings anyone to the Christmas Eve parties," Jeanette says.

"Well, I'm glad he invited me. It's so wonderful to watch how a big family interacts. My family is so small. I like the noise of it all with you guys!" I say.

Interesting. Connor doesn't usually bring a date to these. I'm surprised by how much this pleases me. I'm still reasonably certain I'm not looking for Mr. Right. And yet, something about the knowledge that he has brought me into the fold makes me all warm and gooey. And there is nothing like watching a bunch of committed couples being happy to make one reconsider whether independence is the best choice.

"Well, I'm just glad I'm finally not the only one in the room who isn't Irish!" Ana Maria says.

We all laugh and continue cleaning up with the hum of the five Duncan brothers wafting in from the living room.

⸎

It's just after three when Connor and I finally collapse into his bed.

"Thanks for all your help tonight," he says, pulling me tight against him. "Everyone loved you."

"They're all amazing," I say, snuggling against his chest. "And exhausting! Is it always that draining to spend time with your family?"

"Pretty much. Anytime you have that many personalities in a room, it's bound to be weary-making."

"So what will you all do tomorrow?"

"Well, after a quiet breakfast with you," he kisses the top of my head, "I'll head over to Mom and Dad's. Everyone in the immediate family will be there by noon. We'll open presents, play with the kids, and me and my brothers will begin assembling the crap that comes unassembled while Mom plays general in the kitchen with all the girls. By two, all the aunts and uncles and cousins will arrive, and at four, we'll sit down to dinner. Which means by four forty-five we'll all be stuffed to the gills, half in the bag, and the kids will be cranky from too much sugar. Someone will break someone else's new toy, and one by one the families will peel off toward home."

"Another full day."

"Well, it isn't movies and Chinese food, but it is traditional." He chuckles.

"I think it sounds nice. Family on that scale is something I don't understand, but it always seems sort of magical."

"The grass is always greener. I think the idea of being able to fit your entire family into your car is pretty cool." Connor yawns deeply.

"How about we call it a night?" I'm bone tired, slightly buzzed, stuffed to the gills, and awfully contented.

"Excellent idea. Good night, sweet girl."

This chills me. One of my favorite all-time movies is a darling little film by Ted Demme called *Beautiful Girls*. Great cast, smart writing. Uma Thurman at one point is telling Matt Dillon the way to her heart. "All I need to hear before I go to sleep is four little words. 'Good night, sweet girl.' That's all it takes." And I remember thinking the first time I saw that movie, *She's so right. That is all you really need in life. If you can find the person to express that ideal, you're pretty much set.*

"Good night, sweet boy," I whisper back to him. *Good night, sweet boy.*

Don't Let the Door Hit the Old Year in the Ass

There are certain dates to which we have given an inordinate amount of power. New Year's, Valentine's Day, birthdays, and anniversaries are all potential traps for relationships old and new. And unless you have had a discussion about your expectations, you cannot fault your partner if he doesn't live up to them. No one can read your mind. If you place a great deal of weight on that midnight kiss or heart-shaped box of chocolates, you need to make that known to your partner. You can't blame him for not intuiting that you wanted more; it obviously wasn't something that was forefront on his mind the way it was for you. But since you didn't tell him, then you are the creator of your own disappointment, and frankly, I think you owe him an apology.

—Advice given to a caller by Jill Spingold, July 2006

The phone rings at six.

"Hello?"

"Hey, you." It's Connor.

"Hi! How are you?" It's about flipping time. I haven't heard word one from him since I left his place Christmas morning. *Four days ago.* Not a call, not an e-mail, not a text message. He was so sweet, made me a hearty breakfast, and then sent me on my way with a kiss and a smile, but then, nothing. "Just getting settled in for the evening."

"Sounds nice. Don't go out; it's disgusting out there."

I can see out the window that it is snowing sideways, a

particularly Chicago thing for it to do. "Certainly looks that way. What are you up to?" I ask him.

"Just getting ready to leave work. Me and the guys are heading over to watch the game at Bill's."

"So we both have excellent indoor evenings planned."

"Indeed we do. Anyway, I wanted to check in and talk about New Year's." *Finally!* I couldn't believe he hadn't asked already. I'm getting ready to forgive him for neglecting me.

"Well, Jill and I always do a small dinner party for New Year's. Would you like to come?"

There is a silence. "Oh," he says. "Well, the thing is, I, well . . ."

"You don't want to come."

"It isn't that, it's just, I told Michael and Peg I'd watch the boys so that they could go to a party. I'm not really much for the whole New Year's Eve thing anyway, and since you hadn't said anything yet, I sort of figured maybe you weren't a New Year's Eve girl either, and maybe you'd want to come hang out with me and help babysit."

Babysit? Help babysit on New Year's Eve? Oy.

"Oh, Connor, I'm sorry. I should have told you about the party. I didn't mention New Year's because some people place a lot of weight on it, and you and I just started seeing each other. I didn't want you to feel pressured."

"Well, I didn't exactly check with you first either."

"Aren't we a perfect pair?" My heart sinks.

"Well, it's just New Year's. You'll have fun with your party, and I'll have fun with the nephews. I've got a thing on New Year's Day, but how about dinner on the second?"

"Sounds good." Actually, it sounds like crap. It sounds like I was an afterthought for New Year's Eve, and not good enough to invite to whatever "thing" he has for New Year's Day.

"Okay, then. I'm going to head out. You have a fun night, and I'll call you tomorrow."

"Okay. Have fun at Bill's."

"Good night, darlin'."

"Good night."

Okay. Fine. Regroup. So Connor isn't a New Year's guy. And babysitting three rowdy boys so that Michael and Peg can have a date is very sweet and endearing. And he did invite me. But that "New Year's Day thing" chaps my ass. It's obviously a party of some sort, and one where he doesn't want me tagging along. And I'm trying not to be mad at myself for not broaching the idea of New Year's in enough time to secure plans with him.

*

"Mmmm. I did miss you," Abbot says into my hair. We are snuggled up on my couch, watching a French film about a man who starts a chorus in a reform school right after World War II.

"But it sounds like you had a good trip."

"Oh, yeah. Nothing like a trip home. Mom starts drinking the moment the clock strikes five, Dad keeps running weird errands at all hours so that he can sneak off to see his mistress, and Uncle Joey spends the whole weekend telling racist jokes and complaining about the immigration problem."

"Okay, well, that part isn't so good, but at least you got to see your sister and her kids, and you were smart enough to stay at a hotel."

"True. I'm getting very wise in my old age."

I look up and kiss the underside of his chin. "Not old. Vintage."

"Shhh. I can't talk and read subtitles at the same time."

We watch the rest of the movie, tidy up the plates, and Abbot lights a fire. "So, how are things going at crisis control central?" he asks, refilling my wineglass.

"Okay. Day by day. Up and down. It's been pretty quiet with the holidays, but Kim seems to think there are troubled waters ahead. Can't say I disagree with her."

"And you and Jill?"

"We're pretty good. I'm trying to be a good little girl and really supportive of the wedding plans and stuff, and not pressure her too much on the business fallout. We're editing the new book, which gives us some focus, and still fleshing out ideas for the television thing, but I am really doubting it will happen."

"You need to stop thinking about it for a bit."

"That I do."

"C'mere," he says, motioning to me to join him in front of the fireplace. I had a friend make me a floor pillow almost the size of a twin mattress for sitting in front of the fire, and Abbot has fetched it from its hiding place under the coffee table. I walk over and sit beside him.

"Good job with the fire, Smokey." It is beautiful and crackling and providing a nice bit of heat.

"I have many, many talents," Abbot says, moving in for a kiss.

"Mmmm. So you do."

He moves his kisses to my neck, just under my left ear. I shiver with delight.

"You didn't say that you missed me, too." He cups my left breast and kneads it gently.

"Didn't I?"

His thumb finds my nipple and begins to make slow, firm circles. "No, my lovely girl, you didn't."

"Such an oversight. I do apologize. Shall I show you how much I missed you?" I whisper in his ear, letting my hand wander to his crotch.

He groans. "Well, a gent does like to know he is appreciated."

"Well, then, why don't I appreciate you."

Actually, we are pretty mutually appreciative for the better part of an hour before shifting to the bedroom, where we are additionally appreciative first of each other, and then, of sleep.

I wake up at around two in the morning, sneak out from under Abbot's leg, and go to the bathroom. I take off my makeup, brush my teeth, and head back to the bedroom, to find Abbot dressing.

"Where you going?" I ask him, grabbing my robe off the hook by the bed.

"Honey, I've got to go home. I have a bunch of work stuff that got messengered over earlier today, not to mention the mail and all that."

"Okay. Well, thanks for coming over."

He walks around to the side of the bed where I'm sitting. He leans over and kisses me. "Don't be petulant. You know I'd love nothing more than to wallow in bed with you and sleep in and make you breakfast. Or have you for breakfast. But duty calls."

"All right. I suppose I'll have to forgive you."

"Thank you."

"Hey, Abbot, about New Year's . . ." I've put him off for so long, and after my earlier discussion with Connor, I realize I should have invited him to the party all along. He asked first, and he is the one I am most deeply involved with, and just because there is a new shiny boy paying me some attention shouldn't get me off track with the one who has been making me happy for the last five months.

"Don't worry. I'm taken care of."

Huh? "Taken care of?"

"Yeah, well, I figured since you never responded to my offer of wining and dining you for the New Year that you had other plans, so I accepted an invite to my friend Sol's place in New Buffalo."

"Oh. Well, that sounds like it'll be fun." What is *with* these guys? I must be having some really bad New Year's karma.

"Sol's a good guy, and I like his wife. They've been bugging me to come there for ages. If it's nice, maybe you can come with me for a weekend one of these days."

"Sure, that sounds good."

"Am I allowed to ask what your plans are, or should we include it in the 'don't ask, don't tell' portion of our arrangement?"

I put on a chipper attitude. "Now, now. Nothing like that. Jill and I are having some people over, but I think you'd have been bored to tears. It's the best man and his wife and a couple of friends from college. You'd spend all night listening to two different sets of old private jokes. I thought I'd spare you the tedium."

"Well, thank you for thinking of my mental well-being. And you're right, I probably wouldn't have much enjoyed it, even with your delightful self."

He gathers the rest of his things and heads for the back door without even complaining.

"Good night, honey. I'll call you tomorrow afternoon when my meeting is over." He leans in for a kiss, which I deliver dutifully.

"Okay, then, get home safe."

I lock the door behind him and head back to bed.

So, then, Ben Kohn, this is your lucky New Year's.

The phone wakes me just after nine. Goddammit.

"H'lo?" I say groggily.

"Hey, Jodi. It's Brant."

"So, what's up?" I haven't really spoken to Brant since the get incident. And while it isn't something I miss, I'm just realizing that he has pretty much stopped calling me.

"Well, um, I have some news."

"Okay, what is it?"

"Mallory is moving in with me."

Interesting. Especially that phrasing. Mallory is moving in with him. Not Mallory and I are moving in together. "Well, congratulations. I had no idea things were that serious."

"Well, things are definitely serious. The thing is, she recently got let go by her law firm, so she was worried about living expenses, and we decided it just made sense for her to move in here."

"Wow, that must be difficult. Was the firm downsizing?"

"No, not exactly. She, um, well, she failed the bar again. And her firm was only keeping her on with the understanding that she had eighteen months to pass the bar if she was going to remain with them. So they had to let her go."

"That sucks." Must not laugh at the thought of perfect Mallory getting sacked because she can't pass the bar. "What is she going to do?"

"She's considering all her options. She used to work for a big PR firm when she was in school, so she is thinking she might get back into that."

"That could be interesting, and certainly easier if she has a background in it. Please extend my best wishes to her. When is she moving in?"

"Last weekend."

"That was fast. Are you guys thinking you'll stay there or find a different place?"

"I love this place. Why would we move?"

Duh. "Brant, as a woman, I don't know how comfortable I would be living in the same apartment that my boyfriend shared with his ex-wife. I mean, obviously, in the current circumstances it's necessary, but you might want to offer the idea of looking for a new place for the two of you to set up together. Clean slate, fresh start, that sort of thing." I can't help myself, the need to give advice overwhelms, even though the thought of old Mallory living in my old apartment is sort of delicious. But men in general are so frigging clueless, and Brant in particular, that I have to put in my two cents.

"I never thought of that. But it makes sense. I guess that's why you give advice for a living, huh?"

"Guess so. How's everything else?"

"Good, sort of slow. When the economy is like this, people aren't really upgrading their systems like they used to, so things are a little quieter than usual. But okay."

"I'm sure it'll pick up. We can't live without our computers!"

"I hope so. Especially with Mallory out of work."

Oy. I really need this conversation to be over. "Brant, I'm really happy for you, even if the situation is a little crappy. But I have to start getting ready for New Year's."

"No problem. What are you guys doing tonight?"

"Small dinner party, not a big deal, but I'm cooking with Aunt Shirley this afternoon."

"Well, have a very happy new year. And send my love to Jill and the gals."

"Will do. And you and Mallory have a happy new year as well."

"We will. Talk to you later."

"Bye."

I hang up the phone and flop back onto the bed. I actually did all the relevant shopping yesterday, and Aunt Shirley probably cooked everything last night. By the time I get downstairs there will be nothing left to do except help her get the dining rooms ready. We decided to do a roving party, cocktails and hors d'oeuvres at the aunts', dinner at Jill's, and dessert at my house. We hired a server/bartender and a dishwasher, so that once the party starts, we can all just enjoy and not run around too much.

I snuggle back under the covers and will myself toward sleep.

It is so rare that I can really indulge in a long morning in bed, and I have every intention of remaining right where I am.

And then the phone rings again. What is with everyone this morning?

"H'lo?"

"Hey, Jodi, it's Ben."

"Ben, what is the rule about early in the morning?"

"I can nudge you awake any time after seven, but no phone calls till after ten."

"And what time is it now?"

"Nine thirty."

"And are you gently nudging me awake?"

"Nope."

"I will forgive you this once, but only because my ex is even ruder than you are and woke me up already. What's up?"

"Well, um, I have sort of a problem about tonight." This makes me sit up.

"What sort of a problem?"

"The thing is, when I was in Hawaii, there was a girl I went to high school with there, and we were hanging out and she just moved to Chicago and doesn't know anyone. And when she asked what I was doing for New Year's, I said nothing, 'cause you hadn't said anything, and then we had that whole talk and stuff before Christmas, and I figured, you know, that you were going to make other plans. So she and I talked about making plans to hang out, but she wasn't sure, so we were going to wait and talk when we got back. But she didn't call me, and then you called and invited me over, so I figured everything was fine. But then she just called me to reconfirm for tonight. I guess she thought it was set, and I told her I'd made other plans, but she sounded really down about it. And I thought, I mean, not that I don't want to be with you for

New Year's, but you are going to have all those people, and she doesn't have any plans, and . . ."

"Ben. Ben!" Good Lord, that boy can ramble. "It's okay. Go hang out with her. I'll have plenty of entertainment here, and by the time the party is over, I'm going to want to just crash anyway. It's not a big deal."

"Jodi, you're the best. That is so cool of you."

"I know. I'm amazing. And still in bed. You go, have a nice time, and you'll make it up to me later this week."

"You bet I will! Go back to sleep."

"Happy new year, Benny boy."

"Happy new year to you, too."

Great. Just great. Someone, at some point, will have to explain to me how it is that I can have no less than three men in my life, and I *still* can't get a date for New Year's.

Auld Lang Syne

Being a good hostess is one of the best skills you can develop. It isn't about extravagance, it is about spirit. Pizza and beer can be fine if it is presented with love and attention to detail. If people feel welcome and comfortable in your home, if they feel cared for, it can help to create meaningful bonds. Conversations happen in a living room or dining room that simply don't happen in restaurants and bars. The intimacy created by entertaining at home allows for open dialogue, and that is the basis of solid, long-term friendships. The friendships you develop in your twenties and early thirties are the ones that can carry you through your life, and bringing people into your home for food and drink and convivial conversation creates important bonds.

—From Living Twenty-five *by Jill and Jodi Spingold*

"Anyone need more coffee?" I ask.

"God no. I'm going to be wired as it is," Raj says, running a hand through his thick black hair.

"Seriously, Jodi, instant espresso and chocolate in the cake *and* this Italian roast sludge you call coffee. Is it that you don't want us to sleep until next New Year?" Tim says, waving off the pot. Raj reaches a hand over and rubs Tim's thigh.

"Well, I'll have a half a cup more," Shelly says, handing her cup forward to me in a delicate, manicured hand. "It's delicious."

"Well, of course it's delicious!" Matt says, laughing. "You fill half the cup with heavy cream and four spoons of sugar." He's a large man, with a generous smile, and he reminds me a little of

John Goodman. Shelly is so petite, she looks like she could fit into his pocket. They are easy and affectionate together, and Hunter says that they will probably be engaged by the time the wedding rolls around.

"Well, dear, I'm with you," Aunt Shirley says. "I think coffee is simply a good excuse for cream and sugar."

"Is that a request for another cup?" I ask her.

"Oh no, dear. I'm fine," she says, winking at me.

"Sure she is. Fine." Aunt Ruth snorts. "She's had two cups already, and she won't be able to sleep. We'll go back downstairs, and she'll putter around all night!"

"You're welcome to stay in the guest room at our place if you need to get some rest," Hunter says.

"Kiss-ass." Jill elbows him in the ribs.

"Leave the boy alone, darling," Ruth says, smiling at Hunter. "I happen to like a young man who knows where his bread is buttered."

"So, Jodi, how's it feel to be losing a sister to marriage?" Raj asks me playfully.

"I'm not losing a sister; I'm gaining a brother," I say dutifully, rumpling Hunter's hair as I sit on the other side of him on the couch.

"Aw, shucks," Hunter says, faking humility.

"You are, however, losing a Spinster!" Raj says.

"True enough," I say. "And more power to her!"

"You'll have to hold down the fort," Tim says. "The last surviving Spinster."

"Even if she did take a brief sabbatical to the dark side." Raj laughs.

Aunt Ruth and Aunt Shirley make eye contact over the rims of their coffee cups.

"Hey, marriage isn't the dark side!" Hunter says in mock horror.

"Is it? Are you luring me to the dark side?" He faces Jill, who laughs uncomfortably.

"Of course not," she says and waves her hand in front of his face. "This woman loves you."

Hunter adopts a blank look. "This woman loves me."

"She is not trapping you in marriage."

"She is not trapping me in marriage."

"She needs a Gucci purse for her birthday."

"Even I am not that stupid," he says, kissing her neck.

"Damn," Jill says, the uncomfortable moment gone. "I was so close!"

"Hey, it's almost time," Tim says, checking his watch.

I walk over to the television and turn it on, finding the Times Square festivities. We have less than five minutes to go.

Jill hands around glasses of champagne, a beautiful bottle of Krug that Raj and Tim brought.

"Before we count down," Matt says, "I'd like to propose a toast to the four best hostesses in the world!"

"Hear, hear!" Raj says.

"Beautiful and talented, all," Shelly says. "Thank you so much for including us."

"You are all very sweet," Aunt Shirley says.

"Hey, hey, here we go!" Hunter points at the TV.

The ball begins its journey, and we all count in unison. "Happy New Year!" we all shout, and the ubiquitous kissing begins. I receive my hugs and good wishes from everyone in the crowd and try to think of my blessings, but there is something a little disappointing about not having a man taking me in his arms at this joyous moment. I can see Hunter dipping Jill dramatically, Raj and Tim are holding each other tightly, and Matt has picked Shelly up to kiss her, like a porcelain doll. I wonder what Connor and Abbot and Ben are doing right now.

Everyone begins to straighten up, and I sneak off to my bedroom for a moment. I check my cell phone. Two new text messages.

The first is from Abbot.

Hey honey, happy new year. New Buffalo is great, wish you were here.

The second is from Ben.

Hpe ur pty is gd. HNY.

The boy writes in license plates.

No messages from Connor. I pause. Then I dial his cell number. It rings six times before he picks up.

"Hello?"

"Hey, you. Happy New Year."

"Hi. Happy New Year to you. How's the party?"

"Good. Too much food, too much drink, typical. How are the boys?"

"Too much sugar, too much Xbox, too many Vin Diesel movies."

"What time are Michael and Peg due back?"

"They said by one or so."

I take a deep breath. "Wanna come over instead of going home?" I can't help it. Despite Abbot's attentions the other night, I find that tonight, it is Connor I'm missing, and I'm feeling very much as if I am ready to move that relationship forward physically, even if it means I have to let go of something else.

Connor pauses. "That's a very tempting offer, but I'm going to have to take a rain check. These guys are wearing me out, and

I've got that thing tomorrow. But Tuesday night for sure. I've got good plans for us."

"Okay, just a thought."

"I like the way you think. Hold the thought for a day, will ya?"

"I will."

"Hey, you're missing the movie!" I hear a distinctly female voice muffled in the background.

"I'm coming," Connor says. "Jodi, I gotta go. I'll call you tomorrow."

"Okay." I take a deep breath as I hang up the phone. Who the hell was that? And why do I get the sense that she is the thing he is doing tomorrow?

I head back out to my living room, where everyone is getting ready to go.

"Good night everyone, thanks for letting us old birds come to your party," Aunt Shirley says, making a round of kisses.

"Oh pish, Shirley," Ruth says. "We keep things lively."

"That you do," Tim says, kissing her cheek. "I'd adopt you both if I could."

"And you aren't even Chinese!" Raj says, making us all laugh. "It's not funny! He's been leaving articles about foreign adoption all over the house!"

"It isn't my fault I'm not wedded to the old-world way of doing things," Tim says, waving Raj off. "This one still thinks we'll find the perfect Hindi lesbian to continue the Bijanali bloodine."

"Hey, in just five months you guys can start arguing about kids!" Matt says, clapping Hunter on the shoulder.

"Oh, Lord. Don't even get him started," Jill says, stepping between them. "It's hard enough dealing with Groomzilla over here on the infinite wedding details. I shudder to think about what I'm in store for when it's time for kids!"

"I can't help it if I want the day to be perfect!" Hunter says in his own defense and with an air of weariness. "After all, the perfect bride deserves the perfect wedding, even if the groom is the only one who seems to care."

"Yeah, except I keep waiting for you to come home and tell me that your colors are blush and bashful!" Jill says.

"Shirley, let's get the hell out of here before it becomes a daytime drama." Ruth takes her by the hand and drags her toward the door.

"Wait up, ladies, we'll escort you home," Tim says, and he and Raj each offer them an arm.

"Okay, buddy. You keep these gals in line." Matt gives Hunter a hug.

"Thanks again. It was a great night." Shelly gives me a hug.

They head out, and Jill and Hunter and I flop down on my couch, Jill and I simultaneously kicking off our shoes. Jill puts her feet in Hunter's lap, and he dutifully begins to rub them.

"Another triumph!" he says.

"True enough," Jill says. "Jodi, the cake was amazing."

"Well, your double-baked potatoes were perfect." Hard to go wrong with potatoes, sour cream, and cheddar cheese.

"I think we could have served old shoes next to Aunt Shirley's roast and no one would have noticed," Jill says, rubbing her belly.

"No kidding!" Hunter says. "How the hell did she get it so perfect? Brown and crispy on the outside, but pink and juicy all the way through, right to the very edges." Hunter sighs.

"She is a miracle worker," I say. "Were there any leftovers?"

"She made a smaller second roast and left it in my fridge for tomorrow," Jill says. "She knew we'd want to make sandwiches for the game. Are you coming down?" Jill and Hunter have some of Hunter's poker buddies and their girlfriends coming over to watch the football game tomorrow.

"Yeah, I'll come down. Can I bring anything?"

"No, I think we have everything we need," Jill says.

"Um, Jodi . . ." Hunter says.

"Yeah?"

"Could you do that Ro*Tel Velveeta thing you make?" He asks sheepishly.

"Oh, Hunter, don't you remember last time?" Jill admonishes him.

I made the simultaneously very delicious and totally disgusting cheese dip for our Fourth of July party last year. Hunter ate so much of it that he shat orange for three days.

"I won't have that much again, I promise," he says.

"I'll bring it; you ignore her."

"Thank you, Sis-to-be." Hunter gets up. "You guys sit. I'm going to go downstairs and finish tidying up." Jill moves as if to get up. He pushes her back down. "Nuh-uh, princess. You guys did all the prep work. I'm on the final round of cleanup."

"You're a god among men," she says, sinking back down gratefully.

"I try. Happy New Year, Jodi. See you this afternoon."

"Good night, little brother. Happy New Year."

"Good night, Monkey Ears," he says. Jill shakes her head.

"Keep working," I say.

"Oh well." He closes the door behind him. I turn back to Jill and smile. "He's a keeper, kiddo."

"That he is. Did you have fun tonight?"

"It was fine. A good party. I really like Matt and Shelly."

"Me, too. I'm sorry all your boys bailed."

"Yeah, well. It's my own fault. I waited too long to make plans."

"Because you were waiting for Connor," she says knowingly.

"Because I thought he'd be the best fit for the party, is all."

"Because you wanted him to be here. God, Jodi, there's nothing wrong with liking this guy!"

"I never said I didn't like him."

"But you won't admit that you like him differently than the Father or the Son. Come on, this is *me* here. You can't fool me. Sure, Abbot and Ben have their charms, but Connor has gotten under your skin. And you wanted him to be here with you because you *wanted him with you*, not because he would fit better with us."

"Well, it doesn't matter whether that is the case or not," I say with more vehemence than I intended.

"Why? What's up?" Jill sits up and crosses her legs underneath her.

"I called him on his cell. Invited him to come over after Michael and Peg came home tonight. Thought I'd give him a little late-night New Year's treat."

"And?"

"Well, he said he was going to be too tired, and we have plans for Tuesday anyway, but then . . ."

"Then what?"

"Then I heard some girl tell him he was missing the movie, and he said he had to go. And he has some mysterious plans tomorrow that I'm not invited to."

"So?"

"So?!? So, it doesn't matter how much I like him or don't like him. He clearly has other fish to fry." I know I'm pouting, but I can't help it. Jill starts to laugh.

"You are the best," she says. "Do you hear yourself? You're all pissed that he has some girl over there for New Year's, even though he invited you first. But after he turned you down, you invited *two other guys*, in case you've forgotten, to join you here! And you're mad at both of them for making other plans, even though they both *also* asked you for plans first. You're ridiculous!

You make this whole big stink about your relationships being nonexclusive, but apparently you only mean for you . . . They're all supposed to be at your beck and call!"

"That's not true!"

"Jodi, I love you truly, madly, deeply, but be honest. You like having your little gaggle of guys. Makes you feel all wanton and powerful. But one of those guys is not like the others, and you can't admit it!"

"You're totally off base. And besides, I'd better keep my gaggle of guys, or we'll be out of a job." *Oops.*

"What the hell does that mean?" she snaps.

"Nothing. Forget it."

Her jaw drops. "Are you thinking about what Raj and Tim were saying?"

"They have a point. I mean, we have set ourselves up as the icons for single girls. One of us had better stay single, don't you think?"

She leans over and takes my hand. "What I think is that we have the success we have because we do it together and because our hearts are in the right place. And I hope that you don't ever make your personal life a business decision. You and I can do anything we set our minds to, and our business will grow and change as our lives move forward. My life is so much better with Hunter in it, and I know that the happier he makes me, the better I will be at home *and* at work. And I hope that when you meet the guy who can make you happy like that, whether Connor is that guy or if he is just on the horizon, that you will let go of the persona you think you have to have and just let yourself embrace that happiness. I know you are concerned about the fallout. I'm doing my best to get us through it. But at the end of the day we have to trust in our message and our intentions and let the chips fall where they may."

And even though I can't really believe her, I also can't give in to the desire to yell at her for getting married and potentially spoiling everything we've worked so hard for. So I fake acquiescence. "Ignore me. I know you're right; I'm just pouting. And I really don't want to talk about it."

"Suit yourself. I'm going to bed." She gets up, walks over, and kisses the top of my head. "Good night, Butthead."

"Good night, Moose Face. Happy New Year."

"You, too. Love you."

"Love you, too. I'll see you when I get up."

"You got it."

She crosses the room and leaves.

I swig the last of the champagne out of the bottle and take my sorry self to bed. Alone. Where I try not to think about Connor and who he might be sleeping with.

The Holy Ghost

Look, we're not saying he doesn't care about you; we're just saying that you may have unrealistic expectations of what he may be capable of in this relationship. And more importantly, why are you waiting around for him to start doing the things you want to do? Make the plans, set the dates, organize the events. Then invite him to participate or not as he chooses. But don't sit on your butt and wait for it to all be his idea.

—*Advice given to a caller by Jill Spingold, May 2006*

"Sorry I'm late," I say, sliding into the booth across from Hunter at the Firehouse. "Where's Jill?"

"Running late. She said you'd know what to order for her, and that she would be here in twenty minutes." He grins and shakes his head. "She's stuck in traffic on her way back from the hotel."

"I forgot she was setting up the block of rooms for the out-of-town guests today."

"She wanted to take a final tour of the suites for my folks. For some reason she's certain they won't be good enough." Hunter runs his hands through his hair. "I know they're sort of insufferable. I keep trying to tell Jill she can't be so worried about them; they'll find something to pick at regardless."

"Jill can't help wanting to be good to your family, Rusty; she loves you, and they come with you."

"Well, I just don't want her to feel like I expect it of her. I love them in spite of themselves, but I don't go out of my way for them; it's never worth it."

"I think as long as you stand up for her and make it clear that they have to treat her with respect, you'll all be fine," I say and reach for a menu.

The waiter comes over, and we order three Caesar salads, a grilled grouper for Jill, pork chops for Hunter, and a steak for me.

"Where's Connor, anyway?" Hunter asks after the waiter leaves to get our bottle of wine. "Wasn't he supposed to be coming tonight?"

"Pipe burst in one of his new projects. He's going to try to meet us in time for the play." I'm trying to be light about it, but I'm sort of miffed. We set this double date ages ago, and I pulled in a favor to get house seats for the current production at Goodman.

"That's too bad. Doesn't he have a foreman to handle that sort of thing?"

Exactly my thinking when Connor called. "I think these projects are his babies, and when something this big happens, it would make him too antsy to not be there knowing it was getting fixed properly." I hope.

The fact is, Connor has been running sort of hot and cold since New Year's. He came to a small cocktail party Jill and I had at the office to celebrate our one hundred and fiftieth broadcast late enough that most of the guests had gone home. And then he didn't call me for four days. But last weekend he surprised me with an indoor picnic dinner at his house, followed by one of those amazing nights where you fool around and talk and laugh and fool around again and suddenly the sun is up and neither of you are tired of talking or kissing. Then we slept in and went to the weekly Sunday brunch at his folks' house, and I got to do some bonding with his mom in the kitchen, and apparently impressed his dad with my expansive knowledge of football. The day was perfect, kidding around with the brothers and playing with everyone's kids, and meeting Jack's new girlfriend, Christmas Eve Andrea having been replaced already. It felt so natural and connected, I started to think that if he brought up the idea of exclusivity that I might be up for giving it a shot, but then he dropped off the face of the earth for most of this week and now was skipping dinner in lieu of checking in on work. And what is worse, even though the petting is amazing, he never even asks to go further, and we haven't talked about taking the next step, which is making me think that maybe he isn't all that attracted to me after all. I know that if we take that step, it will mean letting go of Abbot, but just when I think I'm ready to give Abbot up for the promise of something more meaningful with Connor, Connor pulls a Houdini act.

"Is everything okay there?" Hunter asks, probably picking up on my false cheeriness.

"I think so. I hope so. Did you ever go out with someone who kept vacillating between really present and totally absent?"

"Yeah. Once. In college I went out with this girl who was completely amazing when we were together. Great conversation, liked all the same stuff, laughed a lot, great sex. But then she'd sort of check out for a few days after our dates. Once we spent a whole weekend together, and I thought it was a sign that we were really getting serious, but then she blew me off for almost two weeks afterward. Curt phone calls, too busy to see me, that sort of thing. But then she'd finally agree to see me, and it would be the best date ever."

"So what happened?"

"Eventually I asked her for more time, more commitment, and she said she couldn't do more than she was doing, so I broke up with her."

"Did she say why she couldn't do more?"

"No. But I think it was that she didn't want to do more. To make more of an effort."

Which is what I've been afraid of.

"Hey," Hunter says, noticing my lack of response, "we were in college. A nineteen-year-old doesn't exactly have a business to run or a family to be responsible to or any of the pressures of adult life. I'm sure that Connor isn't doing that."

"I wish I were sure."

"You really like him, huh?"

"Yeah. I just, I don't know, I feel very connected to him when we are together. He's the first guy since my divorce that I even have remotely considered having potential."

"Can I ask you something personal?" Hunter asks, chewing on a piece of bread.

"Hey, you're almost family. Shoot."

"Is there any chance that you feel like that about him because he is sort of wiggly?"

I laugh. Hunter has a very interesting way of expressing himself. "Wiggly?"

"Well, look, you have created your world around this idea of being footloose and fancy-free when it comes to dating, right?"

"Yeah . . ."

"I mean, you've probably dated seven different guys in various configurations just in the time I've known you. Right?"

I think back, and mentally check guys off, going backward chronologically to the office project. "Eight, actually."

"Right. And never only one at a time except for some brief weeks between letting one go and acquiring his replacement."

"Well, that sounds a lot more calculated and businesslike than I would like, but I suppose it's reasonably accurate."

Hunter pauses to sip the wine the waiter has poured, and nods his approval before continuing. "Is it possible that, even subconsciously, you are letting yourself feel more for this guy than all the others precisely because he is the least likely to be interested in a commitment?"

"You mean, am I sabotaging myself?"

"Well, let's look at the current roster. Abbot is using patience and charm and a large floral budget to slowly woo you into submission. Ben wants you to have his children . . ."

"My sister has a big mouth." I pretend to be offended.

"Your sister hasn't told me anything you've asked her to keep secret."

"True enough. Please continue." I take a sip of the lovely Barolo that Hunter chose and wait for his diagnosis.

"Connor is, as you say, there when he is there, but sometimes isn't so attentive. So, of the three guys you're dating, you're most interested in the one who is showing the least interest in more than what you have. Is it possible that you're a little gun shy on the commitment thing and are purposely letting yourself fall for the guy who is least likely to step up? You know, for safety's sake."

Before I can answer, Jill swoops in, apologizing and railing at the traffic.

"Two flakes of snow, and everyone in a car loses all sense of reason!" she says, sliding in beside Hunter and kissing him. "Hello, you." She turns to face me. "And hello you, too. How was the meeting?"

"Good. The licensing company is talking to Target next week about placing the new lunch kits, so fingers crossed, we might be able to roll them out in the next three months."

"Excellent," she says as the waiter brings over another wineglass and pours for her. "Where's Connor?"

"Hopefully meeting us at the theater. Work problem."

"That's too bad. What'd you guys order me?" She takes a piece of bread from the basket and slathers it with butter.

"Grouper," Hunter says.

"Perfect. What were you guys talking about?" she asks.

Hunter winks across the table at me. "We were talking about the wedding. I had some ideas I wanted Jodi to weigh in on."

I appreciate his discretion on this, in part because I assume that Jill has already shared her opinions on the Holy Trinity with him and knows that I won't be in the mood for the two of them to gang up on me tonight, and in part because I am sure he knows how strained things are with Jill and me at the moment and wants us to just have a lovely evening. For which I am very grateful. My current boy problems only bring into relief for me how special what Jill and Hunter have is, and how much I am truly afraid deep down that I will never have it. And as much as I love Jill, it is so difficult not to be resentful of that. Especially when she is telling me everything I'm doing wrong in my own love life.

"Oh, Hunter, you know this doesn't have to be some ridiculous production," Jill says in mock horror.

"Well, a boy is only a groom once, dear. Let him have the wedding he's always dreamed of," I say.

"Yeah!" says Hunter. We lean back and let the waiter deliver our salads.

"I give up. Just tell me what time to be there," Jill says.

We raise our glasses, clink, and start eating.

⁂

"Thanks for the play," Connor says, walking me to my car. "That was one of the best things I've ever seen."

"You're very welcome. Thanks for coming." Connor managed to meet us at the theater two minutes before curtain.

"Sorry again about missing dinner."

"No problem. I'm just glad that the damage wasn't too bad."

"Yeah. Once we got the mess mopped up, it was pretty easy to fix." He leans over and kisses me softly. "So, you tired?"

Sigh. He's such a good kisser. "Not exhausted. What did you have in mind?"

"Well, we have two options. I can follow you home so you can get your stuff and drop off your car, and we can go to my place, or I can just meet you at your place."

"I love it when both of my options are good ones. What do you have in the larder?"

"Breakfast? Cereal."

"Aunt Shirley dropped off some risotto cakes today. Bet they'd be good with some scrambled eggs and chorizo," I say. I do love a hearty breakfast after a good night.

"You win. Leave the back door open for me, and I'll meet you at your place."

"Done."

He leans over and kisses me again. "Drive safe, love." He lets me get into my car, closes the door for me, and then waits off to the side as I pull away.

Love, indeed. I pull out of the parking lot onto the street and head for the expressway. I can't get Hunter's accusation out of my head. I mean, yes, I certainly have found the type of relationship situation that I'm most comfortable with, and I haven't been terribly challenged to change it. With my history with men, it is nice to be in the driver's seat for once. And as much as I like Connor and feel happy with him and like I'm getting bonded with his family, I still enjoy the time I spend with the other guys, too. Frankly, getting Connor to the theater was one thing, but he'll never be an opera/symphony/wine-tasting guy like Abbot, and I love the elegance of those events, and how supported and well taken care of I feel with him. And there is something so enjoyable

about being with someone like Ben, who is creative and spontaneous and adventurous, and is always searching the *Reader* and
Time Out for the most interesting things to take me to.

I merge onto the Kennedy and head west. I love the solid feel
of driving this car. It's almost as if it knows the way home and
needs barely any guidance from me. If only my love life were as
easy to navigate.

Paying the Piper

We've found that the key to the success of our partnership is our ability to be colleagues at work and sisters at home. We are both very careful to keep the two relationships separate, and if either one of us crosses a line, the other can gently remind her to get refocused. I mean, don't get me wrong, it isn't like you can't tell we're sisters when you watch us interact at the office, but we have found a good way of communicating in the professional arenas that helps ensure that when it is time for business, we just put on our business hats and get to work.

—*Quote from an interview in* Chicago Social Magazine, *April 2005,*
Jodi Spingold

My cell phone goes off just as I'm leaving the gym to head back to the office. I'm bound and determined to get myself down into a size twelve in time for the wedding. If I lose one to two pounds a week, I should be able to do it. I hired a trainer to help me out, and frankly, I think I hate her more than I have ever hated anyone in life.

"This is Jodi," I say as I pull out of the parking lot.

"Hey, it's Brant."

"Hi. What's up?" Even though I know he's probably calling to wish me a happy birthday. Thirty-five. Good Lord.

"There was something I wanted to talk to you about."

Well, that sounds serious. "Okay."

"I was, well, um, I was wondering about what happens to our financial arrangement if I decide to have children."

I let this sink in a little bit. Our financial arrangement. When Brant and I got married, he brought with him just over $115,000 in student loans. Since Jill and I both had educational trusts from our maternal grandparents' estate, I had been able to cover all the costs of my education, including living expenses. And since the trust had been very well managed and was established with the possibility of covering not only undergrad, but all the way through medical school, law school, or a Ph.D. if we desired, I used less than half the money in the trust for school. After looking at our long-term financial plans before the wedding, we realized that we were going to be better off if we used the rest of the trust to pay off Brant's debt. When we got divorced, Brant insisted on paying me alimony. I said it wasn't necessary, even though at the time I was concerned about what sort of life I was going to be able to make as a freelance writer. But Brant brought up the student loans and said that if I had let that money keep growing during the seven years we were married, it would have nearly doubled by now and I would be more financially secure. So I let him do the math, and we came up with a monthly amount that would allow him to pay off that obligation within eight years. When we signed the divorce papers, it was listed as "maintenance," the new word for alimony, and for the first year of my new singlehood, that cushion helped me get through the months when I didn't earn much.

When Spinster Inc. was born and started to make some money, I thought about telling Brant to forget the rest, but Jill and the aunts talked me out of it. They said that the only reason I had taken on the obligation of paying off those loans was to secure my financial future with Brant. When that future ceased to include Brant, then the benefit was eliminated and needed to be recouped. So I continued to deposit his monthly check into an annuity to let it begin earning back what had been lost. We never talked about it. It came in the mail, I deposited it, it was never late, we didn't bring it up. Until now.

"I'm not sure what you mean," I say.

"Well, I was wondering what happens to the alimony if I decide that I want to have children," Brant says. He and I have never thought of it as alimony. It has always been "the student loan money." Apparently that has changed.

"With me?" Is he suggesting we have a baby?

He laughs. "Of course not with you. I know you don't want kids."

Oh, my God. "Is Mallory pregnant?"

"No."

"Are you guys trying?"

"No, of course not." He sounds slightly defensive.

"Are you talking about getting engaged, waiting a year, getting married, then having a baby? The traditional sort of calendar?" I ask.

"Yeah, something like that."

"And how exactly does our arrangement play into that?" I don't know where he's going with this, but I don't like the way it's started.

"Well, to be honest, I can't afford to have a baby and pay your alimony."

I pull into my parking space at the office and shut off the engine. I'm officially livid. My alimony. The fucker. "Um, Brant, first of all, that isn't true. And second of all, this isn't alimony, it's a repayment of an educational loan. And it has nothing to do with Mallory or what the two of you decide to do."

"Actually, I think it does," Brant says.

I'm trying to stay calm. I know that this has nothing to do with me, and is probably the result of Mallory whispering poison in Brant's ear. But at the moment, this knowledge is doing nothing to mitigate my anger. "Brant," I say calmly, "I don't know what is prompting this conversation."

"What is prompting this conversation is the fact that my monthly financial obligation to you is excessive and will prevent me from having children if I decide to do so."

"Has Mallory found another job?" I ask.

He hesitates and then replies defensively, "No."

"I see. Well let me make a recommendation. If you and Mallory are beginning to discuss having children, then I suggest that she get a job and participate financially in your life together so that you will be able to afford to have them. I don't believe there are any precedents for an ex-wife paying her ex-husband child support for a hypothetical future kid he may decide to have with his new girlfriend."

"Well," Brant snaps, "it's nice to know where your principles are!"

My principles! That shit. I cannot contain myself anymore. "Look, Brant, when you and I split up, we had several agreements between us. It was your idea to pay me back for the money I had laid out to pay off your student loans. You were the one that did the math, you are the one that came up with the monthly amount, you are the one that stood in front of the judge and said that it was important to you to include this in the settlement. And we both agreed at that hearing that neither one of us would seek to alter or change the arrangement in any way. We also agreed between you and me that we were going to work very hard to maintain a friendship between us, and I think so far we have done admirably well. We both also knew that eventually one or the other of us would find a meaningful new partner in our lives and that that would probably change the nature of that friendship. However, it is clear to me that Mallory is so insecure in her relationship with you that she cannot stand that you and I are in healthy communication with each other. Now, if she needs for me to be the shrewish, money-grubbing ex-wife, and to make you believe that, too, in order to feel comfortable and solid in her relationship with you, then I feel very badly for her indeed. And worse for you. But your relationship with Mallory is none of my business. However, your relationship with me is of direct concern, and I think that you are at a point where you should be very, *very* clear with me, and with yourself, whether this is a friendship you would like to continue. It doesn't say anywhere in any rule book that you and I have to be friends. I personally believe that it would be a shame to lose fifteen years of friendship over the pathology of a woman you've only known for four months. But that is your choice. As to the issue of money, I find it personally offensive that someone who takes home a six-figure salary would even dream of claiming that he couldn't afford to have children. We both know that there are single mothers making $30,000 a year supporting not one, but several children and themselves. So it is preposterous for you to even attempt to convince me of that, regardless of whether Mallory is working or not. But I would truly like for you to think long and hard about what is important to you, and if maintaining a friendship with me is important to you, then you are going to have to figure out how to deal with this particular issue."

"Well, it's interesting to know how you feel. I suppose I will have to think about it. In the meantime, I thought I would give you warning that the extra money I usually send is going to stop immediately, and the total monthly amount will revert to what was agreed upon in the divorce settlement."

When we signed the divorce papers, the monthly amount was based on splitting the total into equal installments over the course of several years. At the time, both Brant and I agreed that neither one of us would be claiming the money on our taxes. When the apartment we had shared went condo and Brant decided to buy it, it suddenly became important for him to take the tax deduction available for the maintenance he was paying me. Because we hadn't figured on him claiming it, we also hadn't figured on it becoming taxable income for me. So Brant suggested that he would add an extra $300 per month to the total amount he was sending so that it wouldn't become a tax burden for me. I had agreed to that arrangement, but we never signed anything to that effect. Apparently, he was now going to stop sending that extra $300 a month. Meaning that I was going to have to pay the taxes on the money he was repaying me. The action of a petulant child, pouting because he didn't get what he wanted. Jill's words are ringing in my ears. I have no responsibility to be friends with this man. It doesn't make me a bad person if I cannot maintain a healthy relationship with my ex-husband.

"Brant, I have to go. If you feel that you can no longer send the tax money, that is your choice. However, the arrangement for the monthly amount stands. You have a good long think about the future of our friendship, and you feel free to tell Mallory from me that she can have you. I don't know if you have made clear enough to her that I was the one who sought the divorce. And that I have no designs on attempting to get you back. I am not a threat to her. However, if she really needs for you to hate me in order to feel solid in her relationship with you, and if you need to go along with that so that things are comfy for you at home, then I will be happy to oblige. You call me and let me know what your decision is."

"Fine, I'll do that." And he hangs up.

I click my cell phone off. I'm shaking, I'm so angry. I take a deep breath, grab my purse, get out of the car, and head in to tell Jill about the latest development.

Happy fucking birthday.

❦

"Okay, here it is," Kim says. "Anne Fisher is going to be running a piece next week."

Shit. Double shit. Anne Fisher is a local conservative journalist with a poison pen. Who sort of happened to be in my class at U of C, and whose boyfriend I sort of slept with before they broke up, and who sort of happened to be in a room a few years back where I was sort of referring to her as a talentless hack sort of within her earshot. My first really big PR snafu, and one that had been biting Spinster Inc. in the tush ever since. Proof that you should be careful who you piss off along the way; you never know when they will prove dangerous later. Anne uses us as some sort of negative example at least once a month in her column and makes no bones about the fact that she supports the Christian Right when they take us to task for our advice on relationships. This is sure to be a ferocious lashing out at us.

Mike Thomas got his article printed last week as promised in the Sunday *Sun-Times* Controversy section, a very balanced and brilliantly written feature about the company and Jill's engagement, and he included all kinds of great quotes from our work that talk about how to keep a committed relationship alive, as well as quotes from supporters. He downplayed our "single" stuff and really highlighted our work as empowering women to live their best possible lives, and to determine for themselves what those lives should look like. We love him very, very much.

But we knew that once his piece ran and the press release hit, we were going to get slammed. Conservative radio has been lashing us all week, there has been a small but loud group of protesters outside the offices every day, and Wal-Mart has just informed us that they are considering severing their relationship with us and will potentially be returning all Spinster items to the warehouse. Nationwide. The accountants are guestimating that Spinster will conservatively post a 14 to 18 percent drop in merchandise sales this quarter, and that is before the hit we'll take if we lose Wal-Mart. And while some people have been equally loud in their support of us and our message, it is sinking in that this whole wedding fallout isn't minor.

Jill clenches her jaw. "What else?"

Paige looks at me and then back at Jill. "Krista is having some trouble getting the network guys to return her calls."

"So what does she think that means?" I ask.

Paige's acrobatic eyebrows are stiller than I have ever seen them. "I think she believes that they are not going to talk to you until they see how the wind is blowing. She says we should sit tight, keep on with damage control, and wait it out."

"Okay. Thanks for the update. Keep us posted," I say. Paige and Kim nod and head out of our office.

"This is such ridiculous *bullshit*!" Jill slams a hand on the table. "First, we're antimarriage. Now, when I'm getting married, which they should see as some sort of victory, they are saying we're frauds! I fucking hate these people."

"Deep breath, Sis. We'll weather this storm. They have to wake up every day and be them. How icky is that?"

"And I've ruined your birthday."

"First off, Brant ruined my birthday. And second, this isn't about you; you haven't done anything wrong."

"I still feel shitty."

And I hate that a tiny, bitter part of me likes that she feels shitty. But this is a very bad time to do the I-told-you-so dance.

"Don't feel shitty. We're doing everything we can. Let's get out of here before the traffic gets insane, okay?"

"Okay."

Jill and I finish up our last couple of workday tasks and then head for home.

⁂

"Make a wish!" Aunt Shirley says as I lean over my birthday cake, the same cake I have had since I was old enough to eat cake: Aunt Shirley's famous banana cake with chocolate frosting.

I take a deep breath and close my eyes. I wish for continued health for the aunts. I wish for continued happiness for Hunter and Jill. I wish for Mallory and Brant to go away and leave me be. I wish for the current press crap to resolve itself without irreparably damaging the business. I wish for these last seventeen pounds to miraculously disappear. But when I get ready to blow out the candles, the only wish that really surfaces is for Connor to call. Both Abbot and Ben have made their best efforts to make me feel like a princess today. From Abbot, I got a delivery of flowers so enormous it is practically obliterating my dining room table, with a card promising a real present when I see him Sunday night. And Ben made a mini website devoted to all the interesting things that ever happened on my birthday throughout history. But my wild Irish lad has not been in communication yet today, despite reconfirming our date for tomorrow two days ago and asking what my plans were for my big day. Maybe by the time I get back upstairs there will be a message.

Deep breath.

Whhhoooooosh. All out.

Jill claps. "Happy birthday, Butthead." She hands me a small box. I pull the silky brown ribbon and open the top. Gently peeling the tissue back, I see a pair of the most exquisite chandelier earrings, sparkling with green peridots and violet iolite.

"Jill, they're perfect! I've been looking for a pair like this everywhere." I lean over and kiss her.

"Yeah, I know. I'm usually the one with you when you're shopping, remember?"

"Now this one, darling," says Aunt Shirley, handing me a bag. I take the tissue out of the top and reach inside. Nestled in the snowy, crinkly depths, I put my hand around something smooth and cold. I pull it out. It is a gorgeous crystal wine decanter with an envelope attached. Inside the envelope is a certificate welcoming me to A Taste of California wine club, informing me that six bottles a month, three red and three white, will begin arriving shortly.

"That is so cool!" I go over to kiss her. "New wines every month for a year. I'm going to be an even bigger lush now."

"Well, I spoke to Tracy over at Provenance, and she said that anything you taste and love, you should write down for her, and she'll stock it for you." Aunt Shirley beams. She's always nervous about gifts, sure she's picked the wrong thing, when in fact, her personal magic is always knowing just the sort of thing that is perfect for you.

"Yes, Shirley, we know, it's all been arranged to provide hours of pleasure for the rest of her natural life," Aunt Ruth says, good-naturedly. "Can I give the girl my present before she's another year older?"

"Oh, stick a cork in it, Ruthie. You're just jealous you didn't think of it first." Shirley is preening.

"You two behave yourselves," Jill snaps in mock horror. "This isn't a competition. Especially since, obviously, my present is the best one."

"Respect your elders, dear," Shirley says to her.

"Can. Jodi. *Please*. Open. My. Present. *Now*?" Aunt Ruth begs.

I take the large box gratefully. It is surprisingly heavy. I undo the ribbon and tear off the paper. Lifting the lid, I see an expanse of velvety chocolate brown color. I touch it, a lush, thick toweling, and lift it out of the box. It is an enormous bath sheet, a half-inch-thick Turkish terry, and at the bottom, in lovely celery green embroidery, is the word *Hers*. I look back in the box and take out the second towel. *His*. Then I realize there is still more in the box. I lift out another towel. *His*. And yet another. *His*. I start to laugh.

"I thought your boys might not want to share," Aunt Ruth says with a wicked twinkle in her eye.

"They're fantastic," I say, kissing her. "I love them."

"Such an enabler," Aunt Shirley says.

"The girl is old enough to live her life the way she likes. I'm just being supportive." Ruth is grinning wickedly.

"You'd better keep two of those under wraps at all times, Sis," Jill says. "Someone might mistake you for a ho."

"I'm not bad," I say in my best Jessica Rabbit impression. "I'm just drawn that way."

We all laugh, and Aunt Shirley slices everyone a second piece of cake.

"Thank you all very much for a wonderful birthday," I say around a mouthful of banana-chocolate heaven.

"What's on the docket for the rest of the evening?" Aunt Shirley asks.

"You mean now that I've eaten two pieces of cake for dinner? I have a very exciting date with my couch and the first season of *House*, which the gang at the office gave me. Anyone want to join me?"

"Can't," Jill says. "I have to go meet Hunter. Apparently we're going to Schuba's to listen to some guy who he wants to play classical guitar for the wedding. Anyway, I should go. Happy birthday, Butthead."

"Thanks, Moose Face." Jill kisses the three of us and heads for the door.

"You go have your quiet night. Lord knows you've earned it with everything Brant put you through today," Aunt Shirley says.

"Absolutely," Aunt Ruth adds. "Take all your loot and go enjoy the rest of your night. Many, many more, dear heart."

"I love you both very much. Thank you again for all my wonderful presents." I hug the aunts tight, each in their turn, and kiss their soft cheeks. Then I gather my bags and head upstairs. The hallway smells wonderful, but I can't place the scent. Until I turn the corner of the stairs on the second landing. On the last flight of stairs leading to my door are tiny bud vases with alternating burgundy and golden calla lilies, and little tea light candles in amber holders, giving off a warm, spicy scent. I follow this glowing pathway up to my front door. I turn the handle and slowly open the door. Inside my house, there are candles burning everywhere, and more flowers. That Connor. What a total muffin. I deposit my presents on the table next to the door and call out.

"Hello?"

The sight that greets me is not unwelcome, but it isn't what I am expecting. Abbot Elling. Grinning and holding out a glass of champagne.

"Happy birthday, beautiful."

Such a good man. I'm trying not to think of him as the wrong man, but to relish that I inspire him to such romance. And I'll conveniently ignore that this is probably an attempt to lure me into domestic submission.

"You darling."

"Just wanted to give you a little birthday surprise."

"Well, this is a wonderful surprise, Abbot. Thank you."

"Jill helped," he admits. "I'm an idiot about these kinds of things, usually."

"You seem to be doing just fine so far."

"I'm trying. Want to go sit down?" He leads me to my living

room, where a fire is burning in my fireplace, and there are all sorts of goodies spread out on the coffee table: cheeses and olives and prosciutto, and marinated artichokes and a fresh baguette.

"Oh, my. All my favorite things. You are really knocking my socks off here." I lean over and kiss him.

"I'd better be knocking off more than your socks, missy. I mean, this is grade A prime romance happening here!" He smiles and kisses me deeply, making every hair on my body leap to attention.

"You know what I love about all of these delectables?" I say.

"No. What?"

"They all taste better after sex." I put my glass down and take him by the hand. His hand is warm and firm in mine, I look over at him, and he smiles as I lead him to my bedroom.

Wishing on birthday candles might not work, and Abbot might not be my ideal man, but you surely can't begrudge a girl some birthday nooky.

Valentine's Day Massacre

Oh, now, here we go. Okay, we say this every year, ladies, and this year will be no different. Let the Valentine's Day thing go. We know that, in general, a day devoted to love and romance seems like a great idea. And on paper, it is. But men feel manipulated by the holiday, and the pressure we put on them is the reason. The Valentine's Day blues, the need to get drunk and bitter with other singles on the fateful day, or the overwhelming smothering of the man of the moment is our own fault. Rare indeed is the guy who really gets into the holiday the way we do, and often their best efforts are just not enough. And what is worse, there is always some friend whose boyfriend or husband is the world's most romantic, perfect man, who creates a Valentine's experience for her that cannot be duplicated by our own merely mortal men. Take stock of your current guy, and if he's a keeper, then let him be about V-Day. Please turn to chapter 8 in *The Thirty Commandments*, and follow our advice. Create a Valentine's tradition with a girlfriend or close female relative or best gay boyfriend. Put your energy into looking forward to that tradition, be it a spa afternoon, a museum visit, dinner at a favorite restaurant, or another such thing. Homeless shelters don't just serve meals on Thanksgiving, you know. Just give your man the Valentine's gift he's always wanted . . . permission to simply be a human being. Let him be Kevlar guy on the most mine-filled day of the year.

—*Advice given to a caller by Jodi Spingold, February 2005*

It started first thing when we arrived at the office. The large bunch of roses on the front desk was a testament to Gino's continued presence in Benna's life, despite the snafu at his surprise birthday party. The e-mail on my BlackBerry announcing that Kim's husband has abducted her for the day. The marketing office, as we pass by, is filled with balloons, boxes of cookies, teddy bears, and more flowers, since Maddy, Cleo, and Eileen are all adorable and always dating, as per my sage advice, more than one guy at a time. Bless their hearts. I kept my chin up, headed for the office, Jill hot on my tail. And that was when I saw it.

The basket on Jill's desk.

"What the . . . ?" she says, grinning from ear to ear, dropping her purse and coat on the couch, and practically skipping over to her desk.

"Oh, *please*," I say. "I just wonder what it could possibly be? And who it could possibly be from?" I'm being a little snarky.

"Shut up. I'm entitled." She begins to unpack her gift. A brushed stainless thermos of coffee, already made the way she likes it, with plenty of half-and-half and sugar. A pair of lemon poppyseed muffins. A Tupperware container of sliced mango that I can smell from across the room is perfectly ripe. A single deep magenta gerbera daisy in a little bud vase. Fucking Hunter. I already had to hear about his little morning gift, a handmade photo album of the two of them, chronicling the whole history of their dating. Now he's arranged her most perfect breakfast to be sitting on her desk. I may have to kill him.

"Hey, bitter, party of one?" Jill snaps at me. "Want a muffin?"

"Well, duh," I say. She tosses it over to me.

"I thought we were over the Valentine's Day crap? Didn't Dr. Markovitch cure you?" she mumbles, a couple of muffin crumbs stuck to her lip gloss. For all her delicate sensibilities, my sister is a slob when she eats. It doesn't matter where we go, when they clear the plates, hers always leaves a ring of clean in the midst of crumbs and stains. She doesn't talk with her mouth open or anything disgusting; she just makes a mess.

"My esteemed former shrink did indeed help me work through

some of my Valentine's Day crap, as you call it. But I will have to admit that I may be having a relapse."

"Poor baby. Do you think it's because of Brant being so present right now or because Connor is so absent?" she asks, pouring a cup of coffee out of her thermos.

I think about it as I take the top off my muffin, saving it for last. "Probably both. I mean, Brant couldn't help his shit, and it was my own problem ultimately. But yes, I'm sure that the latest development in my relationship to him is probably dredging up old resentments. And yes, I'm still trying to figure out my hot-and-cold Irishman and wishing he were more toward hot today."

Connor took me out Saturday night for my birthday. The impeccable (count 'em) twenty-four-course tasting menu at Alinea. Followed by a long drive all the way up Sheridan Road and into the ravines, perfectly blanketed in snow and glistening in the sharp night air, and easy, free conversation. Then back to his house, where he had a bottle of vin cuit, a smoky nightcap sort of wine with orangey undertones, and a bar of dark chocolate so deep in flavor that I could practically taste the rain in the fields of Costa Rica where the beans were grown. A first edition of Oscar Wilde's *The Portrait of Mr. W.H.*, which made me cry, Oscar being a personal hero of mine. And then a night of alternate tender kissing and petting and giggly talking. I felt so taken care of that I tried not to notice that, once again, he didn't make any move to take things to the next physical level.

We slept in on Sunday, read the paper with croissants from his neighborhood bakery, and then he drove me home, where he got conscripted by the aunts to help repair a sticking door in their pantry. This degenerated into a full-on afternoon tea, since Aunt Shirley is currently assisting on a cookbook for a British chef. Hunter and Jill showed up, and Hunter and Connor got into an argument about some football player's stats, so the four of us went up to Jill's to check the computer. Jill had one of her impossible-to-ignore cravings for a game of Trivial Pursuit, and by nine o'clock had beaten us all twice, requiring an immediate infusion of Chinese food and Tsingtao beer, which Hunter and Connor fetched companionably. Connor ended up spending the night, and when he kissed me good-bye Monday morning at the ungodly hour of five, I wasn't even mad. It felt like we had turned a corner of some kind. I mean, no guy goes out of his way for a birthday like that, no guy spends thirty-six hours in a row with someone unless he is really into her. Right?

But it's Wednesday, and Valentine's Day to boot, and not only hasn't he called today, he didn't call Monday or Tuesday either. Which, of course, makes me think that spending that much time with me has convinced him that I'm completely insufferable, and he will be breaking up with me any minute.

Just because I give sage advice for a living doesn't make me remotely sane when it comes to my own insecurities.

"And you're still sure that you aren't all in a snit because he isn't jumping through hoops like Abbot and Ben?" Jill asks, slurping her coffee.

"I'd like to think not."

"Well, look, you did spend most of the weekend together, and you said yourself things are really busy for him at work. And it is only nine thirty in the morning."

"I know," I say. Paige knocks on the door, and Jill waves her in.

She flops down on the couch. "I fucking hate Valentine's Day," she says, eyebrows in a sad, straight line.

"What's the matter, kiddo?" I ask.

"Everyone everywhere has someone, even irritating some-ones, acknowledging the day for them. I got a fucking card from *my grandmother*. I mean, no offense to Nana, I love that she sends me valentines, but it is my *only* one. I'm a fucking pariah."

"But at least you're not dramatic," Jill says.

"Fuck you, and your perfect guy, and that perfect fucking rock that is blinding me from here," Paige says.

"If it's any consolation, I haven't had any valentines either," I say.

"Whatever. You have three boyfriends. I'm sure at least one of them will do something incredible today. I, on the other hand, have no boyfriends." Paige is smiling through her misery.

"Having a guy does not mean having a great Valentine's Day, I can promise you that," I say.

"Tell her the story," Jill prompts.

I take a deep breath. I share this tale at least once every Valentine's Day to some forlorn young thing. "Once upon a time, there was a girl who loved Valentine's Day. From the time she was old enough to be aware of the special nature of February 14, she thought the idea of a day devoted to love and romance was the best idea ever. But she never seemed to manage to have a boyfriend for the holiday. Every year, she would end up alone on Valentine's Day, including one year in high school when she started dating a guy on February 15, and he broke up with her the following February 13. Then one day she met a man, and they fell in love. And as their first February came around, she started to let herself get excited to finally celebrate the day with everyone else. She bought him several little presents, food and champagne, invested in sassy new undergarments. Her boyfriend announced the day before that he had accepted an invitation to a poker night with his friends. He gave her a silly card. She gave the presents to her sister to give to her boyfriend instead. The following year, the same boyfriend, now fiancé, gave her a card and spent the night assembling a new computer desk for a pal. She canceled the dinner reservations and gave the impossible-to-get theater tickets to her aunts. They got married, and the first Valentine's Day of their

married life, she made big plans. Bought the fixings for his favorite meal, a bottle of wine way out of her price range. He came
home from work, announced that he was going to work on a project in the basement for a bit, and disappeared. No card. No acknowledgment at all that it was a holiday. She cooked the dinner,
sure the scent would lure him upstairs. He didn't come. She was
too proud to call for him, and ate alone. He didn't come upstairs
till after nine, asking if she had eaten yet, and did she want to order in. She unleashed a stream of venom encompassing nearly
twenty years of pent-up Valentine's Day frustration. She ranted
and raved and threw things and wept and got all snotty. And at
the end his only response was that he was sorry she felt badly, but
didn't she know from his previous behavior that he didn't believe
in the holiday and wasn't inclined to celebrate? And when she
suggested that he get excited about it for her sake, he asked why
she couldn't get unexcited about it for his sake. And she couldn't
argue with his logic."

Paige listens intently to the tale of my former woe. "Did he
ever get with the program?" she asks.

"Nope. I gave up. Started making my own Valentine's joy. I refuse all datelike invitations and spend the evening with my favorite
sister and our aunts, getting drunk on fluffy girl drinks, eating
crap food, and watching old movies. And since you are so blue, my
little peach crumb, tonight you will come join us for our estrogen
festival of love." I walk over and sit next to her on the couch and
put an arm around her shoulder. "Will you come? Bring your jam-
mies, and we'll make it a sleepover."

Paige looks up gratefully. "Really? I won't be an intrusion?"

"Nonsense," Jill says. "You'll be a very welcome addition."

"Don't you have plans with Hunter?" she asks Jill.

"Nope. I'm sending him to Dave and Buster's with some of
his single guy friends." Which was Hunter's idea, insisting that

she keep her tradition with us, and took her for a romantic dinner last night to celebrate "on Australian time." If I didn't have it on authority from Jill that Hunter leaves whiskers in the sink after shaving, has some sort of annoying morning phlegm issue, and an unnatural obsession with the Phillies, I would suspect he was too perfect to live.

"Thanks, you guys, you're the best," Paige says. "Meeting in fifteen?"

"We'll be there," Jill says, and the two of us start getting our stuff together.

⁂

After the meeting we return to our office to find that Hunter has sent two dozen roses in a shade of deep lavender that I've never seen before. I don't have so much as a card.

And the day doesn't get much better. Every hour and a half or so, all day long, something arrives for Jill. An iPod nano loaded with a playlist of romantic songs. A huge chocolate chip cookie with I Heart Jill in red buttercream. I get a text message from Ben wishing me a happy day. He's still pouting that I turned him down for a date tonight. A masseuse shows up at three with orders to give Jill a twenty-minute chair massage and then to work her way through the office, one girl at a time. I get one of Abbot's famous floral arrangements, which have started to be less romantic than they are an easy choice and an offering devoid of thought or heart. At four thirty, she gets a box with a comfy lounging pajama set and a pair of sassy slippers from Cheeky with a card encouraging her to cuddle up and enjoy our evening. Connor is still profoundly missing in action.

I'm trying so hard not to be resentful. I love that Jill found someone so thoughtful and creative and so crazy about her that it inspires him to keep trying to sweep her off her feet. I'm certainly not jealous of the commitment or the natural sacrifices that Jill has to make in order to be a good partner. But I am wondering what it is in me that doesn't inspire the same in someone. I am wondering what I lack that none of the men in my life have ever been driven to consistent demonstrations of romantic love. I am wondering what is so broken in me that I either continue to choose men who won't be romantic or that subconsciously I refuse to let go of the thought that it means that I'm just not good enough.

"Hey," Jill pulls me out of my self-loathing reverie.

"Yeah?" I say.

"I'm sorry," she says. "I know you're disappointed."

"Oh, honey, it isn't your fault my boys are letting me down."

"I know, but I also know that Hunter's attempts to enter himself into the pantheon of most romantic men ever has done nothing but rub it in your face all day."

"I'm not that obviously bitter, am I?"

"Not bitter, Sis. Just human. And having bad V-Day luck."

"Not karma?" I ask.

"Don't be ridiculous. You've done nothing bad to require punishment from the universe . . . unless . . ." she trails off.

"What?"

"Well, maybe in your past life you were involved in the Saint Valentine's Day Massacre!" she says, her face a mask of faux horror.

"Oh, sweet Frito bandito. Can we go home, Helen of Troy, before Hunter wins a war in your honor?"

"Absolutely."

We gather our stuff, say good night to the girls, tell Paige to come over anytime after seven, and head home. I go up to my apartment to change into my comfy clothes and check my mail and messages. A card from Raj and Tim, handcrafted, of course.

An e-card from a college friend. A couple of telemarketing calls, a message letting me know my prescription is ready. Nothing from Connor at all.

I might not have been a Mafia hit man in my past life, but clearly, something about me and Valentine's Day is not a match made in heaven. I shake off the lump in my throat, mentally scolding myself for such silly girlie foolishness, get into my pajamas, and remind myself how lucky I am to have four amazing and supportive women to spend the evening with.

V-Day Redux

At the same time, ladies, remember to support your girlfriends, especially your single girlfriends, on Valentine's Day. It's a great time to send a treat or a card, make that phone call you've been putting off. The day hits us all in different ways, but no one is sad to be acknowledged by someone. Just remember not to call to regale them with how great your guy did at buying the right present or how bitter you are about not having someone to be with. Keep the conversation light and about being happy to know them, and you'll bring a smile to their day.

—*Continued advice given to a caller by Jill Spingold, February 2005*

"Okay, Shirley, your turn!" Paige says.

Our viewing of a documentary about a guy who filmed all of his dates on his search for a wife has prompted the sharing of everyone's worst dates. We've heard about the time Jill was fixed up by a friend from the marketing firm she worked with, and at dinner he continually popped pills for his anxiety problems and made lewd gestures with the loaf of bread. I shared the sad tale of my first date after the divorce. A charming advertising executive I'd interviewed for an article for the *Trib*, who liked the way he came off so much that he asked me to dinner. He took me to Green Dolphin Street. Where we ran into his wife.

Aunt Ruth has declined to participate, saying that she immediately deletes bad dates from her memory.

"Well, let's see now," Shirley says, squinching up her nose the way she does when she is thinking hard.

"I think you should tell them about Junior," Ruth says slyly.

Shirley blushes. "Oh, Ruthie. I don't think . . ."

"Oooohhhh!" Jill says. "Who's Junior?"

"Yeah, I never heard about a Junior," I say.

"Fine," Aunt Shirley says, shaking her head. "In 1956 . . ."

"Fifty-seven, dear heart," Ruth interrupts.

"You're right, it was fifty-seven. At any rate, I had broken off the engagement with Michael, and frankly, none of the boys in the neighborhood were much interested in me."

"It was widely assumed she might be a lesbian," Ruth says matter-of-factly.

"Ruthie, please," Shirley says.

"What? It's true! Any young woman who broke off an engagement to as good a catch as Michael Rueven Goldfarb was definitely assumed to be of the Sapphic persuasion," Ruth offers as explanation. "Plus you and that Himmelman girl were attached at the hip, and she did have a certain androgynous quality—"

"Oh, Lord, can we please not have that discussion again!" Shirley is clearly exasperated, and Paige, Jill, and I are holding back laughter.

"I wanna hear about Junior," I say, faking petulant to get us back on track.

"Me, too," Jill pipes up.

"Me, three," says Paige, never one to be left out.

"Fine." Shirley settles back in her chair a bit. "In 1957, after breaking off my engagement, I wasn't dating much. At the time I was working the register at Manny's delicatessen four days a week. One day a young man whom I had seen a few times before complimented me on my eyes and asked if he might have the pleasure of my company one evening for dinner. He seemed nice, polite, clean-cut, so I accepted. We made a date for the following Saturday night. He picked me up and took me to the Billy Goat Tavern for burgers, the first time I'd been there, and then asked if I wanted to hear some blues. I agreed, and he took me to a place called Club Zanzibar, which was at Fourteenth and Ashland. We went in, got a table—there weren't very many white people there—and my date, Marty, fetched us drinks. The music was amazing, but Marty drank more and more and became, shall we say, rather unpleasant. He asked me to dance and then was less than a gentleman with his hands. When I sat back down, he accused me of being a square. When I said I was leaving, he grabbed my arm and pushed me back into the chair. I didn't notice, but the music had stopped. And suddenly Marty just disappeared into the air. One of the young men who had been onstage had come down into the crowd, grabbed Marty by the scruff of his neck, and simply picked him up and threw him across the dance floor. Marty got up and took a swing at the nearest man, a tall African American gentleman in an exquisite suit, and the man simply reached out and almost gently tapped Marty under the chin. Marty's eyes rolled back into his head, and he fell backward onto the table of another couple. Drinks everywhere. Before I knew what was happening, the place erupted in fighting! The man who had grabbed Marty first reached forward and took my hand, very gently, and said, 'Miss, I think I'd better get you home.' And he led me through the club and around the corner to a car. I was so flustered I didn't know what to say or do. He opened the car door, and I just looked at it. 'It's okay, miss,' he said. 'I'm just going to get you home safe now.' So I got in the car. He was very sweet and made some jokes, and pretty soon we were laughing and getting along like a house afire. I told him how much I liked his music, and this seemed to make him pleased. As we got close to home, I suddenly got very quiet. Because, you know, as liberal as your grandparents were, I wasn't so sure they would be happy to have this particular young man escorting me home. And as if he could read my mind, he asked me, 'Would you like me to leave you at the corner, Miss Shirley, for your folks' sake?' This, of course, made me very embarrassed, so I worked up my courage and said that no, in fact he could leave me at the door. When we got to the house, he stopped the car, walked around to let me out, and escorted me to the gate. He kissed my hand, and thanked me for coming to hear him play, and said he hoped he might see me in the audience again one night, and then he left."

We're all hushed. Paige breaks the silence. "Did you ever see him again?"

"No, I never did," Shirley says almost wistfully.

"But I did," Ruth says.

Three heads whip around. "You saw him when?" I ask.

"A few months later I took a small group to a club to hear some blues, and after the show we got into conversation with the band. One of the musicians talked about how different the shows were when whites came to listen, and teased one of the others about his 'white damsel in distress.' And then proceeded to tell a tale of a bar fight that began when some drunk white man put his hands on his date and this musician boy jumped off the stage to her rescue! So I looked at him and said, 'You're Junior.' And he said he was, and I said that I was Shirley's sister and very grateful to him for his assistance and kindness toward her. And then I came home and smacked Shirley in the head for not paying attention to who exactly had come to her aid," Ruth says. "I mean, it isn't every day Junior Wells saves your bacon!"

"Junior Wells!" I yelp.

"Aunt Shirley, why have you never told us this story? That is classic!" Jill says.

"Okay, I'm an idiot," Paige says. "Who is Junior Wells?"

"A legendary bluesman, dear," Ruth says. "He played with Muddy Waters."

"Wow. That's amazing!" Paige says, realizing the connection.

"He was just a very nice young man who helped me out of a pickle," Shirley says.

"No vision, my sister," Ruth teases. "You could have been Mrs. Junior Wells had you played your cards right."

"Maybe," Shirley admits. "But then how lonely you would have been all these years," she finishes with a wicked smile.

"I'd have survived," Ruth says, pouring another round of wine. "Now, Paige, dear, that just leaves you to share a tale of woe."

Paige takes a sip of her wine and thinks a moment. "Okay, how about this one. I meet this guy at the gym. Nice, cute, seems normal. One day we're walking out at the same time, and he asks if I want to run over to Jamba Juice with him to recharge the batteries. I figure, sure, no problem. We have a nice half hour over juice, and he asks me to dinner. I say sure. He takes my number. When he calls me to make plans, I tell him that I had received a gift certificate to Charlie Trotter's from a raffle at a benefit, and ask if he wants to go there. At which point he launches into a ten-minute tirade about how much he hates stacked food!"

"Stacked food?" Jill asks.

"You know," Paige says. "Vertical presentations at schmancy restaurants."

"Like the base of rice with a layer of spinach with the lamb loin fanned on top with a chive sticking out sort of thing?" Shirley asks.

"Exactly. Stacked food. It's pretentious, he says. He hates having to deconstruct his dinner, he says. Why should putting all the food in one teetering pile warrant charging double for it? Food doesn't need to be in fanciful shapes, it should just be shaped like food, he says."

"What did you say?" I ask.

"I said I'd see him at the gym some time, since I couldn't imagine a world without stacked food, and clearly we weren't destined to eat together," Paige says. "And then I took my brother to Trotter's and had a spectacular meal! Stacked all over the place!"

"Really, where do these men get their strangeness?" Shirley mutters.

"Parents, mostly," Ruth says with an authority that belies her own lack of experience in this arena.

"Well, I'm grateful I'm not still out there," Jill says. "No more nightmare dates for me!"

"It isn't nice to gloat, darling," I say.

"Says the woman with three attractive men on her dance card!" Paige elbows me in the ribs.

"Want one?" I ask. "I'll make you a nice deal!"

"Tut, tut," Ruth clucks at us. "If Shirley and I have learned one thing, it is that there is no one way to be in the world. And no one's life is any better than anyone else's, just different, and with their own unique joys and challenges. Time for our Valentine's resolutions."

Another Spingold tradition, we do resolutions for each other.

"Me first!" Shirley says. "I resolve that Paige should do at least one thing every week that she couldn't do if she were in a relationship. I resolve that Ruth should remember not to leave half-filled teacups all over the house. I resolve that Jill should have the wedding she didn't even know she was wishing for. I resolve that Jodi should sit down for one hour and really ponder the idea of monogamy." She looks very pleased with herself.

Ruth nods thoughtfully. "I resolve that Shirley should get over the damn teacups. I resolve that Jodi should continue to seek her happiness in the way that fits best for her. I resolve that Jill should not ever apologize to her new in-laws for who she is or where she came from, but should bring their family the same joy she brings to ours. I resolve that Paige should not be afraid to throw herself into the dating pool with abandon and be open to men outside her normal comfort zone."

"Okay, I'll try," Paige says. "I resolve that Jill have a wonderful marriage. I resolve that Jodi should dump Ben and Abbot and settle down with Connor. I resolve that Aunt Shirley start going to blues clubs again. I resolve that Aunt Ruth show me some of the Chicago I haven't seen yet. How's that?"

"Excellent, dear." Shirley pats her hand.

"My turn," I say. "I resolve that Aunt Shirley should bake a batch of poppyseed cookies before the week is out. I resolve that Aunt Ruth should take a one-week sabbatical from sniping at her sister. I resolve that Jill should not make me wear periwinkle as her maid of honor. I resolve that Paige should take us up on our tuition reimbursement plan and get that damn MBA she doesn't know we know she's been researching." Paige's eyebrows shoot straight up in the air.

"I ditto Jodi's Paige resolution," Jill begins. "Just apply already! We'll figure out the logistics later. I resolve that Aunt Shirley should start doing more things for her own enjoyment and not make such a huge percentage of her life about doing for others. I resolve that Aunt Ruth should be in charge of telling us what we should do for all the ancillary events the weekend of the wedding. I resolve that Jodi should not worry about how things look to the world and just do what is in her heart in all things."

We toast, clean up, hug and kiss all around. We head upstairs, and once I get Paige settled in my guest room, I head for bed.

Jill resolves for me not to worry about how things look. I can't tell if she means about the business or my personal life. Or both. And while I love the sound of it, I know I can't necessarily live up to it. After all, what my heart wants right now is to call Connor and ask him to be my valentine. But I know that what I want more than that is for him to want it. And the fact that he obviously doesn't bothers me more than I like to admit. Because, despite Hunter's assertion that I probably only want him because he's the one I can't get, nevertheless, I do want him.

Beeep beep beep. My cell phone. I have a voice mail message. I dial in and enter my code.

Then I hear Chet Baker singing "My Funny Valentine." The whole song. I listen, letting the perfect words flow over me. As the song fades out, I hear the one voice I have been waiting all day to hear.

"Hey. It's Connor. I'm generically shitty at Valentine's Day. I get sort of paralyzed at the very idea of being romantic, and I ignore it for weeks and get swamped in work instead, and the day of, I procrastinate so long trying to think of something cool and not cliché, that all the florists are sold out and the candy stores are closed and all I can think to do is hold the phone up to my hi-fi. I know. Makes me totally lame. I'll try to make it up to you. I'd say that I hope you're out having a lovely evening, but frankly I hope you're not with someone who is better at this stuff than I am, since that will make me an even bigger loser. I'll call you tomorrow. Good night, sweet girl."

I didn't even know that I yelped out loud until Paige came running into my room.

"Are you okay?" she asks, breathless and wild-eyed.

"Listen." I press the button to repeat the message on my phone and hand it to her. She listens. She smiles. She listens more. Then her eyes well up with tears.

"Fuck you," she says, wiping her nose on her sleeve.

"Hey, that's not very nice." Really.

"I know. I'm just jealous." She sits on the bed. "Do you think he might be the one?"

"The one what?"

"Don't be obtuse." She smacks me on the leg. "*The one.*"

"Oh. *That* one." I think for a minute. "I can't really say. I mean, I don't really know. He could be. But he might not be. But he might. I'm not sure."

"Do you want him to be?"

"Maybe. Then again, maybe I don't want anyone to be. I like my life. I like my freedom. I've been down that road before, and I'm in no hurry to be there again. And there are a lot of things I'd have to give up if Connor Duncan were, as you say, *the one*. I don't know that I'm ready for that."

"Do you think you could lose him if you don't take a step forward soon?" Paige's eyebrows dance around a minute before settling back down. "I mean, obviously he knows you are dating other people; he referenced it in his message. And I know you aren't having sex yet, and it has only been two and a half months, but how long is that going to be okay with him?"

"That's just the thing, Paige. He hasn't given me any indication that it isn't okay with him. Maybe he's in the same place I am. Maybe he isn't going to want more than what we have."

"And is that okay with you?"

"Um, well, no, actually. It isn't." Which is the first time I have voiced this out loud.

"Wow. You really like this guy."

"I know. And it scares the crap out of me." I can feel everything surging upward. "What do I do if he doesn't want to take the next step? I mean, the kissing and petting are great, but he isn't exactly trying to rip my clothes off. I'm starting to think that maybe he isn't that attracted to me at all and doesn't really care about sex with me. I'm also thinking maybe he has his own female version of Abbot, which makes me insane with jealousy, even though I know I have no right. I feel trapped. I can't exactly suggest moving forward myself, not with Ben and Abbot hanging around. I mean, it's one thing if he asks to be exclusive and I say okay, or if he pressures the physical side and I acquiesce. But if I ask and he says no, then I'm a moron. And I certainly couldn't ask if I hadn't already told Ben and Abbot that we were over, and if Connor turned me down, then I'd be all alone, and—"

Paige slaps her hand across my mouth. "Boss Lady, you have lost it. Take a deep breath." She removes her hand.

I inhale.

"Better?" she asks.

"Better."

"Now, for someone who is one of the smartest, sanest, most clearheaded women I have ever met, you are an idiot."

"Paige, you're fired."

"Right. You give the best relationship advice of anyone in the world. Why can't you get your head around this situation?"

"Because I can't be objective about my own life. And my subjective self is, as you point out, an idiot."

"What would you tell a caller if she posed this scenario to you?"

I think about this for a moment. "I'd tell her that she is clearly going through a paradigm shift in her wants and needs personally, and that any reward worth having is worth risk. I'd tell her to dump the two placeholders and present herself free and open to the guy she really wants. I'd tell her that she can't keep a backup plan just because she doesn't want to be rejected. I'd tell her—"

"Go big, or go home," Paige says, one of my favorite tag lines.

"Go big, or go home," I repeat.

"This is what I'm saying," Paige says. "Jodi, go big. For what it's worth."

"Thank you, Paige girl."

"My pleasure, Boss Lady."

"Can I ask you something?"

One eyebrow raises as if on hydraulics. "Yes?"

"Are you really so sad about your dating drought?"

"Really, truly?"

"Truly and really."

Paige pauses and runs her fingers through her hair. "You have to promise not to tell Jill, but I wasn't feeling so bad until she got engaged. I mean, that whole single woman united thing at work, even when people are dating seriously, it still feels like we all come first. Even Kim, our only married hen, she and Marc have so many problems, she's practically single herself. But then Jill got engaged, and Benna is on this crazy are-you-the-father-of-my-children-to-be? hunt, and you have your gaggle, and Kim does have Marc, however fucked up they may be, and the marketing girls have their endless adventures, and I'm starting to feel like the last girl picked for dodgeball."

"Poor Paige. You know you're just in a rut, right? I mean, you know you are exceptional and gorgeous and smart and sexy and lovable, right?"

"I know. I know. But I can't seem to make the guy thing happen, and it really didn't used to bother me, but now it kinda does."

"I have an idea. Why don't you sign up for one of those high-end exclusive professional dating services. On the company. We'll use it to see if they really work, so we can know whether to recommend it to callers. What do you say?"

"You guys would pay for that? It's like thousands of dollars."

"I know. You're worth it. And it's tax-deductible as a business expense."

Paige leans forward and gives me a hug. "Thanks, Jodi. You're the best. And thanks for that whole MBA thing. I'm still thinking about it, but it's nice to know you guys approve of the idea."

"Hey, you're happy, we're happy, the company's healthy. Easy decision."

"Speaking of the company, we have work tomorrow, so I better go to bed. Good night, Boss Lady."

"Good night, Paige girl."

"I'm glad he called."

"Me, too."

Paige tiptoes out the door, shutting it behind her. I settle into the dark and then reach for my phone. I just want to hear that song one more time before I go to sleep.

The Ides of March Madness

Anger isn't necessarily a sign of weakness. But screaming obscenities and name-calling is! Anger can be a useful emotion. It can help us find strength to remove ourselves from unhealthy situations. It can drive us to succeed. It can spur us to honesty with each other. When we talk about anger management, we don't simply mean not to hit people. We mean learning how to tap into that emotion and express it in ways that help you and those around you. To use it to its best advantage. As women, we are told in subtle, insidious ways that it is basically unattractive to have any emotion that manifests itself in an obvious way. We're told it isn't ladylike to get angry. Which poses the question, what's so great about being ladylike anyway?

—*From an article for* Cosmopolitan *magazine about expressing emotion,*
April 2004, Jill and Jodi Spingold

"You off to the airport?" I ask Jill across our office.

"In about fifteen minutes," she says, still focused on her computer. "I'm starting to wonder if we've done this book in the wrong format." She's looking puzzled at the draft of *Facing Down Forty*, which is due to our editor next week. She's cleaning up the last two chapters, which I cranked out over the weekend, to get it ready for the one-two punch of the aunts' edits.

"What do you mean, wrong format?" Jill always does this. She comes up with the single most brilliant idea at the single least convenient time.

"Well, right now it's sort of haphazard. What if we organized the chapters into sections, like Romance, Career, Travel, Adventure, Finances, Friendships, Family, Personal Growth. I mean, all of the chapters seem to fall into one of those categories pretty neatly. It would help lump all the advice pertaining to them in one section, and we would just have to write a brief introduction to each section. What do you think?"

"I fucking hate you."

"It's not that bad an idea, Jodi, yeesh."

"No. I fucking hate you because you're right, and now I have to write eight fucking section headers while you gallivant off to O'Hare to fetch your clenched mother-in-law-to-be."

Jill laughs. "So, it's good, right? We should do it that way?"

"Yes, you insane bitch. Just once in our lives could you *please* have the genius idea at the beginning of a project instead of ten minutes before it's due? Good grief, you've been doing this to me our whole lives!" This is true. Every science fair entry, history fair paper, and art project, Jill always came up with the idea that took it to the next level at the eleventh hour. I would never admit to her that those are some of my favorite memories, those long all-nighters making the suddenly necessary changes. Never once was it an option not to take her idea and implement it. Something about knowing it could have been great and letting laziness prevent the improving just isn't in the Spingold code. But Jill was a hands-on adviser, and if she gave you a great idea, you knew she'd be helping you execute till the final minutes, Aunt Shirley coming around with sandwiches the minute you felt your energy wane, and Aunt Ruth sweeping by for five minutes of some secret Thai acupressure to make your cramping neck unclench.

"Sorry. I could do the section headers, and you could go to the airport . . ."

"No, thank you. I have to get this done and then go home to help the aunts with the shower prep." Jill's bridal shower is tomorrow, hence the imminent arrival of not only her future mother-in-law, Grace, but Hunter's paternal grandmother, Grammy Ella; Grace's sister, Aunt Bunny; and her daughter, Cousin Twish. Not Trish. Twish. I'm not exactly envious.

"It's not going to be a nightmare, right?" she asks, imploring me with her eyes to assure her.

"Hey. You have us, your friends, there are going to be forty women there celebrating you and giving you awesome presents. The fact that Hunter's family is likely to maintain a stoic distance from any fun should be only a blip on your shower joy."

"They aren't going to embarrass me, are they?"

"Oh, yeah. Be prepared. There are a couple of great games planned, a video presentation, and some really revealing toasts and roasts." Actually this is a lie. No games, no roasts, just elegant and perfect, and I think exactly what she would have planned for herself.

Jill sighs deeply. "Oh well, it's just an afternoon. And at least there will be booze. I'm shooting you an e-mail with my notes on these section headers. We can work on whatever you don't finish on Sunday afternoon after everyone is gone." She clicks away at her keyboard for a few more seconds, then shuts it down and gets up. "I'm going to head out. I'm supposed to just hang out with them at the hotel and get them settled, and then Hunter is meeting us for dinner. Are you sure you can't come?"

"No can do. Much prep on the first floor, and then Connor is coming over for a late supper."

"Really? That is the third time in five days. A new record."

"I know. I actually had to blow off Abbot to accept the offer. Thank God your shower made for a perfect excuse to back out."

Jill smiles a knowing smile. "Maybe you should blow Abbot off permanently. Since Connor has been so attentive of late, I have to assume we are reconsidering the idea of devoting ourselves to just one man."

"We are waiting for him to broach the subject, and if he does, we are prepared to accept him."

Jill shakes her head. "While you're doing the section header on romance, Sis, reread your brilliant prose on ensuring one's romantic future, would'ja?" She crosses the room and opens the door. "Have a great night. I'll talk to you later."

"Love to the Gentiles!" I call after her, and open her e-mail to get down to work.

∞

"Honey, we're fine." Aunt Shirley is trying to shoo me out of her kitchen. "Go get ready for your date."

"He's not due for another hour. Are you trying to get rid of me?"

"Of course not, kiddo," Ruth says, gliding past with an armload of gift bags. "We just want you to know that whenever you need to go, you should go."

We've been prepping all evening. Well, prepping and drinking. The sparkling pink Prosecco Aunt Ruth found for tomorrow was much in need of testing. It will be gorgeous on its own or with the blood orange juice for a decadent pink mimosa. We'll be in a private room at the Peninsula, so most of the food is taken care of there. But Aunt Shirley has made a ridiculous number of cupcakes, Jill's favorite, dark chocolate with vanilla buttercream icing, sprinkled with silver and lavender dragées. These aren't the dessert but part of the gift bags. We found a company that makes a contraption called a Cup-a-Cake, a plastic container specifically designed to hold a single cupcake in perfect portable stillness so as not to mush the frosting. Each guest is receiving a single cupcake in one of these cute containers, which we've personalized by having them imprinted with each woman's name. Also in the gift bags, a set of photo coasters with pictures of Jill as a kid, a small foil container of toffee, a little pot of red currant–scented Parfumeria lip balm, and a little makeup purse in brown corduroy with a pale blue ribbon detail that we designed at 1154 Lill Studio custom bags.

"You seem to be doing better these days with the whole Jill-getting-married issue, if I'm not mistaken?" Aunt Ruth asks, taking the last load of gift bags out to the living room.

I stick a finger into the bowl of icing, as Aunt Shirley tries to smack me away. "It isn't about Jill getting married; it's about what may happen to the business as a result of her being married. It's about what happens to our credibility with our primary audience and how much fodder it gives our ever-growing list of detractors."

"Things getting any better on that front?" Aunt Ruth asks.

"Not really. There have been a few small local pieces, three nationals, some Internet snarking. The volume of ick mail has neither increased nor decreased. Nothing has gotten more violent or threatening, nor less. Security is on high alert, we doubled the number of cameras in the office, and the local police have been wonderful at managing the picket crowd. And I'm trying to just not think about it and enjoy Jill's happiness. Jill is handling the PR stuff pretty well. We're just moving forward."

"But your concerns are still very deep for the life of the business, not to mention your personal relationship with Jill," Aunt Shirley says. "You should talk to her about your fears for your connection."

"I have to put my own neuroses aside right now and let Jill focus on being a happy bride and on keeping the business moving forward. The rest will wait." I can't talk to Jill about the damage it might do to us; I can't even get my own head around it right now.

"If you think that's best, dear," Aunt Shirley says.

"Don't listen to the guilt, darling; I've thought about it, and I agree with you. Just let Jill get married, and deal with your concerns if they still remain afterward." Ruth pours the last of the Prosecco deftly into our glasses, and Shirley finally sits down with us at the table. We clink and drink.

"Well, Ruthie, I still say they should talk it out sooner rather than later, but you'll do what you think best. Now truly, scoot, go get ready for your date!"

I drain the last sparkling sip and stand up. "All right, I will. Good night, ladies. I'll come down at eleven to head over to the Peninsula." I kiss them both on the cheek and go to primp for the evening.

I nestle into Connor's chest, feeling his arm snake around me, his hand making its lazy way from shoulder to hip and back again. For the first time, I feel irresistible with him. We've just made love for the first time, and the waiting was well worth it. In less than ninety minutes Connor has erased all my doubts about his physical attraction to me.

"Mmmm." He sighs. "Nice skin."

I lift my head and kiss his skin, slightly moist and salty from our exertions, and replace my head over the spot as if to seal the kiss between us. "Thanks. I've got miles of the stuff."

He chuckles, low and deep. "And I'm fond of every square inch." He kisses the top of my head.

"Really? Every inch?" I tilt my head up to his and receive a kiss on my lips for my effort.

"Every. Single. Inch." Connor rolls over and begins to kiss me and stroke my body. I'm tingly everywhere.

"Mr. Duncan! You can't possibly . . . ummm . . . oh my." But apparently Mr. Duncan could, possibly, making me feel frankly wicked and beyond sexy.

After such a delightfully unexpected second act, we couldn't be blamed for feeling completely starved, in spite of having had something of a Middle Eastern feast from Reza's a mere three hours ago. Confirmed by the mutual gut rumblings that have just erupted.

"I think we're going to need sustenance," Connor says. "May I suggest pancakes and bacon somewhere nearby before I head home?"

"You're not staying over?"

"Um, let's see . . . you're going to settle in all curled up next to me and then begin a nightlong twitchtravaganza in anticipation of tomorrow's festivities. Then you're going to get out of bed at some ungodly hour to begin a festival of primping and prepping, which I prefer remain a mystery." Connor reaches over and with one finger under my chin, closes my mouth, which is apparently gaping open. "C'mon. Get up, throw on some clothes, and we'll go have a midnight breakfast to replace the one we won't have tomorrow." Connor gets up and heads for my bathroom. I stretch and pull on a pair of jeans and an old sweater.

I'm very nervous that Connor's decision to not spend the night is somehow reflective of his feelings for me. Or lack thereof. On the other hand, I'm somehow tickled by the fact that he knows me well enough to know that I'm unlikely to have a restful evening's sleep. And I do kind of like that he's confident enough to simply go home, as opposed to staying because it seems the thing to do. And I like that he and I have been spending so much time together of late. It was something of a revelation when he called to suggest a late dinner tonight that my first instinct was to cancel my plans with Abbot. Something about it felt good and right. I'm feeling like I am on the verge of something, and when Connor looked at me and said he really wanted us to make love, I didn't hesitate to say yes to him. I think about what Jill was saying earlier. I think about making personal decisions for professional reasons. And I'm beginning to think maybe it is time for a paradigm shift.

"All yours," Connor says, coming back into the bedroom and breaking me out of my reverie.

I smile and touch his cheek. "Be right back." I head into the bathroom to tidy up so that I can go have pancakes with my guy.

⚘

"Thank you all so much for everything, truly. I'm just so touched!" Jill smiles at the assembled crowd, having managed to open all forty-two of her shower gifts with grace and dignity and transparent gratitude. And it was quite a haul, huge generosity from everyone, beautiful housewares and expensive kitchen appliances. Even Hunter's family had a good time and only seemed shocked by a couple of the lingerie gifts.

"I really need to pee," she whispers to me.

"Come on," I say. "I think we can sneak through the back."

Jill and I head through the crowd toward the ladies' room. "This was so perfect, Jodi. Thank you so much. It absolutely was the shower that I wanted." Then she giggles. "I can't believe you said there were going to be games! You had me so scared."

We're laughing as we enter the bathroom, distracted enough that we don't notice the redhead checking her lipstick in the mirror.

"Well, well, what a surprise and coincidence. If it isn't the Spingold sisters."

Jill and I turn at once toward the voice to find none other than Mallory.

"And to think I was planning on calling you on Monday! Such a small world. We haven't officially met." She turns to Jill. "I'm Mallory. Brant's girlfriend."

"So nice to make your acquaintance," Jill says. "I've heard a lot about you."

"I don't doubt that's true," Mallory says. "And I've heard a lot about you. For example, I've heard that the two of you have managed to get yourselves into a negative publicity pickle. It's pretty amazing when you attain the level of fame and success that the two of you have, that you haven't had such a big backlash before. Especially since it seems that no one in your organization has ever given any indication to the public that you're anything less than well, frankly, perfect."

I can feel Jill begin to seethe next to me, but she maintains her smile and her calm composure as she responds. "Why, Mallory, it's true that we've been fortunate enough to not be the focus of any seriously negative PR before now. In no small part because we do everything within our power to run a good, fair, honest business and actually to present ourselves to the world as human, and therefore flawed. In fact, if you read any of our books or listen to our shows, you will find that we use ourselves as examples, frequently of how not to do something. And we are very clear with our audience about the fact that part of what makes us good at our job is the fact that we have made many mistakes. That we learn from them, and seek to not make them again, and try to prevent other women from repeating them by sharing the details."

Mallory's smile is entirely devoid of warmth. "Oh sure, you've talked openly about your little dating mistakes, your white lies with friends, your occasional career faux pas. But let's be honest. You haven't been as forthcoming as you might, and there are certainly things from your collective pasts that would not reflect so well on the business."

"What exactly are you implying, Mallory?" I ask. "Clearly you have an agenda. Why not just put your cards on the table?"

"All right, if you want to know my position. I think Brant may have told you that I've decided not to pursue a law career, but instead to return to my first love, which is public relations."

"Actually," I say, "what Brant told me was that you were unable to pass the bar for the third time and were let go by your law firm."

Mallory blanches. And then turns a deep shade of red, which clashes ferociously with her hair. "Regardless," she says, clearly intending to ignore my remark, "I have made an application to return to my old PR firm. They have made it clear to me that I need to be able to demonstrate that I still have connections in the press. Which means I need a news item that I can plant that will get publicity, to indicate that to my company. I think that my former contacts would be very interested in some of the information that I have about the two of you. Especially in light of Jill's impending marriage and all the hoopla it has created. After all, it does seem a bit incongruous that suddenly a divorcée and a married woman are going to be telling the single women of the world how to live their lives, don't you think? Better everyone have all the facts."

"Mallory, you can tell your connections at the press whatever you damn well feel like," Jill spits out sharply. "We know who we are, we know how we run our business, and the women who turn to us for guidance and advice will continue to do so, because the guidance is honestly given and the advice is intelligent and sound. But I will be surprised if your potential new employer will be impressed by any sort of additional negative publicity that you might attempt to create around our company, piggybacking on the sad workings of a few loudmouths. Surely, the crux of their business is to enable and encourage positive press placements for their clients. And if the only thing you have to offer them are lies and half-truths that shed a negative light on someone, I'm hard-pressed to believe that they will find that an attractive package for a new employee."

"Regardless of whether it is the kind of information that will get me the job," Mallory says with a smirk, "I find that it is the kind of information that will blast itself across tabloids, make the cut for *Entertainment Tonight*, maybe even get a *Saturday Night Live* spoof. Or maybe Dave's top ten reasons not to trust a Spinster Sister. Even if it's mostly print media, it will force your own PR firm to do some serious spinning on the old Spinster Inc. image. It's likely to cost you a pretty penny to undo the damage that could be wrought."

Jill begins to laugh. "Oh my God, Dr. Evil, this is the holdup? You are threatening us with negative publicity in order to get something out of us. Pray tell, Mallory. I can only imagine. What exactly is it that you want?"

Mallory sighs as if we have offended her delicate sensibilities. "It isn't about me. But Brant has suffered." She snaps her head around to look me in the eye, glaring with a fierce intensity and hatred. She begins to jab her finger in the air in my direction. "How would it look to your readers and listeners that you continue to take alimony payments from a man who makes so much less than you, and who is struggling to make his bills, while you rake in millions! A man who didn't get his bonus this year, and was just given three months' notice that he is likely to be downsized if the business doesn't pick up. How do you suppose it makes him feel to be the brunt of your jokes? Your example of a failed relationship? Brant is too nice a guy to tell you how hurtful that is. Just like he's too nice a guy to tell you how awful it is for him to try to meet his obligation to you, knowing that every check he sends you negatively impacts his own financial well-being. All the while he sees the level of financial success that you are enjoying. It seems very clear to me that you would not currently have your business at all were it not for your relationship with Brant, and I personally find it unconscionable that not only does he not recoup any personal financial gain from the company that in essence was sparked by your relationship with him but that you continue to participate in his financial downfall. And yet you purport to be his friend, to care about him and want his happiness! What a fraud you are, Jodi, really, so very sad. And not so flattering a portrait to have on the front page."

I take a deep breath so that I may remain calm in light of this attack. "Mallory. My relationship with Brant and any financial connection between us is quite simply none of your business. I think it is very interesting that this is all coming up at a point in time when you yourself are not participating financially in your life with Brant. It strikes me that of the two of us, you are the bigger financial obligation, since you are living off of his salary. Living in his condo, with him paying all of your bills. I'm sure that Brant has shared with you that our financial arrangement, as you call it, is quite simply a repayment of a student loan, which I paid for him at a time when I was making next to no money, in order to secure our future. I am equally sure, considering the seriousness of your relationship with Brant, that he has shared with you that it was, in fact, his idea to repay that loan. As far as my business is concerned, Brant has never been any part of this endeavor. He was not present for the conception. He did not participate in any aspect of the creation of the business, and we had been divorced for over a year before the business even launched. To even remotely imply that he is entitled to any compensation from Spinster Inc., let alone eliminating the repayment of his debt, is preposterous. I cannot for the life of me figure out what it is in you that makes Brant believe that you are the best person for him. But his relationship with you is his own business. I find it difficult to imagine that Brant would condone your threats, which you appear on the surface to be presenting as your protection of Brant's interests. And I will let you decide whether or not to share with him the details of this meeting. But let me make perfectly clear that there is nothing you can say or do that will inspire me to forgive the rest of the loan nor make any compensation to Brant out of the Spinster Inc. success. I hope I make that perfectly clear."

"That is your prerogative," Mallory says. "But I would suggest that you speak to your own PR firm and think about the potential ramifications of broader negative publicity before you make any final decision. By the end of the week I intend to have some interesting conversations with some of my media connections, unless I hear from Brant that his financial picture has changed materially. I'm so glad we ran into each other. Have a good day."

Mallory smiles her twisted, cold smile and exits the bathroom. I'm shaking I'm so angry. Jill reaches over and takes my hand.

"Don't even think about it," she says. "There's nothing she can do to harm us. And she and Brant are in for one hell of a fight if they pursue this line of extortion."

I turn to Jill. "We do have to talk with our advisers about this. She is right about one thing. Negative publicity is still negative, even if later it's proven to be manipulated or outright untrue. It doesn't positively affect the business, that's for sure, and considering what we've been dealing with, we have to have some outside advice on how to handle her threats. We're at a very tenuous place with the television deal. That contract is not yet signed, and you heard Krista say that they are reconsidering their options and holding off for now. If something like this really blows up, they could very well decide once and for all that they don't want to work with us. Our deal is up in nine months with XM, and once *Facing Down Forty* is finished, we've fulfilled our publishing contract. We could literally be one hundred percent out of work if everyone decides we're a bad publicity risk!"

"I know it's upsetting, but let's try not to think about it today. When we go in on Monday, we'll gather the troops, explain what's happened. And we'll talk through all the possible outcomes. But I would rather lose the television deal and maintain our dignity and our integrity than pay that troll and your idiot ex any hush money. I feel very badly for Brant. I'm sure he cannot possibly imagine that the woman he is living with would behave in such a manner. You really should tell him."

"I can't. It comes off bitter. He'll take it however he wants to take it, and Lord knows she'll do everything in her power to manipulate it and turn it around to make me even more the evil ex-wife. Brant is going to have to figure out on his own that he is living with a heartless, gold-digging she-devil."

"Your choice. Now, I really have to pee before we go back to my beautiful party."

"I'm so sorry. I hate that this is going to be a mark on your special day." Poor Jill. Embroiled in my sick drama with my ex-husband's psycho girlfriend.

"No worries, it takes a lot more than idle threats from a butt-munch like that to ruin such a spectacular party."

Jill heads into one of the stalls, and I take a cloth from the side of the sink, run it under the cold water, and pat my face. It's easy to get on my high horse and play righteously indignant in the moment. But I think back to every deep, dark secret I ever shared with Brant during the course of our friendship and marriage and wonder how many of them I would actually be comfortable seeing in print. And Mallory is correct about one thing. Seen from a certain light, my continued acceptance of the student loan money through the filter of my enormous financial stability can be easily portrayed as greedy or vindictive. With the company on the line, not to mention my existing concerns about the impact Jill's marriage will ultimately have on the business even without the smear campaign, I do believe that there is cause for worry. The stall door opens, and Jill exits, straightening her skirt. She washes her hands, touches up her lip gloss, and gives me a megawatt smile.

"What do you say we go back to my party and have more bubbly?" she asks.

I smile back at her. "I think that's an excellent idea." I hold the bathroom door open for her, and arm in arm, heads held high, we go back to the celebration.

Inconvenient Truths

Just because a relationship isn't exclusive or serious does not mean that you won't have occasion to have important and serious conversations with your lover about the relationship itself. However casual the connection may be between you and your lover, it is necessary and essential to your health as a human being to tackle any issues that may be impinging on the quality of that relationship in a straightforward manner. Avoid accusations, and eliminate the words "we need to talk" from your vocabulary. Choosing the appropriate time to bring the subjects up can ensure that our relationships are smooth, happy, and healthy. We strongly discourage having these conversations either immediately before or immediately after a sexual encounter. A man who believes he is about to have sex is thoroughly unprepared for serious talk about other aspects of his life. And it is generally considered inhumane to begin a serious relationship discussion with a man who is naked.

—*From* The Thirty Commandments *by Jill and Jodi Spingold*

"How is your chicken teriyaki?" I ask Ben over dinner at Hachi's Kitchen.

"Excellent," he replies. "Wanna bite?"

"No thanks. I'm getting full, and I haven't even finished all my sashimi yet." I've been sort of avoiding him since New Year's, and, strangely, he hasn't been complaining. But it is nice to see him.

"So what do you guys think you're going to do about Mallory's threats?"

"There's still some debate," I admit. "All the girls at the office agree with Jill that we should stand firm, not do anything, and let Mallory do her worst. But Krista, our agent, is concerned about how it could affect the television deal, which is already shaky, and our PR firm has been very up front about the fact that we are ripe for a massive negative PR campaign."

We've run this company for nearly five years without any terribly serious backlash. There is some validity to the idea that the media could smell potential weakness in the two of us personally and in the company in general. It was one thing when it was just general snipes from the conservatives and the Christian Right, attacking our values. But the latest stuff is evenly split between our usual detractors and some disheartened former fans, and that is dangerous. And while everyone is in agreement that any accusations or implications would be baseless, and ultimately we would be exonerated, it's difficult to respond to such an attack and not look defensive. Considering the planned expansion for the company, the new merchandising deals, and the television contract, which could open up a whole new area of business for us, they are recommending at this point that we strongly consider some sort of financial settlement with Brant. Ultimately, it will be Jill's and my decision, but we have a lot of people who are counting on us and need this company to retain its success. If we go down, it isn't just the two of us that are affected. There are nine women full-time in our offices who are counting on our sustaining the viability of this company, not to mention literally hundreds of others in a less direct way. It becomes very difficult to consider taking a stance out of our own pride and self-righteousness that could ultimately destroy not only what we worked so hard to build but also put at serious risk the livelihoods of the people who have helped us get where we are.

"How much money are your people talking?" he asks, forehead wrinkling.

"Ultimately, we're not sure. It will require our lawyers broaching the idea of a settlement with Mallory and Brant and seeing if we can get them to name a figure that we can respond to." Which is, in itself, a delicate thing. I have no idea if Brant even knows that Mallory has threatened us. And I've been advised not to have any conversation with him until the matter is settled, so I can't even talk to him to determine if he has a hand in this or if he's in the dark. If he doesn't know, and suddenly our lawyers call him, he could end the whole thing and break it off with her, giving her even more reason to go after us. The problem is that there's no turning back if we broach a settlement. We have to move forward with negotiating that settlement, because if Mallory takes to the press that we came to them, attempting to hush them up with money, and then in any way reneged, it will make us look worse in the long run. It's a fucking mess.

Ben reaches across the table and takes my hand. "Jodi. I'm so very sorry. I know that this is a horrible time for you, and I wish there was something I could do to make it easier."

I steel myself for what I'm about to say. Ben has unknowingly given me the perfect opening for the speech I have been practicing all afternoon.

"Actually, there is something you can do, but I'm hesitant to ask you, because I don't think it will make you happy."

Ben takes another bite of his chicken. "You want to stop seeing me," he says quietly.

"It's not that simple," I say. "I like you very much, and I love hanging out with you. You're smart and funny and kind. You always have interesting ideas, you're a good listener, and I think we've had a great time together. But the fact is, you and I both know that this relationship, however much fun, isn't going to last forever. You and I want different things for our futures. I have a tremendous amount on my plate right now. Jill's wedding is only seven weeks away. The business is always crazy, and now we have the additional stress of our current predicament. I'm feeling pulled in too many directions, and I also feel that it would be very selfish of me to continue with you."

Ben smiles a huge grin, which is not exactly the response that I was waiting for. "Actually, Jodi, I couldn't be more relieved. See, the thing is, remember that girl? My friend from high school that I spent New Year's with? Well, we've been hanging out kind of a lot, because she really doesn't have too many friends here anymore, and well, a couple of weeks ago we were at my place, watching a movie, and, I don't know, she said something, and I laughed, and she punched me in the arm, and we made eye contact, and it suddenly just hit us both that there was something more going on between us. The truth of the matter is that I had a huge crush on her when we were in high school and never had the nerve to confess. And she finally admitted that she had a crush on me, too, even though she was dating somebody else at the time. And, well, the thing is, I was actually going to tell you tonight that I think we should stop seeing each other. Because I really like this girl. And I really want to offer myself to her without any other encumbrances. So I guess we were both on the same page, and we just didn't know it! Kind of funny when you think about it. So, anyway, you shouldn't worry, because we're totally in sync and no hard feelings. I've had a great time hanging out with you, and I hope that we will honestly stay friends."

I shake off my surprise. "I hope so, too, Ben. And I'm really happy for you and your girl. What a fantastic and romantic way to find somebody to be with. How cool it is that you have made this reconnection! I hope that you guys are just as happy as anything."

"Thanks, Jodi, that means a lot to me."

"Well, I think this calls for more sake." I wave over our waiter and order us a surprisingly celebratory round.

We finish our dinner, with only slightly stilted conversation, after which he walks me home. Promises to call soon, but not too soon, with a wink. Gives me a big hug, unlocks his bike from my front porch, and rides off into the sunset.

For what was supposed to be an uncomfortable conversation, that went surprisingly well. Considering how many potentially uncomfortable conversations are imminent, I hope it isn't downhill from here.

⚜

"Hey, Boss Lady, can I talk to you for a minute?"

I wave Paige in, and she shuts the door behind her.

"What's up?" I ask her.

"Um, I sort of wanted to talk to you without the other boss lady here, if that's okay."

"Of course. Jill's off with Hunter, tasting menu options at the caterer. She won't be back for ages. What's on your mind?"

"It's this whole thing with Brant and Mallory. I wanted to say that I'm starting to maybe reconsider my original thoughts about fighting the good fight. But I wanted to talk it through with you before telling Jill."

"She does get a little Norma Rae now and again. What have you been thinking?"

"Well, I wonder if it might not be better to offer them a version of the profit sharing you offer us. That way, the company wouldn't have to take a hit in terms of cash outlay, and in any year when the company doesn't post a profit, they get nothing. It could even be a limited time structure. Kind of like alimony, five years of one percent profit sharing or something like that. I mean, it's just such a weird time, and there's the whole television thing, and I hate that I feel like I'm backing down from my principles, but I also have to think of the bottom line and the health of the company. I did some research over the weekend, and there are at least ten companies our size that went under after a public scandal in the last couple of years."

"What sort of scandals were they?"

Paige pauses. Then blushes. "Okay, they were mostly embezzling, drug, or sex scandals. But those are just the ones who had to close up shop. I mean, there have got to be others who have survived but taken a big hit."

"I know. It's obviously on my mind as well. So you are changing your vote to payoff, huh?"

"I guess I'm changing my vote to let's further explore the possibilities of a payoff that doesn't kill us."

"Duly noted. You know, you're going to have to have this discussion with Jill." I smile at her.

"I know. I think I just wanted to test it out on you first."

"You did a good job. Just explain it to her the same way you explained it to me, she'll listen, and we'll both take it under consideration."

Paige smiles, obviously relieved. "Okay, I'll tell her when she gets back. Thanks, Jodi."

"My pleasure. Thank you for caring that much about the company."

"What's on your docket this afternoon?" Paige asks, stealing a handful of M&M's out of the bowl on my desk. I can't get through the day without my dosage of vitamin M; I order them in custom colors to match the office.

"I'm going to pick up the prototypes for the lunch kits out in the burbs, and then hopefully get back in traffic in time to meet Jill for her dress fitting at six."

"Well, I'll speak with her while you're gone, and then the two of you can talk about me later."

"Sounds like a plan."

"Okay, I'm going back to work. Thanks again, Jodi."

"No, thank you."

"No, thank *you*!"

"Oy, get out of my office, you goose!"

Paige closes the door behind her. I wonder how many others are having private little doubts about this situation. Jill's passion is extraordinary and infectious but also difficult to argue with. I think I'd better take the temperature of the rest of the staff before having any more discussion with her about this issue. I get up from my desk and head out into the office to do a little reconnaissance.

❧

I tear ass into the bridal salon twenty minutes late, having slogged through an hour and ten minutes of rush-hour traffic. "Did I miss it?" I ask the aunts, who are sitting on a settee, sipping champagne.

"Catch your breath, sweetheart, you haven't missed a thing," Aunt Shirley says.

"Here, drink this." Aunt Ruth hands me a flute, and I swig half of it in one gulp. This makes me burp a little.

"Such a delicate flower," Aunt Ruth says.

"Hey, is Jodi here yet?" Jill's muffled voice wafts out of the dressing room.

"I'm here," I call out to her.

"Okay, here I come!" The door opens, and Jill steps out. My eyes well up with tears. Aunt Ruth begins to cough. Aunt Shirley puts her handkerchief up to her eyes. My little sister is wearing the single most hideous wedding dress I have ever seen. It is a yellowish shade of ivory, shiny satin with huge puffy sleeves, a sweetheart neckline trimmed in iridescent beads, a princess waist, and eighteen miles of skirt. She is beaming at us.

"It's quite a dress, darling," Aunt Shirley says.

"It's really something," I mumble.

"It's the ghastliest thing I have ever laid my eyes on," Aunt Ruth says. "Take it off at once, young lady. Have you entirely taken leave of your senses?"

"Ruthie!" Aunt Shirley scolds. "Really, behave yourself! She didn't mean it, honey, she's just trying to be funny."

"No I'm not. That dress is a disaster," Ruth says.

"*Ruth!* I mean it, stop that this minute!"

I look over at Jill, who has her face buried in her hands, her shoulders shaking. I walk over and put an arm around her. "It's okay, Jillybean, it'll all be okay." Jill looks up at me, which is when I realize that she hadn't been crying at all, but rather, was laughing hysterically.

"I. Cannot. *Believe*. You. Thought. I'd. Buy. This. Dress," she stammers between giggles.

"Well, I'll be," Aunt Shirley says, plopping back down on the couch.

"You evil thing!" I say, beginning to laugh.

"You little bitch," Ruth says. "That is no way to treat the women who love you."

The four of us collapse in relieved mirth, and finally, Jill disappears to get into her real dress. When the door opens again, our three reactions are nearly identical as before, but this time for the right reasons. Jill is stunning. A vision in champagne silk. A simple scoop-neck bodice with wide straps, fitted to show off her amazing collarbone and tiny waist. The skirt is tea length, with just enough petticoats to give it some shape. A ribbon belt. The silhouette is almost a 1950s feel, and she's wearing an ephemeral fingertip veil so gossamer sheer that it is practically invisible, and a pair of kitten-heeled pumps.

"It's perfect," Aunt Shirley says, dabbing tears.

"You're stunning," I say, grinning like an idiot.

"Well, that's more like it," Aunt Ruth says.

The tailor swoops in, making tiny adjustments here, little pinches there. The dress is going to fit her like a glove. After she gingerly gets back out of the dress so as not to disturb the pins and markings, she comes back into the waiting room.

"And now, your turn, ladies!" The salon owner wheels out a rack, which has three hanging bags on it. "Who is first?"

"What's this?" Aunt Ruth asks.

"A surprise," Jill says. "I wanted you all to have the perfect outfits. Tell me if I did okay."

The salon owner hands each of us a parcel and directs us to dressing rooms. I unzip the bag and see the most perfect shade of green that God ever invented. Not quite a sage, not quite a mint, not quite an olive. The color of a shady meadow in Wales or something. Fairy green. I pull out the dress, a flowy satin with enough weight to give it substance. The top has sort of a crisscross effect with a V-neck, short sleeves, and a similar skirt to Jill's but with an overlay of chiffon, giving the skirt a dreamlike quality. I put it on, and it fits like a glove, the green making my eyes really pop and my fair skin look porcelain, just the right amount of cleavage and totally camouflaging my ass and tummy. It's perfect. I walk out into the main room. Jill is grinning like the Cheshire cat.

"You look awesome, Butthead."

"Thank you for my princess dress, Moose Face. And it isn't periwinkle!"

A door opens, and Aunt Shirley walks out. Her Chanel-styled suit is in a perfect deep pewter, setting off her silver hair and blue eyes to perfection. She is smiling as wide as Jill.

"Oh, honey, it's the most amazing thing I've ever had." She comes over to kiss Jill. "And aren't you gorgeous in that green! Oh, Jodi, you're beautiful, sweetheart." She claps her hands delightedly.

"And what am I, chopped liver?" Ruth says behind us. She's in a sheath of deep eggplant purple with a duster of lighter purple chiffon over it. She looks like a queen.

"Oh hush, Ruthie, you're gorgeous, too, all right?" Aunt Shirley says.

We all admire ourselves and each other, as the tailor makes his adjustments on us as well. When we are done, we get back into our street clothes and head home, Jill riding with me, and Ruth driving Shirley.

"One helluva day, huh?" I ask Jill in the car.

"I know. Especially with all the muckraking around the office."

"Muckraking?"

"You know perfectly well that everyone is talking about us caving in to Malcontent and your ex-idiot. Little Paige is even devising payment plans, the sneak."

"Jill, people are worried about the business. They're entitled to be concerned."

"Concerned yes, unprincipled, no."

"That's a little harsh."

"I don't think so. I mean, we explained to them all what was going on. I can't believe they want to cave to extortion! Just to prevent a little negative publicity."

"Jill, look at it from their perspective. They want to protect us and protect the company. There is a lot at stake right now, and we are already open to plenty of public scrutiny as it is."

"What do you mean?"

I take a deep breath. I've already had one difficult conversation this week; time for another. "I mean that with you getting married, people obviously have an opportunity to speculate that the company may not be as viable as it once was, as we have seen these past weeks. Maybe they're not wrong to question us."

Jill looks over at me as I drive. "Are you still on about that crap? Not enough spinsters at Spinster Inc.?"

"I'm not on about anything. But you have to admit, it will change the dynamic, and if our detractors continue to latch on to it, it will be something of an ongoing challenge. Adding this crap with Brant and Mallory on top of it just might not be the smartest thing right now, that's all."

"I see," Jill says curtly. "And this isn't about you at all."

"What does that mean?"

"Nothing."

I stop at a stoplight and turn to look at her. Her jaw is clenching and unclenching. "What does that mean?" I ask again.

"It means that it seems very interesting that in a time of crisis brought on by *your* ex, and in the middle of your own existential angst about relationships, *suddenly* my *marriage* is the thing mucking up the works. I can't stay single for you. I won't stay single for you or anyone else. Not for the aunts, not for our fans, not for anyone. I can't be your playmate twenty-four hours a day. You're thirty-five years old, and you need to figure out your own shit."

This makes tears sting my eyes. "You think I would want you to stay single to keep me company? You really believe that?"

"I don't know what I believe, except that we weren't raised to walk away from something because it was hard. And just because you won't face the things that are hard about relationships in your personal life doesn't mean I'm going to let you do that in our business."

"And why should I let you throw our business under the bus so that you can retain your sense of moral superiority? We have people counting on us!"

"I count on us," Jill says quietly.

"Well, I do, too."

We ride in silence all the way back home.

Before Jill can get out of the car, I reach over and grab her arm. "I love you, Moose Face."

She looks at me with deep disappointment. "I love you, too, Butthead. But you're really making me angry right now. Let's talk about it later when we both cool off."

"Okay. Should we get the aunts in on it?" Frequently we force them to moderate our disagreements.

"I think this time, it had better be just us."

"Fine. Let me know when you're ready."

We walk into the house, and I hope the foundation is strong enough for the storm that's approaching.

Taking Care of Business

Business relationships are in many ways very similar to familial relationships. And they should be handled with the same care, thoughtfulness, and sensitivity. If you manage other people in your line of work, it is important that they see you as an authority figure but also as someone who is aware of their own professional practice and willing to admit to mistakes and be a team player. Making the people who work for you feel as if they work *with* you is the surest way to have success in business. And while we can't please everybody, we can ensure that everybody respects the fact that we have listened to all possible ideas and made decisions that we feel are best for our business.

—*From a speech to the Chicago Chamber of Commerce, Jodi Spingold,*
May 2004

Jill looks up at me from her desk. "You ready?"

I smile over at her. "You bet."

"Well, then. Let's go get 'em."

We both rise from our desks and cross the room. I hold the office door open for Jill. "After you, Moose Face."

"Thank you, Butthead."

We head down the hall to the conference room, where our team is assembled, looking nervous and whispering anxiously among themselves. When we walk in, they all look up guiltily. Jill begins.

"Okay, guys. Here is the deal. We wanted to have this meeting to talk about the situation with Mallory and Brant. But we also want to use this as an opportunity to really explore some other is-sues that people might be concerned about regarding the busi-ness. Jodi and I are both aware of how hard you all work to make this company what it is, and how much you each have at stake personally in the success of this business. We would not be where we are without all of you, and so we do not want to make any de-cisions about the future of this company without hearing from you. We want to hear your open and honest opinions about what is best for us as a team. We all know this is not a democracy, but Jodi and I like to think of ourselves as benevolent dictators, and we hope that we have shown you in our years together that we re-spect each and every one of you and truly do listen to your coun-sel. I'm going to let Jodi say a few words, and then we're going to open things up for discussion. What's most important about this meeting is that, first and foremost, everything that is said in this room today is one hundred percent confidential. But more than that, everything that is said in this room today can be said without any fear of repercussions. If you disagree with any of the sugges-tions that we are going to make, we want you to voice that opin-ion. We can't promise that we will act on it, but we can promise that we will hear you. Jodi, why don't you start."

"Thanks, Jill. I don't have very many memories of our father. But one memory that does stick out for me happened just a few months before he passed away. Our dad, for those of you who don't know, worked in manufacturing. He was the vice president of a company that built office furniture. He took me to work with him one afternoon and gave me a tour of the plant. And one of the things that I noticed was that as we were leaving, he went up to an older gentleman who was sweeping the floors, intro-duced me, and asked about the man's wife and children. As we were leaving the plant, he looked at me and said, 'You know that man that I just spoke to who was sweeping the floor? That whole company couldn't work without that one man.' I remember giggling as if my dad had made a joke. How silly it was to imagine that the man sweeping the floor was what made the company work. But my dad stopped me and said very seriously that he had not made a joke, that it was always important to remember that any company was only as good as its lowest-paid employee, and that he would not be a good manager unless he remembered every single day that the work that he does is only made possible by the work of that old man with the broom. Jill and I have always run this company on that principle. She and I don't ever forget that this organization is only as successful as all of you make it. The only reason that she and I are free to talk on the radio and write books and make appearances and think of weird merchandising ideas is because all of you make the company run day to day. And we are as grateful for that as we have ever been for anything. Your loyalty and commitment is a daily gift to us. And we both hope that we are reasonably diligent about making that clear to you on a regular basis. For the first time in this young company's life, we are faced with a serious dilemma, a problem, and we know that the decision we make about how to deal with this problem affects each and every one of you. We also know that you all are hesitant to hurt our feelings or disagree with us. But we need to put something on the table today and really hear from you what you think and feel about what lies ahead. I want to start by apologizing to all of you for having married a man who would remotely align himself with the kind of woman that Mallory has turned out to be."

The assembly laughs.

"I'm not entirely kidding," I say. Obviously, I could not have foreseen when I got married to Brant that someday I would divorce him, and several years later, he would meet the devil incarnate, and move her into his apartment. However, it is technically my fault that we are all in the pickle that we are in. And for that, I am genuinely sorry and horribly guilty.

"We all know that negative publicity, even when manipulated or half-true or outright false, can significantly damage the health of a company," I continue. "We are in no position to know at this point in time how serious Mallory is. We do not know if Brant is aware of what she has threatened. And we don't know how good her contacts are. We have to make a decision, and on both sides that decision is a risk. If we make the decision that no matter what happens we are going to stand firm and fight whatever comes, it is entirely possible that it may be a serious fight, and that it may take years to bounce back from the damage that could be done. There is no shame in making a financial settlement with someone in order to prevent that kind of damage to a company. It is done all the time, far more often than any of us even know or can imagine, and frequently board members and directors of companies make those decisions in order to make problems go away. One of the things that Jill and I did very early on in starting this business was to align ourselves with an incredibly talented insurance agent. And if it comes down to the need for a financial settlement, we are insured against that sort of damage. In other words, the actual settlement itself would be covered by our insurance, and while our premiums would go up, it would not materially damage the fiscal health of the organization. Paige has also done some research and has figured out an alternative to a cash settlement in the form of profit sharing, which is another option that we could consider if we decide to essentially throw some money at this problem to make it go away. There's no shame in making this payoff, and there's no shame for any of you in asking us to make this payoff if it is what we all believe is best for the company."

Jill jumps in. "Look, guys. It's my turn to apologize. I know that I can get a little overzealous when my principles are challenged, and I know that I came in here last week and gave a very impassioned speech about our integrity, about our intelligence, about the need to stand up and fight the good fight. And I realize that by making that speech, particularly by making it before asking you all for your initial thoughts and opinions, I was in no small way influencing the nature of the communication that followed. I still believe very strongly that this company can withstand any attempt by the likes of Mallory and Brant to damage our credibility. I genuinely believe that we are in a position to fight this openly and honestly, to stand our ground and to not just survive but thrive. But I also know that it isn't a risk I can take on my own. And ultimately, I'm not so interested in being responsible for making that decision without you all. I won't be angry with anyone if, after today, you change your vote to making a settlement. As Jodi said, there is no shame in that personally or professionally. If we go in that direction, it is because we honestly believe that it is the best thing for the company, and we will move on and continue to grow together. I also want to acknowledge that some of you may be having some concerns over the impact that my impending nuptials may ultimately have on the business. I know this is a crazy time. And I know that in most businesses, the marital status of the CEO is completely irrelevant. But it has been brought to my attention recently that when the name of your company is Spinster Inc. and the mission of your company is to empower single women to live their best lives, marital status suddenly gets put on the table for business discussion."

There are murmurs around the room. A couple of people nod their heads, and a couple of people look away.

"Look, guys," Jill continues, "I know you all care about me, and I know that you all are excited about my wedding for my personal sake. And I'm sorry that I was dismissive when somebody tried to tell me that perhaps it ought to be up for discussion. Not whether to get married, but how to handle it in terms of the business. And while I'm not going to cancel my wedding just to retain my spinsterhood for the sake of the company, I do want to ensure that there isn't any sort of backlash. We are putting two things on the table right now for open discussion. The first is the Mallory/Brant issue. We would like any of you who would like to weigh in with us on whether you are more in support of fighting the fight or more in support of making a settlement to make your voices heard. The second topic has less of the decision-making air to it and simply is more of a brainstorming session. What do you see as the potential negative ramifications of one of the Spinster Sisters not being a spinster anymore? And what, if any, are the potential positive impacts of that? We want to take this time to think through how best to handle the situation. And hopefully to turn it to our favor." Jill looks over at me. I smile and turn back to the team.

"Guys, we're not leaving this room until we make a decision about Brant and Mallory, and until we figure out the best way for the company to support Jill's marriage. Are you guys up for it?" Around the table heads begin to nod.

"All right, then," Jill says. "Who wants to begin?"

❦

Jill holds her wineglass out to Hunter for a refill. "I really think it was the best meeting we've ever had," she says. "Don't you think, Jodi?"

"Absolutely," I say. Once everybody got over their nervousness, people were very open and honest about their concerns. But it also became very clear how much those concerns were truly about the impact to us personally and the general success of the company and really very little about protecting their own interests. They hated the idea of Jill and me being dragged through the mud, and more than that, they all believe so strongly in our message and are so certain that we really do help people that they wanted to be sure that we could continue to do that effectively. It was truly amazing.

"Well, dears," says Aunt Shirley. "I'm not in the least surprised. You have such wonderful people working with you. I would have been shocked if you had found anything different."

"I agree," says Ruth. "But let's cut to the chase. Ultimately, what did you decide?"

"Well," says Jill, "we debated the PR issue pretty extensively, and even though a few people still have some reservations," she winks at me, "we all agreed that it is a clear connection to the message of our company to fight if it comes to that. So we have decided not to offer any sort of settlement and, in fact, not to have any communication with either Mallory or Brant for the time being and simply to see how it plays out."

"I still think Brant may not be fully aware of what Mallory is up to," I say. "And I also believe, when push comes to shove, that Mallory may in fact back off to protect her relationship with Brant once she realizes that we aren't going to cave. At least, I really hope so."

"And what about the other issue?" Hunter asks. "Am I about to be lynched by the entire staff of Spinster Inc. for taking one spinster off the market?"

"Actually," Jill says, "I'm glad you bring it up. I've decided for the sake of the company not to marry you."

There is a deafening silence as Hunter's head whips around to look at her. Jill smiles at him and winks.

"You are so mean," I say.

"You've got to stop playing these pranks. They're going to give one of us a heart attack," says Ruth.

That discussion, while slightly shorter than the other, was probably the most meaningful. It turned out that the underlying message that we send has far less to do with someone being single and far more to do with someone being true to themselves and is aimed at empowering people to live a life of joy, abundance, and personal success. It was interesting that Maddy actually brought up that she and Cleo had had a few ideas that they had been hesitant to bring to us, because she felt so strongly that it was sort of a top-down organization. That when it came to the big picture, Jill and I were in charge of ideas and the team was in charge of executing. But once we started, it became clear that we have assembled a team that is as passionate about our ideas as we are, and what's more, a group of people who are creative and intelligent and have wonderful ideas of their own.

"Well," says Jill, taking a sip of her wine. "What we figured out is that the company has grown to a point where it has to stop being so centrally focused on Jodi and me. That actually being a Spinster Sister has nothing to do with your marital status. Nor with your being blood related to one of us. Being a Spinster Sister is about attitude and lifestyle, and we have an office full of Spinster Sisters who embody that ideal just the way we do. So we are going to begin a marketing campaign that starts to make some of the other team members a part of being the face of the company."

I take a sip of wine and jump in. "Paige and Kim came up with the idea of a campaign that opens up the company in, I think, a pretty exciting, and more important, inclusive way. So we're going to start with a series of ads in magazines and on billboards and signs on buses that say things like, 'Are you a Spinster Sister?' 'Be a Spinster Sister.' And the second round of ads is going to have pictures of all the girls on the team with the tagline, 'I'm a Spinster Sister.'

"We're also going to change the website to include sections where the team members each get their own page and their own blog, and where our fans have opportunities to engage with and ask questions of any particular person in the company, not just Jill and me. We think, if we handle it right, that the new face of the company is going to be the entire company. And in that way we'll be able to reach an even broader market and have a more inclusive message. If we can convince everybody that *Spinster Sister* is an attitude and not a legal term, it will eventually really broaden our market to be more accessible to women who aren't single. Jill and I are going to propose that the next book we write is *The Spinster Sisters on Marriage*. Jill will cover the points of being newly married. I will cover the points about being married for a longer period of time, as well as some of the trials and tribulations associated with getting divorced. And we're actually going to work with a third author for this book, someone who has been married for a very long time and is successful so that we have that demographic represented as well. It'll open up a new ability to address the issues connected to sustaining relationships."

"Well, I think it's a brilliant idea," says Hunter.

"We're hoping to use the new campaign as a preemptive strike against Mallory," Jill says. "In fact, Kim and her team decided to stay late tonight to get the initial round of ads and billboards designed so that we can start as early as next week getting them in place. Hopefully, by the time Mallory can plant her poison in the press, everybody will be too focused on the rebranding to pay much attention."

"I'm very proud of you girls," says Ruth. "I know that both of these difficult things have brought up some serious issues for you. It is very impressive that the two of you can work through them openly and honestly and not have it damage your relationship."

"Well, we learned that from the best!" says Jill.

"Hear, hear," I say. "I'd like to propose a toast to the original Spinster Sisters who taught us that sisters make the best friends, the best support, and the best business partners."

We all raise our glasses in praise and drink to our health.

The Dynamic Duo

Does it feel greedy? I don't think so. For me, dating more than one man is no different than having more than one favorite restaurant. Don't forget, it is always my assumption when I'm dating more than one person that the men I am dating are also dating other women. I certainly don't ask for exclusivity from someone with whom I am being nonexclusive. I don't think that dating more than one person takes anyone off the market for anyone else. And in general, I find that the nature of those types of dating relationships tend to be between people who are both in the same place in their lives. I always try to be open and honest with my partners and encourage them to be open and honest with me. And I genuinely believe that it doesn't do any harm to play the field. I find that sometimes women who only date one man at a time tend to settle in making permanent connections to partners because of the amount of time they have invested in one person, and how daunting it is to end a relationship and start over from scratch. Whereas dating multiple people allows someone to feel comfortable about ending relationships that aren't working and also to recognize that truly exceptional singular partner when he does come along.

—From an interview in Jane *magazine, Jodi Spingold, September 2006*

"You take the last bite," Abbot says, pushing the crème brûlée across the table to me. "I'm stuffed."

"Well, if you insist," I say, spooning the last delectable morsel of custard into my mouth. Abbot waves at our waiter for the check and then smiles at me.

"So, I've been having an idea, and I wanted to get your take on it."

"All right," I say. "Shoot."

"Well, from all reports, being the maid of honor is an exhausting business in the best of cases, and certainly in your situation, considering everything that's been going on, I have to assume that by the time the wedding duties are done, you are going to be much in need of some R & R. I have a client with a beautiful little villa in Tuscany, on a charming piece of property, with its own olive grove, in a village only an hour outside of Florence. He's been offering it to me for years, and I thought that perhaps this summer might be a good time to take him up on that offer. He has informed me that it is free the first two weeks of June, and at my disposal. What would you say to allowing me to whisk you away for two weeks of wine, pasta, and relaxation after the wedding?"

My jaw drops open. "You're serious."

"Of course," Abbot says.

"Two weeks?"

"Well, it could be less, but frankly, I would think a minimum of ten days to fully enjoy the amenities."

My head reels. Two weeks in Tuscany. I'd only been to the region once before, nearly ten years ago, and then only for four days. It was magical. The thought of being able to get away to such a beautiful place is thrilling.

"But Abbot, you and I have never spent longer than three days together. Are you sure that we should jump to such an extended vacation? And in a foreign country, no less?"

Abbot looks at me with a very serious air. "Jodi, I'm a very patient man. When you and I first began our relationship nine months ago, you were very open and clear with me about the nature of the relationship, and certainly that matched what I felt able to commit to as well. It has become clear to me over our time together that you and I are very, very good together. You are the first woman since my divorce who has made me believe that it is possible to find someone with potential. Someone that reminds me how wonderful it could be to be seriously committed to one person. But neither one of us will ever know unless we take a step forward. I'm suggesting this trip for a few reasons. First, I think we would have a wonderful time. It's a beautiful country with much to explore and enjoy. But I also believe that spending that kind of time together would give us both a clear indication whether this is a relationship we would like to pursue in a more serious vein. If we find at the end of the two weeks that we are not compatible in that way, then at least we know that and will have had a great time and wonderful memories.

"I'm forty-eight years old, Jodi, and for the first time in a decade I see genuine potential in a relationship. And I'm tired of the two of us playing chicken with each other. To see which one is going to broach the idea first. It's going to be me. You don't have to decide right now, but I would like you to give some serious consideration to my offer. Come to Italy with me. See how we do, and if it is as wonderful as I genuinely believe it will be, then I would like for you to consider moving forward with me. Exclusively."

Holy shit. "Abbot, that is one of the loveliest things anyone has ever said to me. And you are right. I do think we would have a wonderful time, and I do think it would give us a clearer idea of who we are to each other. You are also right in that it is the kind of offer I will need to seriously consider before giving you a final answer. But I want to thank you so very, very much for making it."

"That is all I can ask," he says. But his demeanor belies his casual comments. Everything about him seems to imply that, of course, I will say yes. "Shall we?" he asks, having signed the bill.

I smile at him. "Absolutely." I can feel the warm pressure of his hand on the small of my back as he gently guides me out of the restaurant.

Of course this throws a wrench into my plans to suggest we take a break. My conversation with Ben went so smoothly, it empowered me to think that it was time to end things with Abbot, too. My newfound intimacy, emotional and physical, with Connor has simply changed the dynamic. But with Abbot's offer on the table, and no equal offer from Connor, I start to wonder. As we stand in the chilly night air waiting for the valet to bring his car, he takes me in his arms and looks deep into my eyes.

"You are the kind of girl I could fall in love with, Jodi Spingold. Give me a chance to prove to you that I'm the kind of guy you could love back." He leans over and kisses me tenderly and deeply, and everything from the neck down begins to melt.

"No way," Jill says, stealing a piece of my bacon.

"Way," I say, snagging a forkful of her pancakes. We are indulging in a decadent Sunday brunch at the Bongo Room.

"Are you going to go?" she asks.

"I honestly don't know. I mean, it's a pretty spectacular offer, and I know that I would have a great time."

"But . . ." she prompts.

"But I also know deep down that Abbot probably isn't the guy."

"What makes you so sure?"

"For starters, his neat-freak thing. And he'd never in a million years move in with me in our building. And I find his apartment cold and sterile."

"And?"

"And I think despite what we have in common in terms of culture, he also isn't a night owl the way I am. He's a lot older than any of our friends and probably wouldn't mix as well . . ."

"And?"

"And what?"

"And what about Connor?"

"Connor hasn't been offering to take me to Italy. Connor actually hasn't been offering to take me much of anywhere. Our last six dates all involved DVDs and take-out food."

"But I thought you've been having a good time with him?"

"I have. I love being with him. We can talk about anything. He makes me laugh. I sleep so well with him. The sex, as we have recently discovered, is fantastic. But Connor is far more likely to offer to take me to a cabin in the north woods than he is to a villa in Tuscany. And I gotta be honest, I kinda like the whole villa in Tuscany thing."

"Put the vacations aside for just a minute," Jill says. "Between the two of them, which one are you generally more compatible with? As a person, forget entertainment."

I think about this for a moment. Abbot and I talk mostly about business and the issues of the day. But with Connor, I can talk about hopes and dreams and fears and funny stories about family and childhood in a way that I can't with Abbot. When Connor and I spend the night together, some part of him is always touching some part of me. He holds my hand, he puts a leg over mine, he spoons up behind me. It doesn't matter how I shift or turn in the course of the night. There is always some tangible connection between us. When Abbot and I sleep together, he cuddles with me for about twenty minutes after we have sex, but eventually he rolls over to his side of the bed and remains there until morning. Connor is spontaneous and will call me last minute if he gets a free evening. Abbot, with the notable exception of a couple afternoon abductions for sex, has never in my memory called me in the middle of the day to find out what I had on the docket for that evening. I look at Jill, who's waiting patiently for my brain to settle down. "Okay, if I put aside the entertainment things, like the kind of places I like to go and the kind of vacations I like to take, as a person, I think I'm more compatible with Connor."

"Well, then, isn't that your answer?" Jill asks.

"It might be if Connor had also proposed that he and I take things to the next level. But at the moment, there's only one offer of exclusivity on the table, and it didn't come from Mr. Duncan."

"Well, maybe it's a topic you should bring up with him."

"What if it's too soon?" I ask. "I've been seeing Abbot for nine months. I've only been seeing Connor for just over four, and we've only had sex once! What if he hasn't talked to me about exclusivity because it takes him longer to figure that kind of stuff out, and I scare him away by bringing it up too soon?"

"You know, if you turn Abbot down for this vacation, your relationship with him is over. He's not going to want to keep dating you if you tell him that you're not ready to go away with him."

"I know."

"And you can't possibly be considering saying yes to him, with him believing that the vacation would be about exploring the potential for getting exclusive, if you already know that that potential isn't there?"

"That would be really bad, huh?"

"Yes, that would be really bad."

"I honestly don't know what to do. I know you're right; I can't go to Italy with Abbot. Not unless I tell him that I'd only be going to have a great time and that I don't think we have a future. And I think the chances that he would still want to go with me at that point are slim to none. I also know that I really do like Connor, and I really do sense potential with him. But I don't really sense that he senses the same potential. Do you know what I mean?"

"You mean because he still disappears for a few days and then sees you every day for three days and then goes away for a week? That sort of thing?" Jill adds more cream and sugar to her coffee.

"Yeah, I guess. I think when he's with me, he's really with me. But I think when he's not with me, he's not necessarily thinking about me in the same way that I tend to be thinking about him, and that really makes me nervous."

"Is that what makes you nervous, or is the idea of being completely alone what makes you nervous?"

"What do you mean?" I ask.

"Well, let's look at the facts. Putting Connor aside, you know you have to turn Abbot down, and you know that if you turn Abbot down, that is going to be the end of your relationship with him. That means that Connor will be the only man in your life. Your choice is to either start actively recruiting a replacement for Abbot, which kind of goes against what you're feeling for Connor, or to actually look at Connor and be honest with him about your feelings. And take the risk that he will not feel the same and therefore end his relationship with you, at which point you would be entirely without a guy. It just makes me wonder if a part of the fear isn't about being alone. Perhaps even more than being fearful of losing Connor specifically."

I steal another forkful of her pancake. "It's been a really, really long time since I was vulnerable like that with a man. I'm not sure I entirely remember how to handle it."

"It's like falling off a bike. As I recall, your cure usually involves champagne, a lot of ice cream, Cheetos, and a couple of one-night stands with completely inappropriate men."

I laugh. "You suppose I should market that in a package somewhere for the heartbroken women of the world?"

Jill smiles at me. "We can certainly try to fit it into the next book."

"What am I going to do if I lose them both right before your wedding?"

"Well . . ." Jill thinks a minute. "There is always Worth. He's not bringing a date. I'm sure he'd oblige you during the slow dances."

"You're kind of a cunt, you know that?"

"I learned it from my big sister."

"We're definitely going to need more bacon," I say and wave for the waitress.

⚬⚬⚬

"Jodi?" Benna squawks at me through the intercom. "I have Brant on the line. What do you want me to do?"

Sweet Stay Puft Marshmallow Man. "Put him through," I say. I take a deep breath and pick up the phone. "Jodi Spingold."

"Jodi, it's Brant," he says curtly.

"Brant, I'm really not supposed to speak with you."

"Says who?"

"Our lawyers," I say.

"Why would your lawyers tell you not to speak to me?"

"That's probably a question for Mallory," I reply.

"What are you talking about?"

"Look, Brant, I am only at liberty to say that, on advice of counsel, I am not supposed to have any contact with you, and if you would like to know why, I recommend that you ask your girl-friend."

"Fiancée," he says.

"Excuse me?"

"Fiancée. We got engaged. It's why I'm calling. I wanted you to hear it from me."

"Well, let me be the first to offer you all the luck in the world. Is that all?"

"Is that all you have to say to me?"

"Brant, I don't know what else you would like me to say. It's been pretty clear of late that as far as you and I are concerned, our friendship is ended. And frankly, if you genuinely have no idea why it is that someone might suggest to me that communicating with you would be against my best interests and the interests of my business, then might I suggest that you and your fiancée have a very serious talk. In the meantime, all I can offer you are my very best wishes for a happy life."

"You just can't stand to see me happy, can you?" he says.

"Brant, I have to hang up now. Whatever you believe, all I can tell you is that I have never wanted anything but for you to have a happy life. And if you believe that you can have a happy life with Mallory, then all I can hope is that that turns out to be true."

"Well, then I guess all I can do is wish you a happy life as well. Good-bye, Jodi."

"Good-bye, Brant." I hang up the phone just as Jill comes into the office.

"Benna said Brant called. Is that true?" she asks.

"Yep, just hung up."

"What did he have to say?"

"He and Mallory are getting married."

"Does he know about her threats?"

"It wouldn't appear so."

"Well, did you tell him?"

"I didn't think it my place. I simply told him that on advice of legal counsel, I wasn't supposed to be in communication with him, and that if he wanted to know why, I recommended he have that discussion with his fiancée."

"Wow. I bet it's going to be a long talk at the old Summit house tonight!" Jill giggles. "You think he'll marry her once he finds out?"

"If I know Brant, she'll manage to convince him that she was just trying to help him out, and that she never really intended to go through with it but that it was all for his sake and the sake of their future."

"And don't forget the future of their future children."

I laugh.

"Seriously," Jill says. "What do you think he's going to do when she tells him?"

"Honestly, I don't know." I think it could go either way. She clearly has him poisoned against me. So it isn't impossible to believe that if she explains her scheme to him that he might in fact choose to go along with it, and we could still be in trouble. But I would like to hold out some hope that there is a little bit of Anakin Skywalker left in the Darth Vader that my ex-husband has become. Just enough to make him realize that trying to create a smear campaign against our business and me personally is something he won't be able to participate in.

"Hopefully, now that Mallory has her future with him secure, she'll simply let it go," I say.

"I hope you're right."

"Yeah, me, too. Let's talk about happier subjects. Are you ready for your big bachelorette night?"

"I am indeed. Hunter's leaving tomorrow for his bachelor weekend in Vegas, and I'm ready to get my groove on with the girls."

"I think we're in for a great time. I've booked out the whole Kiva Spa, so everybody's doing a circuit of massage, facial, manicure and pedicure, hair, and makeup. You and Paige and I have the most ridiculous suite at the Hilton, and the rest of the girls all have rooms one floor down. We have two limousines at our disposal. Dinner reservations in the private room at Nomi, followed by live band karaoke at the Redhead Piano Bar, and the brunch scheduled to be catered by the hotel on Sunday morning. The aunts and I finished the gift bags yesterday."

"Did you get them to come?" she asks.

"Nope, couldn't convince them. The most they will do is join us for brunch on Sunday. They say they're too old to be a part of bachelorette night."

"I suppose it will be better to have them at brunch and be able to tell them all the wild tales of the night before."

"That's what I figure. It's going to be a fantastic weekend."

"Are you seeing Connor tonight?"

"Yes, apparently we're actually going out for dinner. It's a small miracle."

Jill clucks at me. "All right, now. Don't get all geared up to be irritated just because he doesn't do that man-of-the-world wining and dining the way Abbot does."

"I know, I know. I have to remember that ultimately, perfection is boring."

"Exactly. Except when it comes in the form of your younger sister."

"Well, that goes without saying."

"What do you say we wrap things up and head on home?"

"I think that sounds like an excellent idea."

"And Jodi?"

"Yeah?"

"You said you can talk to Connor about anything; remember that."

"I know."

"I'm just saying."

"I'm working on it; let's just get through the weekend first. The discussion isn't really going anywhere; it'll keep till next week."

At least I hope it will.

Two Steps Back

We always hope to make good decisions. We hope that we are the kind of people that can process new information, assess potential impact, and make a decision informed by our knowledge as well as our hearts. Sometimes, in an effort to lead us in the right direction, the advice of those closest to us is fairly conservative. It's important when seeking outside counsel to recognize that nobody wants to be the one who advised you to take a big risk, because they don't want to be in a position for there to be resentment or blame if the risk doesn't pan out. However, when we speak to women who are in their mid to late thirties, often they talk about regrets. These women will point to the things they didn't do, the places they didn't go, the risks they didn't take in love and business and life. When you come to a crossroads in any of these areas, and a choice has to be made for one path or the other, don't dismiss the riskier path out of hand. While taking risks may ultimately not pan out, there are always things to be learned on those journeys.

—*From* The Thirty Commandments *by Jill and Jodi Spingold*

I realized when I was younger, and dating a lot of different guys (particularly guys who were far less into me than I was into them), I found myself falling prey to some pretty common traps. I was big on compliments, and no matter what the man I was with looked like or said or did, I always managed to praise him. I very rarely voiced a negative opinion, because usually, I was afraid that they would leave me. I think one of the things that drew me to Brant, way back when, was how at ease I was in his company. How much I felt that I could be honest with him. Even about things that came off as negative, I never felt like I had to placate or flatter. Of course, my comfort with sharing with Brant all of the things that I didn't particularly like about him eventually turned into my dictating many things about our life together. And I'm still feeling somewhat guilty that one reason Brant is going to marry a woman who is a manipulative shrew is due in no small part to all of the years that I didn't let him fully participate in major decision making.

By the time I got divorced, one of the things I had to recognize about myself was that I could never again be in a relationship where I felt the need to be obsequious. In the time since I've been single, and with all the men that I have dated, I have never felt less than free to express a differing opinion, to make a gentle recommendation on anything from hairstyle to lifestyle.

But it is amazing to me how quickly bad habits can return to one. Earlier tonight I was so excited that Connor had actually planned an evening out (as opposed to another night on a couch) that I completely went overboard in a festival of flattery. He took me to Heaven on Seven, which is a great place if you like Cajun and Creole food. Which I do not. In fact, I can barely eat anything with the least amount of spice in it. With any other man, I would simply have said, "I'm so sorry. Thank you for making a reservation, but unfortunately I can't really eat spicy food. Would it be all right with you if we made another choice?" But did I do this last night? Nope. Last night I went to Heaven on Seven, attempted to order the least spicy thing on the menu, and drank exactly four enormous glasses of sweet iced tea to compensate. The result was not just that I had to pee every twenty minutes for the rest of the evening but also that I had the very embarrassing situation of having to go number two at Connor's house for the first time.

It is amazing, even to myself, that as a woman who advises

other women on how to be themselves, on how to embrace everything that is natural and beautiful about them, on how to engage in honest, open relationships with other people, I would be nervous about such a thing. I, nevertheless, fall prey to some of the same insecurities as any other woman. And while I know intellectually that Connor Duncan is fully aware of the fact that I shit, I was entirely embarrassed to have to do it anywhere near his presence, let alone in his bathroom.

When my lower intestine made its need known to me, I engaged in a quick plot to create subterfuge. I suggested to Connor that he turn on *SportsCenter*. I waited just a couple of moments until he was engrossed and then offered to fetch him a beverage. He thanked me and requested a beer. I told him I was going to powder my nose and then get his beer and that I would be back in a moment. I headed off to his bathroom, ran the water on high in the sink, and attended to the unavoidable dirty business that I was there to do, grateful for the can of Febreze air freshener next to the toilet. I washed up, got his beer, and returned to the couch. The whole thing took less than two minutes and thirty seconds. I was very pleased with myself, as if I had somehow pulled off a *Mission Impossible*–level heist. My smugness didn't last long. As soon as I was settled on the couch next to him, Connor turned to me and said, "Is it terribly toxic in there, or dare I go take a leak?" I looked at him in utter amazement.

"What? How did you know?" I sputtered.

He smiled at me. "You are the fastest-peeing woman I have ever met in my life. I've never known you to be gone to a bathroom for more than forty-five seconds. Plus you smell like air freshener."

I dropped my face into my hands, mortified. Connor laughed at me.

"Jodi? I don't understand. Why are you embarrassed about this?"

I looked up at him. "Because no girl wants to think that the guy she's about to have sex with is going to be imagining her pinching a loaf in his bathroom."

"Pinching a loaf?" he said.

"Dropping the kids off at the pool, going to see the Browns play in the Super Bowl . . . Whatever you want to call it, it's not exactly a sexy image."

Connor leaned over and kissed me deeply on the mouth. "I think you're incredibly sexy, even if you did just pollute my bathroom." I punched him on the arm. He tweaked my nose, kissed me, pulled me against him to finish watching *SportsCenter*. When we finally went to bed, I was feeling comfortable. Very, very comfortable. Comfortable enough that I decided to take a risk.

"Connor?" I asked. "Would you escort me to Jill's wedding?"

"When is it again?"

"Saturday, May nineteenth," I said. "Two weeks from tomorrow."

"Sorry, darlin', I can't," he said, and my heart sank. "Mike and I are going up to his cabin to fish that weekend with the boys to give Peg a little break.

And did I look at my lover and say, "It would really mean a lot to me if you came"? Did I tell him, "You're the only one I want with me, and do you think maybe you could either schedule another weekend or Mike could take one of the other brothers with him?" Did I look at him and say, "I feel like things are moving in a great direction, and I'd like for us to talk about making this relationship exclusive"? Nope. I reverted 100 percent back to my eighteen-year-old self, who thought that expressing any opinion would make a boy dump her, and said, "Well, I'm sure you guys will have a good time."

After that brief exchange, Connor rolled over and began kissing me. And I let him, even though the romantic mood I had been in was somewhat deflated. And for the first time in our brief physical history together, despite his skill and honest efforts, I couldn't come. And so I did what my eighteen-year-old self had always done in that situation. I faked it. It took me a long time to fall asleep. And now a mere six hours later, I'm awake again, watching him sleep and thinking to myself, *How very, very handsome he is, and how very, very much he has disappointed me*. And mostly I'm embarrassed for my own behavior.

I slip out of the bed and down the hall into the bathroom, where I make a very quick morning toilette and then return to the bedroom where I get dressed silently. I lean over the bed and kiss Connor's forehead. He opens his eyes.

"What the—? Hey, you're dressed already?"

"I know, sweetie. I didn't wanna wake you; I just wanted to tell you that I have to go."

He rubs his eyes. "Wait. What's going on?"

I touch his cheek. "I have to get ready for Jill's big bachelorette day. I have a million things to do, and I've gotta get home and get myself ready, and it's Saturday. I didn't want you to have to get up."

"Don't be silly. Give me a second to throw some clothes on, and I'll drive you home."

"Don't you be silly. It's your day off. Stay in bed, sleep in, do whatever you want to do. I'll grab a cab."

"Are you sure? It's no trouble."

"I'm positive. Go back to sleep." I kiss him on the mouth, tuck the blankets around him, and head home.

And in that moment, I'm sure of one thing. Connor Duncan is nowhere near ready to pursue a committed relationship with me. Which suddenly makes Italy a less impossible prospect after all.

⚜

Hey, Butthead, you asleep?" Jill whispers outside the door.

"I'm up. Come on in," I say.

She tiptoes into one of the three bedrooms in our swank Hilton penthouse and climbs on top of my bed.

"Can't sleep?"

"I can't shut my head off," she says. "It was too exciting a day."

"Have you had fun at your bachelorette party?"

"This was by far the best bachelorette party anyone ever had. Thank you so much for all that you did to make it perfect."

"You're very welcome."

"You seemed a little quiet, though. Is everything okay?" she asks.

"I've just been thinking a lot lately. And I'm thinking that maybe I've been too hard on Abbot. You're always telling me that I am slightly strict when it comes to my demands. Perhaps I used the fact that I am not willing to settle as a way of avoiding the kind of relationships where I might have to compromise. And I know that we are always telling people that there are ways to compromise without giving up what's important to us. I mean, Abbot is a wonderful man and treats me like gold. Why am I so willing to break it off just because he has a couple of things about him that aren't a perfect match? I mean, he's smart, he's funny, he's successful, he and I like a lot of the same things, we enjoy each other's company. We have a good sex life. Why shouldn't I give it an opportunity to grow and develop? Just because he's a little OCD about cleanliness, like it would be a bad thing if I learned how to be a little neater and more organized in my own life? He makes me happy in many ways, and I've never thought much about taking things to the next level. But he obviously has and is willing to make an effort. Why do I think that he wouldn't be willing to compromise on some of the things that are giving me hesitation?"

"Is this about Italy?"

"Not about Italy in specific, but about the concept of Italy, in general. I mean, think about it. Here is a man who has put up with all of my rules and restrictions and strange little quirks and foibles and has never asked me to change anything about myself to suit him or his needs. And he's presenting an opportunity to me, for the two of us to really explore what we could be to one another. Why am I so afraid of doing that?"

"Because you're in love with Connor?"

"I'm not in love with Connor. I'm in very deep like with Connor. There is a difference. Do I think I could fall in love with Connor? Yes. But why couldn't I fall in love with Abbot?"

"Because you can't decide on paper who is an easier choice and force yourself to fall in love with him."

"It isn't about an easy choice. It's about a smart and logical choice. Abbot wants me to give him a chance to prove that he is the right partner for me. I've been with him longer. Why shouldn't I give him that opportunity?"

"What the hell happened last night?"

"Nothing. It's just something I've been thinking about. And the more I think about it, the more I think that perhaps it would be a good thing to give Abbot this chance."

"And then what do you do about Connor?"

"I think I have no choice under the circumstances but to break up with him."

"Something did happen last night."

I take a deep breath. "Remember how I used to get with all those guys, the ones I wanted more than they wanted me?" I confess all of the previous evening's ridiculous behavior, without leaving anything out. From my own retarded overreaction to the natural need to use his bathroom, all the way through to my Meg Ryan performance in the bedroom. She listened intently. "I mean, Jill, he didn't even hesitate to say that he was too busy to take me to your wedding. There wasn't a moment of question. There was just 'I'm going fishing with Mike and his boys.'"

Why am I working so hard for a man who simply doesn't feel the same way about me that I feel about him? It's ridiculous. And it's a wake-up call. I've been ignoring everything that's right and good about Abbot because I have this fantasy about Connor, but ultimately, Connor is no different than any of those guys that I was so wild about in the past who just weren't that excited about me. I've always wanted to win. I've always wanted one of those guys to not want to lose me. Connor's just the latest one. And I've worked very, very hard over the years to not turn back into that girl. Jill and I have built an entire business trying to help other women not be that girl. And Connor, through no fault of his own, is turning me back into that girl. But I'm not that girl. And if I hadn't run into Connor in the grocery store over Thanksgiving, right now, I'd be picking out clothes to go to Italy without a second thought.

Abbot is out of town on business. He gets back on Friday. The plan was to see him next Saturday night and to tell him that I couldn't take him up on his offer. But I don't see now that I have any reason to not take him up on his offer. Instead, I'm going to take a risk. I'm going to openly and honestly give Abbot a chance to do exactly what he said he wanted to: prove to me that he is the kind of guy I could fall in love with. Maybe it won't work; maybe we'll come back from Italy and realize that we just aren't meant to be together. But I'm not going to throw away an opportunity to reach for happiness with a good man because I'm insane over not getting the guy I never could get.

"Jodi," Jill says quietly, "I love you very much. And I want for

you to be happy. And I know that what happened last night with
Connor hurt your feelings. I know that you wanted him to jump
up and down and say, 'Of course I will take you to the wedding.
I'm so thrilled that you have asked me, and by the way, don't you
think it would be a good time for us to talk about being exclusive
with one another?' And I am so sorry that he didn't do that. But in
all our good advice giving, some of that advice is also about not
expecting someone to have ESP. It's two weeks until my wedding.
You waited until essentially the last minute to ask him to be your
date. You can't expect him to assume that this is very important to
you, and that it will disappoint you if he says no, if you treat it like
an offhand, casual offer. There is a reason that we asked people to
RSVP like three weeks ago. Because, in general, people need at
least six weeks' notice to commit to an event like a wedding. How
do you think it made him feel to know this whole time that the
wedding was coming up and for you to casually mention it to him
like a throwaway offer? You didn't give him enough notice, he has
other plans, he committed to his brother to help for a weekend
with his kids so that his sister-in-law can have a quiet weekend
without having to take care of a bunch of people. That sounds to
me like the kind of thing that you would normally praise in a guy.
His willingness to help out and be a good, dependable guy to his
family. And you know that if you had made a commitment to the
aunts or me, and then someone asked you to be their date for
something, you would have said no. It isn't like he said, 'I don't
feel like it; I was thinking of going to a movie that night.' He's going to be in the north woods of Wisconsin."

"But he should've—"

"Uh-uh. No." Jill puts on her stern face. "You should have.
You should have looked at him and said, 'I'm kind of disap-
pointed, because I would really love for you to be there with me.'
You should've asked him weeks ago to be your date. You should've

looked at him and said, 'I really like you. And I've been thinking lately that maybe we ought to discuss taking this relationship to the next level. I would love to know what you think about that.' But you didn't do any of those things. And so your misery right now isn't Connor's fault. It's your fault. And I really, really hope that you are not going to give Abbot a false sense of your intentions because you want somebody to make nice to you. I'd rather see you alone at my wedding, standing proud and firm in your decision, than on the arm of somebody who you are using to lick your wounds."

"Jill, it isn't like that. When I left Connor's this morning, it just struck me. He likes me. He just doesn't like me the same way I like him, and he doesn't see the same potential that I see, and before I get myself all worked up into a frenzy, I need to take an opportunity to step back and look at what I really want and what I really need. Abbot didn't ask me to make a big commitment to him. He just asked me to open my mind and try. I'm not moving in with him; we're not getting married. It's just taking a next step. And the more I think about it, the more I think that I've been too closed off from that possibility, because I was in this fantasy haze with Connor. But there are just as many things about Connor that don't quite fit as there are with Abbot. And since Abbot is the one who is offering himself forward, I think it would be short-sighted of me to not at least try. It would be different if both of them were making this offer. But they aren't. And so, all things being equal, I do think I'm ready at this point in my life to at least consider a more serious relationship, and the relationship that is being offered to me is with Abbot."

"Jodi, if you really think it's what you want, I will support you. Just please, please promise me that before you make a final decision that you will seriously consider being honest with Connor. I would hate to think that your desire to avoid a potentially awkward conversation would prevent you from having the relationship you want with the man who is your first choice. If you are so certain that he's not in a place to be more to you than he is right now, at least give him an opportunity to be the one to tell you. Will you promise me that you'll think about it?"

"I promise."

Jill cocks her head at me.

"I promise! I will think about it."

"Okay, I'm done lecturing you for the night."

"Only two more weeks. Are you ready for this?" I ask.

She laughs. "It's weird. The closer we get, the more excited I get. And the closer we get, the more nervous Hunter seems to get. You should see him. He's like a chicken with his head cut off. He's started talking in his sleep, and everything that he says is related to our wedding details. I swear! I wake up, and he's mumbling about centerpieces and place cards and hors d'oeuvres."

I laugh. "He's one of a kind, your husband-to-be."

"Yes he is, thank goodness," she says.

"You wanna crash in here with me?" I ask.

"Yeah, can I?"

I lift the covers, and she snuggles in beside me.

"Good night, Moose Face," I say.

"Good night, Butthead," she says.

I roll over and pull the covers up to my chin, burying my head in the soft, fluffy pillow. Despite what Jill has said, I'm not so sure that talking to Connor is a good idea. It isn't his fault that I allowed myself to create a fantasy around him. And I close my eyes and imagine the life I could have with Abbot, a life unfettered by familial responsibilities, a life of elegance and luxury and beautiful music and lovely trips. It isn't a bad life. There is much about it that I like. Jill's just being overprotective, because I dragged her into my own wild imaginings where Connor was concerned. But

I think I'm coming down to earth now. And I believe that my thinking is finally clearheaded for the first time in months.

"Hey, Jodi."

"Yeah?"

"What are we having for breakfast?"

This makes us both giggle, and soon, sleep.

"Hey," Connor says, answering the phone. "How was the weekend?"

"Okay," I say, stalling for time. "How about yours?"

"Pretty boring, mostly doing the quarterly taxes for the business. Whassup?"

"Nothing, I, um . . ." Shit. I fucking hate this. "I just have to cancel our date for tomorrow."

"Okay."

"Okay?" *That's it?*

"Yeah, okay. No problem."

He sure is making this easy. "Well, I'm glad it doesn't inconvenience you."

"Not at all."

"Don't you care?" I ask.

"Hey, I'm sure something came up. It isn't the end of the world, right?"

"Fine." I don't know what else to say.

"Are you mad about something?" he asks.

"No," I say.

"Don't pull that shit, Jodi. Talk to me. I hate that passive-aggressive crap. What, is it in the genetic code? It's fucking manipulative."

"There is no reason to yell, Connor."

"Well, there is no reason to not acknowledge your feelings. If you're mad about something, just tell me."

"I'm not mad."

"Okay, I'm hanging up now. If you want to call me back and tell me what you're pissed about, I will be very happy to listen. But I'm not going to stay on the phone listening to your wounded breathing and play guessing games as to what I've done wrong."

And then he's gone.

Fucking hung up on me.

I call back.

"Yes?" he says, obviously irritated.

"That was extraordinarily rude and juvenile, and I really didn't appreciate it," I say, trying to be calm.

"Well, I don't appreciate being manipulated."

"I'm not manipulating you."

"Look, Jodi, you may not think I know you, but I know you enough. You're upset about something, and Lord knows I probably did something stupid to cause it. If you tell me what it is, I can apologize and try not to do it again. But if you play this silly-ass game of making me guess and drag it out of you, I'm going to be less inclined to apologize and more inclined to be angry myself. And if you don't want to have an adult conversation with me, then I am going to get back to work."

"Look, Connor, while I am sure the whole universe does indeed revolve around you, at the moment, you are not the major source of my displeasure. At least you weren't. However the pompous audacity with which you accuse me of playing some junior high game of 'guess the problem' has shot you right to the top of my list. In case you hadn't noticed, I have a great deal going on right now, which might be reason for me to sound less than chipper, none of which has anything to do with you. I was calling to see how you were, to find out about the rest of your weekend. Instead you hang up on me and accuse me of dishonesty. You know what, Mr. Duncan? Fuck you."

I hang up, shaking. Not just because I am so furious, but because he was right. He was goddamned *right*. I was mad at him, still wounded about his turning me down for the wedding, still stinging from his hot-and-cold routine, still hating that he could make me feel so unsure of myself and my place in his life. And I was manipulating him, testing him, canceling our date to get him to ask me why so I could admit to a date with Abbot so that he could tell me he wanted me to stop dating other people. Once again, the wisest source of sage advice makes the worst possible personal decision.

What the fuck is wrong with me? I want to call him back and fess up. I want to tell him he was right and that I'm a mess. I want to tell him that I'm broken, but worth sticking with. But I can't. And when the phone rings, I can't force myself to answer it.

The Harder They Fall

I miss the American dream. It used to be that the ideal in this country was to work hard and attain success on your own with strength of character, intelligence, and ambition. It used to be that the ideals upon which this country was founded, that anyone could achieve the highest level of success, was connected to their ability to have a great idea and put it into practice. Somewhere in the twentieth century, that idea began to get muddy, and more and more the American dream became about instant gratification and overnight success. Suddenly, fame and wealth could be attained in a matter of moments if one could win a reality television contest, buy the right lottery ticket, marry the right person. This concept came into clear relief for me earlier this week. I received a phone call from an individual who claimed to have important information about a local celebrity. The kind of information that sells newspapers and magazines and tabloids and gets names mentioned on television. I listened to the information that was presented to me and was struck by how truly insidious the person was who was claiming to offer me an opportunity to share that information with the world as if it were for the common interest. I will not use names for the purpose of this column, but I will present the following scenario: A young couple, after years of struggle, decide to divorce. Sometime after the divorce, the wife achieves a level of success that is staggering. This success comes with a certain amount of fame and a significant amount of money. When the business that she has worked very hard to build starts to really achieve its potential, the ex-husband acquires a new fiancée. And the life that the two of them can afford seems paltry in comparison to the life that his ex-wife now enjoys. Is the response from the ex-husband and his new woman to seek, through their own labor and intelligence and ambition, to try to create something on their own? To attain a matching level of success? No. Their response is to call a member of the media in an attempt to place a negative article about the ex-wife in the local newspaper. Now any journalist who has been working in the business for a reasonable amount of time knows that when a tip of a negative nature comes your way, the first thing you are required to do is to consider the source. What does the source have to gain by this information going public? Are they genuinely trying to perform a public service, or are they potentially attempting to do something for their own gain? It is amazing to me that the desire to keep the public face of a company clean frequently results in an enormous financial payout to people who threaten public disgrace. When I got off the phone with my new source, I immediately called the person whose integrity had been questioned. And was in no way shocked to find that indeed, the person who had phoned me had done so in an attempt to shore up a case for personal financial remuneration. We all want to believe that there are people in the world who will reach out to the press when they are in possession of information that the public genuinely needs to know. The public needs to know when our politicians are doing things that are illegal or immoral. The public needs to know when we are being failed in some way by the people who are supposed to be serving our common needs. And the public is going to assume that when we journalists give them information, it has a level of import. It is essential for us, in serving the public good, to maintain our own integrity by not allowing ourselves to become puppets for those seeking to line their own pockets out of greed and malice. I spent the last two days doing something that I felt, as a journalist, was a genuine public service. I contacted every major media outlet that I could think of, spoke to every colleague whose number was in my Rolodex, and gave them the name of the person who had called me, the essence of what was going on, and a sense of my personal outrage that this person had attempted to manipulate me into using my own reputation and good name to support her own greed. I had more interesting and meaningful conversations with my fellow journalists in the last few days surrounding this issue than I have had in a very long time. And for that, I am actually grateful to the money-hungry lowlife who called me originally. And to the woman who was the victim of

the potential attack, I say to you, you are safe, and I
hope that you will continue to do the work that you
do, and continue to stand your own ground, should an
attack like this ever come again. And to anyone who is
reading this column who has a thought about striking
it rich by extorting hush money out of people who
have worked hard to attain their success, I say shame
on you. Shame on all of us for creating an environment that allows for that possibility to begin with.

—*Jordan Blank, Op Ed in the* Chicago Tribune, *May 12, 2007*

"Congratulations," Abbot says, toasting me with his whiskey. He's
just finished reading the piece from this morning's paper. We've
already sent an enormous gift basket over to Jordan. When he
called to fact-check the little bit of evil that Mallory had spoken
to him about and heard the true details of the story, he was obviously enraged. And when I told him that he should feel free to
print it, that the company had already decided to stand our
ground where the threats were concerned, and that we were prepared to face anything, that rage increased to a level that has
clearly served our purposes very nicely. We appear, for the moment, to be safe on that front. The rest of the PR crap continues
at its petty pace, a few other retail outlets have dropped us, particularly in conservative markets, and the new forecast financially
is an overall 22 to 24 percent drop for the fiscal year. But not total disaster, and if we can maintain, hopefully the new book will
help an upswing come next spring.

"Have you heard from Brant?" he asks.

"Not a peep." And Brant never reads the papers, so I doubt
that he's seen this, and even if he did, I don't know that he's smart
enough to understand that it is about us. Especially as Mallory has

been less than forthcoming with him as to what the situation is. Frankly, I think the whole thing is for the best. It forced me to look at what role Brant was playing in my life. And, as it turned out, it wasn't a role that had any true meaning. It also forced the company to come together and make a decision about who we are and where we're going, and ultimately I think both the company and I personally are going to be better off and stronger as a result.

"Well, let's hope he stays peepless!" Abbot says.

The hostess comes over to where we're sitting at the bar. "Your table is ready, sir. Madame, right this way."

We carry our drinks over to the table in a quiet corner of Trattoria 10.

"Do you have theater tickets this evening?" the hostess asks us.

"Yes," says Abbot, "eight o'clock curtain."

"At which theater?"

"The Palace."

"We'll have you out of here in plenty of time," the hostess says. "Enjoy your dinner."

We scan over the menu, place our orders, and nibble on their delicious Parmesan crackers while waiting for our salads to arrive. While Abbot talks about his trip, I examine him. He's looking particularly handsome in a dark gray suit, his salt-and-pepper hair clipped close to his head, and as I watch him and think about the time we've spent together, I'm filled with a sense of certainty that I haven't had about much of anything in a very long time. I know, with every fiber of my being, that I have made the right choice for me. The best possible decision for us both. And I am suddenly really looking forward to sharing it with him later tonight.

"Jodi, dear, more wine?" Aunt Ruth asks me.

"No thanks, I'm good," I say.

"I'll take more," Jill says, holding her glass out, and Ruth reaches over with the bottle and tops her off. It's our last Thursday cocktail hour before the wedding, and we are all exhausted. Hunter's family arrived yesterday in surprisingly good spirits and regaled us during dinner last night with all the details of the party plans for next weekend. Ice sculptures and a martini fountain and three different bands. Apparently, approximately 250 of Cleve and Grace's friends, family, and colleagues are all eager to meet our quaint little family. Both Jill and Hunter were amazingly even-keeled, in spite of the fact that everything about that party seems to go against the sort of event that they themselves would ever have planned. But they are so happy and excited about the wedding that ultimately, whatever sort of over-the-top display is going to be made out East, all they can focus on are the perfect details of what will happen in two days.

"So, Miss Jill," Aunt Shirley says, "we have something for you." She walks over to the sideboard and takes out a simple white box tied with a white ribbon. She hands it to Jill.

"More presents?" Jill asks. "Really, it's very unnecessary." Her grin is in direct opposition to the protests coming out of her mouth.

"Oh, just open it already," I say.

She unties the ribbon and lifts the top off the box. Gently moving aside the tissue, she reaches in to find a small, ivory-beaded clutch purse. "It's beautiful," she says. "It's just perfect."

"It's the purse our mother carried when she married our father," Aunt Ruth says.

"I found it last week when I was looking through a box for some old recipes," says Shirley. "We had no idea it was even down there."

"It's the perfect something old," Jill says. "Thank you."

"Open it," Shirley says. Jill undoes the clasp and looks inside. She pulls out a small linen handkerchief embroidered with blue forget-me-nots. It's the handkerchief our mother carried at her wedding to our father and the one I carried when I married Brant. Jill recognizes it immediately.

"Well," she says, "that means all my requirements are met. I've got the something old. The dress is new. I'm borrowing Jodi's diamond bracelet, and now I've got my perfect something blue. All I need is a groom and a justice of the peace."

"You seem very happy," Shirley says, "and we are very happy for you."

"We wish you all the love in the world." Ruth raises her glass.

"Hear, hear!" I say, and the four of us clink glasses and toast to Jill's future.

"Is Abbot coming with you to the rehearsal dinner tomorrow night?" Jill asks.

"No," I say and take a deep sip of my wine. "Actually, Abbot won't be able to come to the wedding either."

Three heads snap around to look at me.

"What do you mean?" Aunt Shirley asks.

"Are you okay?" Jill says.

"Relax, relax everyone. I'm fine," I say.

"I thought the two of you were going to Italy?" Aunt Ruth says.

"We were. I told him last weekend that I would accept his offer of going to Italy. And ever since then, my stomach has been in knots. I really thought it was the right thing to do. He's a good man, and I enjoy his company immensely, and he's been nothing but lovely to me."

"But you're in love with Connor," Jill says.

"This isn't about Connor," I say. "This is about me."

My relationship with Brant was not a good or healthy relationship for me to be in. And when it was over, I needed to take some sort of action regarding my romantic life, which has worked pretty well up until now. This situation forced me to look into my heart to decide whether I am in a place now to really consider being someone's partner again. To give up the freedom and autonomy that I have worked so hard to achieve in order to have someone at my side in a more permanent way. And I discovered that yes, I am ready. I naturally thought that since the answer to that was yes, and Abbot was the one who asked me to consider that possibility with him, that he was the one that I should be saying yes to.

"Because you love Connor," Jill says again.

"No, Jill, not because I love Connor but because I don't love Abbot. I meant what I said; this isn't about Connor. It isn't even about the idea of Connor. This is about me. There's no way I could have been that enthralled to be with Connor if I was really supposed to be making a commitment to Abbot. I thought about it long and hard and realized that I couldn't force myself to explore this idea of commitment with the wrong man. So I spoke to Abbot and apologized and told him that I changed my mind. And I was very sorry to have to ultimately decline his offer, and I hoped he would understand."

"And what did he say?" Aunt Ruth asks.

"He was reasonably understanding. He said he was very sorry, that he wished it was different, that he had been excited at the prospect. But that as he hadn't made any definite arrangements, it didn't put him out, and that he wished me a wonderful life."

"How very gentlemanly of him," Aunt Shirley says.

"There's no question that Abbot is always a perfect gentleman," I say.

"So what did Connor say when you spoke to him?" Jill asks.

"I haven't spoken to Connor," I say. "I'm not exactly sure what I could tell him. Hey, I thought you'd want to know, somebody else offered to date me exclusively, and I turned him down, but the idea got me thinking?"

"That might be a good start," Aunt Ruth says.

"Look, the truth is, Connor and I had a fight. A really stupid fight about exactly nothing. And we talked, and we both apologized, but I'm not sure what he thinks about me right now. And he is off fishing, and by the time he gets back, we'll be out East, and so we are supposed to get together when I get back. I don't even know if we're technically still together or not right now, and I can't think about it. For right now, I'm just going to live in the world and see what happens." I really like Connor. I genuinely care about him, but I have to tread very lightly here. Just because I have recently come to the decision that I'm open to having an exclusive relationship with someone, and just because I was smart enough to recognize that it wasn't Abbot, doesn't mean I should suddenly throw myself at Connor and ask him to make all kinds of commitment. And now that things with Connor are all catawampus, I have to go on the assumption that I may very well be starting from scratch.

"I think that's very wise," says Aunt Ruth. "You have come to this knowledge in your own time and in an organic way, and frankly it's only fair that you give that boy an opportunity to do the same."

"Well, as long as you don't wait too long," Aunt Shirley says. "Sometimes those men need just a little push."

Jill reaches over and squeezes my arm. "I'm very, very proud of you."

I smile at her. "You know, I'm kind of proud of myself." Which I am. Not to mention sad, and fucking terrified, and more than a little lonesome. But, you know, in a proud way.

"But then who are you bringing to the wedding?" Shirley asks.

"I'm going solo," I say. "After all, there is no shame in that."

"Of course not," Ruth says.

"Are you sure there isn't a friend or someone you'd like to call?" Aunt Shirley says.

"I think at least one Spingold Spinster Sister ought to be represented at this party, and just because the three of you have dates doesn't make it a requirement for me." Shirley is bringing Gerald, a local illustrator who did the pictures on the last cookbook project she worked on. And Ruth is bringing Robert, an investment banker and former client who was recently relocated here from D.C. and relied on her to help him find the right apartment. She has been advising him on everything from where to get his shoes resoled, to where to take clients for business lunches.

"I think it's just fine," says Jill.

"So do I," I say.

And I do.

Do You Take This Man?

❧

I am my beloved's, and my beloved is mine.

—*From the* Song of Songs, *attributed to Solomon*

"It gives me great joy to present to all assembled here for the first time, Mr. and Mrs. Hunter Charles," the justice of the peace says, and the crowd erupts into delighted applause as Hunter and Jill kiss a second time and walk back down the aisle.

Worth looks at me, offers his arm, and we follow behind them. Aunt Ruth and Aunt Shirley are dabbing their eyes and smiling broadly. Hunter's mom is collapsed in her husband's arms. It couldn't have been a more beautiful ceremony. The vows that Jill and Hunter wrote themselves were both deeply moving and very funny, including things like Hunter promising not to tease her about her addiction to Dairy Queen with rainbow sprinkles, and Jill promising to try to learn how to play at least one video game.

We all head out into the reception and mill around accepting hugs and kisses from friends and family and being sure to introduce Hunter's family to everyone they didn't meet at last night's rehearsal dinner. It is a whirlwind of hugging and talking.

"You look like you could use a drink," says a voice behind me. I turn to find Connor, holding out a glass of champagne.

"What are you doing here?" I ask him, completely flabbergasted. "You're supposed to be in the North Woods!"

"I was, and this morning at five A.M., sitting in a boat in the middle of the lake with Mike, waiting for the fish to bite, I casually mentioned to him that Jill's wedding was tonight. He asked if I was angry at not being invited. I told him I was invited, but that I couldn't go because he and I had made these plans, and he yelled at me."

"He yelled at you?"

"Yep. Told me I was a complete asshat and he was ashamed to have me for his brother. I asked him why, and he said that inviting someone to be your date at a wedding of a close family member was a very important invitation. He said he noticed I've never brought a date to any of the family weddings. Ever. And that if I had had any sense, I would've called him up and told him to take somebody else this weekend. He said he bet you were really pissed. I said I didn't think you were angry, that you had taken it in stride, but then we had that fight, and that maybe this would explain it. And he said all the more reason that I shouldn't be there with him. I should be here with you. He said that any woman so upset that you won't be at her side at an important family event is the kind of woman you don't want to let slip through your grasp. And I realized that he was right. So I made him row me back to shore, I packed up my gear, and I called Jill to ask if you were bringing someone else to the wedding. She said you weren't and that it wasn't too late. And I got on the road, and here I am. And I'm sorry that I didn't make the right decision when I should've made it. It's been a very long time since I was involved with someone that I wanted to be responsible to, and I'm so used to putting my family first that I forgot to pay attention when you invited me to be your date. And Mike's right. You had every right to be angry with me." He leans over and kisses me softly.

"I was trying to manipulate you into asking me why I was mad.

I was playing the petulant victim, and when you called me on it, instead of being an adult, I acted even more idiotic."

He leans over and kisses me again, deeper this time. And then takes my face in both his hands, looks me deep in the eyes, and sighs. "I'm really, really sorry. I'm kind of an idiot about a lot of things, especially relationships. Promise me in the future that you'll just tell me when I'm doing something that hurts your feelings so I can fix it."

"Done," I say. "Thank you for coming. It really means a lot to me to have you here."

"It really means a lot to me that you asked. Even if I didn't know it right away."

I take a sip of my champagne and look at him. "I'm just going to say this because I'm feeling particularly brave right now. I know that when we began I made myself out to be the kind of woman who wasn't interested in a serious or committed relationship. But lately, I've started to change my mind about that. And as a result, I wanted you to know that I have officially stopped seeing any other people. I'm not suggesting that that is where you are, and it's fine with me if you're not. But I did want you to know."

He grins at me. "Want to know a secret?"

"Sure," I say.

"I haven't been seeing anyone else since before Christmas."

"What about New Year's girl?" I ask.

"What New Year's girl?"

"When I talked to you New Year's Eve, I heard a woman's voice calling you back to watch the movie."

He laughs. "That was my nephew Jimmy's girlfriend."

"Oh," I say. "I have to tell you you're pulling a real Jake Ryan on me here."

Conner laughs. "I love *Sixteen Candles*," he says.

"You're kidding?"

"Not kidding. I love to watch it at about three in the morning." Jill will be very relieved to hear that, I think.

"Hey, you two," Jill says, coming up behind us. Connor kisses her and slaps Hunter on the back.

"I'm so glad you could make it, man. It's good to have you here," Hunter says, glowing more than any bride.

"How was the drive?" Jill asks.

"Seven hours door-to-door. I even had time to take a nap."

"Hey," Hunter says. "Come here and meet my crazy family." And he whisks Connor across the room to introduce them. I turn and look at Jill, who is beaming at me.

"You couldn't give me a little warning?"

"He and I thought it would be a good surprise."

"It is. A really good surprise. I told him. I mean about wanting to be exclusive."

"And what did he say?"

"Apparently he's been dating me exclusively since December."

"I guess that makes you the ho in this situation."

"True. But let's be honest. In almost any situation, I'm probably the ho."

"Not anymore," she says and raises her champagne glass to mine. We clink and drink.

"How do you think our fans will react?" she asks.

"React to what?"

"If neither of the Spinster Sisters are spinsters anymore?"

"You know what?" I say.

"What?"

"We'll just have to tell them to walk it off."

"I think that's an excellent plan, Butthead."

"I think so, too, Moose Face."

"Well, well, well. Looks like you're not solo anymore," Aunt Ruth says from my right elbow.

"Dears, I think we're supposed to go sit down at our table, or they won't be able to get anyone else to sit down for dinner," Aunt Shirley says, coming up next to her sister.

"Well, then we should do that," I say, and the four of us head over to the next part of the celebration.

"Hey, Jodi? You sleeping?" Connor whispers in my ear.

"No, not really," I say.

"You don't happen to have *Sixteen Candles* on DVD, do you?" he asks.

I sit up in the bed and look over at him. "I'll get the DVD set up. You go get that leftover wedding cake out of the fridge."

"Deal," he says, kissing my cheek, and gets out of bed.

Whoever said you can't have your cake and eat it, too, never met a Spinster Sister.